# "You have to be careful who you trust."

"I can trust you."

"How do you know that?" Dane asked, slightly impatient.

She looked at the hand still holding hers. "I don't think I have anything you want."

Was that what she thought? Did she think so little of herself, or too much of him?

Dane shook his head in amazement. "What I want, I can't have," he said ruefully.

Taylor fixed her gaze on his face. "What is that?"

His fingers on the side of her face wove their way into her hair. Dane's mouth shifted a hairbreadth to kiss her lips, but gently and so briefly that it was like a feather's touch: a mere hint—a promise.

"It's you," he whispered against her mouth. "I want you."

# ABOUT THE AUTHOR

Sandra Kitt is a librarian with the American
Museum-Hayden Planetarium in New York City.
She is also an artist and graphic designer. Sandra
lives in Brooklyn with her husband, Thomas.

## Books by Sandra Kitt

### HARLEQUIN AMERICAN ROMANCE

Don't miss any of our special offers. Write to us at the
following address for information on our newest releases.

Harlequin Reader Service
901 Fuhrmann Blvd., P.O. Box 1397, Buffalo, NY 14240
Canadian address: P.O. Box 603,
Fort Erie, Ont.  L2A 5X3

# THE WAY HOME

SANDRA KITT

# *Harlequin Books*

TORONTO • NEW YORK • LONDON
AMSTERDAM • PARIS • SYDNEY • HAMBURG
STOCKHOLM • ATHENS • TOKYO • MILAN

To Thomas A. Lesser,
for love, understanding
and support

Published January 1990

First printing November 1989

ISBN 0-373-16327-4

# Chapter One

She'd forgotten that she never slept well in planes. Of course, she had to also admit her traveling experience was limited and she'd never learned how to doze in inconvenient places or contorted positions. She only knew that seven hours transatlantic flying did terrible things to her back and the state of her clothing.

As Taylor walked through the unending passageway that led from the international arrival gate to the main terminal and baggage claim, she also remembered that the outskirts of London near Heathrow Airport invariably appeared dreary at seven-fifteen in the morning, as they did through the terminal windows now. It had been a long time since her last trip to London, but some things never changed.

Stifling a yawn, Taylor momentarily squeezed her eyes shut against the burning grogginess of insomnia and tried to shift her carryon, handbag, winter coat and a small, but heavy parcel to a luggage cart. She wheeled it to a point in front of the conveyor belt, and waited along with a hundred or so other bleary-eyed travelers for her bag.

It might have been a while, but the routine was familiar. It was just strange to be here once again; Taylor remembered, with a twisting of her insides, that her last trip to London on simple business had changed her life and sent her into a tailspin of confusion. And now she was making a simple business trip again in the hope of straightening out her life. Taylor thought it simply ironic that she had to travel to another country to gain control of her existence, when she wasn't even sure how she was going to accomplish it.

Twenty minutes later she maneuvered her cart into a line to pass through Immigration Control. The young man at the desk barely gave her a glance as he opened her passport to review and stamp it. Taylor sighed as she watched him, knowing how close she'd come to forgetting it, along with the receipts and papers for the package she was carrying, and the envelope that contained all the information she had on Michael. Perhaps she could begin this afternoon to look for him.

Taylor began calculating how long it would take to get through Customs, make her way to ground transportation and the quickest way into the city. She knew that even though she'd landed at the crack of dawn, she rarely reached London before eleven o'clock, which meant that half the day was lost in merely getting there. And since it was February, it was going to be very cold walking around the city.

"Have you any other identification?" the young man asked.

"Yes, of course," Taylor answered, smiling faintly at his precise speech. She found her New York State driver's license and passed it to him. "It's not a very good picture. These things never—"

"Would you mind removing it from the casing?" he interrupted. He was polite, but all business.

Taylor grimaced and did as she was asked. He was being too businesslike, she thought, and it was adding unnecessary minutes of delay to an already long night and morning. Then, dazed though she was, Taylor sensed the immigration officer looking at her carefully; she frowned.

"Is anything wrong?" she asked.

"When was your last trip to the U.K.?"

The question surprised Taylor. The agent had only to check the last stamped date on her passport. But the question also triggered a memory causing her heart to skip a beat.

"About three years ago," Taylor answered softly. "It was business."

"And the purpose of your visit now?"

"Business," she replied firmly. She blinked at him. "Is there something wrong?"

The agent looked at her without any particular feeling, opinion or understanding in his eyes. He was only doing his job, she realized. "I'm afraid so, madam. I'll have to ask you to step to one side. This way, please—"

Taylor felt stunned. "But—"

"This way, please," he replied. Already he was signaling for another agent, who approached with an equally expressionless demeanor, took Taylor's papers from the young man and motioned to her.

"Can't you tell me . . . ?"

"Just follow the officer. Someone will explain everything to you in a few minutes." He turned to the next passenger waiting to be processed. Taylor felt dismissed and forgotten. She had no choice but to obey his directive. Pushing the cart with her things, Taylor walked behind the other officer. He wore soft-soled shoes, while hers made hollow tapping sounds on the marble floor that echoed in the corridor. Taylor had a wry thought that this was what it must feel like to be taken off to jail.

It was all so intimidating. Suddenly she had no power, no control. She couldn't think what the problem could be, but in her mental effort to assess this unexpected development, she became completely alert, and her earlier exhaustion quickly vanished.

They seemed to walk forever down quiet, narrow hallways before the officer finally approached a door, opened it and waved Taylor inside. She wheeled her cart into an office with gray walls, furnished with a long gray metal table and several gray chairs. Without windows or pictures on the wall, and only one fluorescent fixture on the ceiling, it was dreary and uninviting. With a sinking heart Taylor wondered how long she was going to have to be here.

"Please sit down. Someone will be with you soon," the man said, and Taylor turned anxiously to him.

"I just want to know—"

"Sorry. I can't tell you anything." And he closed the door.

Taylor realized in some alarm that he had her identification, all she carried that could prove who she was. She tried to think what to do, but knew at once that was futile, since she didn't know what was wrong. Her frustration gave way to anger and a growing sense of injustice. She didn't like not knowing what was happening. She had vivid memories of things being kept from her, information that came piecemeal or was misleading—answers to questions that were incorrect, leaving her confused. She thought of Michael and of her family.

Taylor understood her family's natural tendency to protect her. Part of it was due to being the youngest born to older parents in a family of much older brothers. She had been the pampered baby, the one to be watched over—the one who followed or had to be led—the one who was never old or big enough or who knew enough.

Such concern had been endearing but irritating. It sent Taylor out into the world on her own at twenty, to prove that she could take care of herself. Five years later she'd met Michael, who'd proved that maybe her family had been right, after all.

It was almost an hour before the door opened again, and for an instant Taylor was still so deep in thought that she never noticed. When she raised her eyes, she felt more bewilderment, had more questions. A middle-aged woman was standing there, who began to smile kindly at her.

"I know you're very confused, but I can assure you that everything will be quite all right."

For a moment Taylor, still immersed in her recent past, thought the woman had somehow sensed what was on her mind.

"How do you know?" she questioned blankly.

The other woman laughed. "There's no problem that can't be solved sooner or later. If you'll come with me, someone will see you now. Have you got the keys to your luggage?"

Taylor took the keys from her purse and silently handed them over, hoping the solutions would come soon. In more ways than one, she'd waited long enough.

"You still have to pass Customs, but while you're being interviewed, we'll take care of it here. Just leave your things."

The woman was friendly and reassuring, but Taylor knew that all her instructions were to be obeyed—and she wasn't reassured at all. She stood up and lifted her chin.

"I really think there's some kind of mistake."

"That's entirely possible. Now come along."

Taylor, taking her purse and the wrapped parcel, left the room behind the other woman. Again there was a maze of halls and doors, until they stopped in front of yet another office. All of this shifting from room to room finally brought Taylor to the breaking point. When she was ushered inside, her eyes were gleaming with impatience, and her mouth was a firm, closed line of suppressed anger. The door closed softly behind her, and Taylor found herself facing a huge desk; a man was seated behind it. He more or less lounged in the chair and didn't look as though he was conducting business. There was a window behind him, so the weak winter light it admitted put Taylor at a disadvantage; she couldn't see his face. But that didn't stop her.

"Look, this is ridiculous," she began. Her voice was strong and clear, but she kept her tone even and low. She was not often given to losing her temper, and even then she never yelled.

"It's almost eight-thirty in the morning. I haven't been here two hours yet, and already I've walked miles in this terminal and seen more gray rooms than I want to.

"It was an exhausting flight, and the man next to me snored. I'd love a bath and change of clothes and something other than airline food. I haven't been to England in almost three and a half years, so I can't imagine how I've managed to get into trouble in just a few hours."

Having gotten her angst off her chest, which was heaving slightly with indignation, Taylor met with only silence.

Then very slowly the man moved and, with the stealth of an animal, stood up to face Taylor across the desk. He was very tall, or maybe just seemed to be because she wasn't. Five feet, four inches usually put her at a disadvantage with other adults. She'd never allowed that to intimidate her before, but somehow didn't feel on an equal footing with this man. She couldn't see his eyes, because they were shrouded behind dark glasses. He gestured toward the chair in front of the desk.

"Won't you sit down? It's Mr. Hillard you want to complain to, I'm afraid. Not me."

Taylor could only stare, somewhat hypnotized. His voice was deep and quiet and gravelly in texture, as if he were hoarse all the time. His quiet response made Taylor feel a little foolish, and she blushed. The man before her did not identify himself, but walked away from the desk as Taylor took her seat. Her eyes followed him, and it was then that she saw the other man, who was pulling papers from a file cabinet. The man with the dark glasses silently took a chair off to Taylor's right, almost out of range of her vision. The second man closed the file cabinet and sat down heavily at the desk.

"Your passport's expired," said the pleasantly modulated voice of the man in front of her, apparently ignoring her outburst of a moment ago. Given his announcement, it seemed insignificant, she reflected.

Taylor looked completely blank for a moment, then her anger dissipated.

"What?" she whispered.

In his forties, and graying, the man was dressed in a neat dark suit, but he didn't look very comfortable in it. He eased his large frame forward to lean on the desk to study some papers, including her passport, which lay on top. Taylor waited stiffly for him to speak again.

There wasn't any other sound in the room, so Taylor slowly turned her head to the right and looked cautiously at the man seated in the leather chair. He was very still and seemed to be watching what was happening between the official and herself. But Taylor couldn't tell for sure because of his glasses. She resented the idea that he might be watching her now, recognizing that in another way this man was much more imposing than the one at the desk. She felt her eyes widen in fascination. The ankle of his right leg rested on the knee of the left. One arm was negligently draped along the low back of the chair. The other hand, the right one, large and long-fingered, hung over the end of the armrest. Taylor's eyes were drawn to the puckered skin on the back of the hand, and to the movement of the fingers as he rhythmically squeezed a small leather ball.

The sight of that strong hand held Taylor's attention, and then she raised her gaze to his face. It was long and strongly chiseled. Hard-planed features with a prominent square chin. His nose was long, almost aquiline, the mouth wide and well shaped. His hair was very dark, combed back from his forehead, with a slight tendency to wave. It was a hard, imposing face. Cold. Taylor felt a curious chill of uncertainty wash over her. He was dressed in a black turtleneck sweater and dark gray slacks. He also wore a dark brown leather jacket. Everything about him seemed dark, secretive, and except for the flexing of his one hand, he didn't move at all. But Taylor found herself blushing, because she sensed that he was watching her very carefully.

"I'm Roger Hillard. I'm in charge of Immigration at Heathrow. What is your name, please?"

Taylor reluctantly turned her attention back to the official.

"You have it there on my passport," she said with a frown.

Mr. Hillard looked at her quietly for just a moment and gave a slight smile. "I'd like you to tell me, anyway."

Taylor dropped her gaze to her hands, feeling her insides begin to churn. It was a completely benign question, but it suddenly seemed impossible to give an answer. As a matter of fact, she wasn't sure what her name was...or should be. She was acutely aware of the man to her right. She had no idea who he was or what part he was playing in this little encounter, but she didn't want him to hear her make a fool of herself, as she knew she was about to.

"It's—it's Taylor Evans," she answered tonelessly.

Mr. Hillard raised his brows at her evident reluctance and wrote something on a form in front of him.

"You said my passport is expired?" Taylor questioned.

"You told the agent that it's been some three years since you were last here?"

Taylor nodded. "That's right."

Mr. Hillard lifted the passport, looked at it, then at Taylor. Holding it up, his large fingers deftly flipped it around to show her the opening page.

"Who's Taylor Ashe?"

She felt the color drain from her face and twisted her hands together.

"I am," she replied softly.

Mr. Hillard arched a brow and waited. Taylor tried to ignore the silent man to her right.

"Ashe is my—my maiden name," Taylor added.

"Your maiden name, hmm?" Mr. Hillard repeated in a skeptical tone.

Taylor raised her chin defensively. It really was very simple, but not so simple to explain all the details, and she didn't want to.

"I have another passport. It's in my...under Evans. I guess I just took the wrong folder. I was in such a rush," she added when Mr. Hillard sat back in his chair and regarded her with heavy speculation.

"Have you been married long?" Again Taylor blushed. Another difficult question. She swept a hand nervously through her dark hair and took a deep breath.

"No." Her voice was barely audible.

"I beg your pardon?" Mr. Hillard leaned forward slightly, forcing Taylor to look directly at him and answer again.

"I said no. I haven't been...long."

Mr. Hillard was again writing on the long form. "You realize that you cannot enter the country without a valid passport, no matter which name you're using."

The full implications of her plight hit Taylor. She'd planned and waited so long, had endured a miserable, restless night, months of planning, what had seemed like endless years of waiting....

"Oh, but..." Taylor stopped and swallowed. How could she make him understand? Again she hazarded a look to the right. The other man was slowly beginning to straighten and sit forward, so silently that he might have been an apparition. He bent forward until his forearms were balanced against his spread knees; his hands gently tossed the leather ball back and forth. The leather jacket was pulled taut across his shoulders.

Taylor took a breath. She wasn't going to be intimidated. Not anymore. She turned to face Roger Hillard once again. "I'm here on business. I was asked to deliver firsthand several rare books from an auction house in New York."

Taylor opened her purse and pulled out an envelope. She passed it to the official.

The envelope bore the imprint Strafford House and gave a lower Fifth Avenue address. He withdrew several sheets of paper—a cover letter, a pink receipt and looked them over.

"I work in the antiquarian book division. I do repairs and restoration on books and documents. The purchaser is here in London. His name is Philip Mayhew Johns. I believe he's a banker," Taylor said.

"Your company sends you to deliver books by hand? A bit much, isn't it?"

"Well, the books are very valuable and need to be handled carefully. The postal services aren't known for their delicacy in handling fragile parcels."

He nodded, making notes, and then looked quickly at the other man. Nothing was said between them, but Taylor got the distinct impression that something had been communicated.

"How many trips have you made for your company?"

"Only three. This is my third trip here."

"Mmm," Roger Hillard said vaguely. "Why none in the last three years or more?"

Taylor stared at him for a moment. "I got married. And..."

She saw him look at her for a moment, clearly assessing the hesitancy, detecting the flush in her face. "Did your husband not want you to travel?" he inquired.

"Yes...that's right." She nodded, but didn't meet his direct, questioning gaze.

He silently reached across the desk, and after a moment Taylor handed him the brown-wrapped package. He pulled the cord and the wrappings fell away.

"Original?" he asked as he lifted the first volume with its rich leather corners, heavily corded and gold-embossed on the spine. The lettering read Charles Dickens, *The Life and Adventures of Martin Chuzzlewit*.

Taylor shook her head. "A second issue of the first edition. It sold for $4,500."

He put the book down. "Why did your husband change his mind about you traveling?"

Taylor conceded that this man was very good at his job. She wondered how many people had tried to lie to him...and succeeded. She didn't try. She simply didn't tell him everything.

"I...needed my job," Taylor responded evasively. "I made the decision to return to work."

"And your husband didn't object?"

Taylor hesitated. "No, he didn't."

Roger Hillard appeared to consider Taylor's response and lifted the form on which he'd been writing.

"There's still the invalid passport. Bit of a problem, I'm afraid."

"Isn't there something I can do?" Taylor asked anxiously, suddenly afraid he would simply put her on the next plane back to the States.

He nodded, rocking his chair back on its springs. "Actually there is. I could contact the American consulate in town to begin processing a new passport for you."

"Oh, thank you."

"In the meantime, perhaps we can get some information verified. I assume your husband is not traveling with you?"

Taylor shook her head.

"Then we'll have to phone him long-distance and—"

"That's not possible," Taylor said softly. "He won't be there."

There was an awful silence in the room again. She knew she had to explain, and her mind, still fogged for want of a good night's sleep, tried to test all the possible answers. There were too many to even count, so she made it simple.

"My husband and I are separated," she said clearly and in a flat tone.

"I see," Mr. Hillard commented dryly.

Taylor looked at him quickly. *No, you don't,* her eyes said, *because even I don't see.*

"It's the middle of the night in the States, so there's not much to be done for a few hours. In the meantime, we'll contact the consulate and get things going from this end.

"I'll need to see any other identification you have. Was someone to meet you here?"

"No. I don't know anyone here. I'm just to deliver the books and—" She stopped.

She saw Roger Hillard look at her sharply. "And what?"

"And...finish the business transaction and return home."

He nodded and slowly stood up. "Well, I'm afraid you're stuck here for a while. We'll put you in a lounge and try to make you comfortable. There's a sofa. Perhaps you can catch up on sleep. I'll have your luggage brought in to you."

"How long do you think it will take?" Taylor asked anxiously.

"Can't say, really. Depends on the information we receive from the States, whether it corroborates what you've told me. We'll have the passport agency in New York fax a copy of your application, but all this takes time."

Taylor nodded tiredly and rubbed her temples. She stood as Mr. Hillard came around the desk. She turned in the other direction, only to find that the other man was on his feet as well, a short distance away.

He wasn't as tall as the immigration official, but she still had to look up into his hard-edged face. His dark hair was a little long, touching the collar of his leather jacket. Although it was smoothly combed, there was a sense of subdued wildness about him, some energy and force that seemed to be held in check. And there was an odd sense of calm about his presence that made Taylor feel for a quick moment that somehow everything was going to work out.

"Come with me, Mrs. Evans. I'll take you to the lounge."

Taylor winced slightly at being called Mrs. Evans, and with a final curious glance at the silent stranger, turned back to the official and nodded.

"I can promise you it won't be another gray room."

"Oh, the books—"

"Leave them for now. I'll rewrap them and bring them in."

They left his office, and a casual glance over her shoulder showed Taylor that the second man had not followed; she felt disappointed. But there was no time to pursue the matter. Another door was opened, to yet another room that was more comfortable than the first. It held a long sofa and a chrome-and-glass coffee table. There were several comfortable chairs, a few reading lamps and a round table near the one window, with an electric coffee maker and fresh water for instant coffee or tea.

"The loo is through that door. I'll have your baggage brought round." He looked about him. "It won't be so bad here."

"Yes, it will," Taylor said with a sigh of resignation. She saw Roger Hillard raise his brows; was he hiding a smile? she wondered.

"I'll be back later," he said, and left.

Taylor stared at the closed door. Another thought occurred to her. Supposing he'd locked the door? With a strong sense that the beginning of her trip did not bode well for the rest of it, Taylor carelessly dropped her white winter coat over the arm of a chair and put her bag onto the coffee table.

The room was not particularly warm, and she hugged herself, rubbing her arms briskly as she slowly wandered over to the window. It was busy outside; the operations of the large metropolitan airport were in full swing. She watched the hurried coming and going of people just beginning on a trip or just ending one. There were expectant looks, as hundreds of eyes searched the crowd for the comforting familiar faces of family or friends. Taylor stared blindly, remembering the day when she had last waited for a plane to arrive, and a particular passenger to disembark.

Michael had not been on that plane, or any other arriving from Europe that day. Or the next. Or even the day after that. Just as frightening had been the information that Michael Evans was not listed on any of the passenger rosters for any airline making the trip from London into New York that August three years ago. Yet the real panic had only set in when Taylor realized how little she actually knew about Michael Evans, who'd come in and gone out of her life like a gust of summer wind.

In her purse was a manila envelope that contained all the information she had; it was an embarrassing collection of mismatched data on the man she had hastily married against the advice of her overprotective family.

Taylor wasn't sure where he was from, although it was in London that they'd met during her last courier trip three years ago. She wasn't sure what his business was, although he apparently had something to do with stocks and bonds and financially did very well. She didn't know where he stayed when he traveled, but he seemed to have no permanent home in the United States. He would only say he was originally from Illinois, and Taylor didn't even know if he had family there.

She only really knew that from the moment she'd walked into Bolton's Antiquarian Book Store, where it was apparent that he was acquainted with the manager, he'd cheerfully pursued her, all the way back to New York.

Michael traveled a great deal and to many different places, and there never seemed to be a connection between one trip and another. Taylor also had to admit that she never exactly knew where he traveled to or with whom. He wired her flowers, called her constantly at work, at home in the middle of the night. He'd show up unexpectedly in New York to overwhelm her with his attention, with his laughter and constant good cheer, never sitting still for long, flitting around her, sweeping Taylor into a whirlwind courtship that didn't allow her to think. She had been kept breathless, busy, excited, off balance, flattered by the sheer force of Michael's personality, which was always on. She knew he was fun to be with—but that was all she knew.

Taylor recalled with renewed amazement that there had never been a chance that was "right" for him to meet her parents or two older brothers. There had never seemed to be enough time together to just sit and talk. Michael had always avoided talking about himself. Even after four months that could now best be described as mere fun and games, Taylor had been nonplussed to try to describe their relationship. It had been an effervescent thing, cloaked in defiance on her part and physical attraction on his; strong enough to make picky details like love, commitment or stability seem unimportant.

Then he'd wanted to get married, and Taylor couldn't remember if she'd ever thought about saying no. Michael had insisted on a civil wedding, and it had been fast. She remembered her disappointment that he didn't want to wait until her family could be part of the occasion. No time to dream or plan, not even to shop or celebrate afterward. There'd been no honeymoon. Her wedding band had been an extravagant confection of a string of diamonds along the top surface of a gold band, and it was the sole memento she had of the occasion.

It was only after they'd settled into her small apartment in Riverdale, just north of New York City, that she realized how few possessions Michael seemed to have of his own. He dressed well and expensively, but didn't have a lot of clothing. And when he traveled on business, which he still seemed to do with frequency, he took everything with him. When he was away, Taylor used to feel that she wasn't really married at all. Other than her wedding ring and the license, there was no evidence to show that she was. She had no wedding pictures and no photograph of Michael. She never knew where to reach him if she had to, although he would call her when she least expected.

Taylor had told Roger Hillard the truth about Michael not wanting her to act as courier for Strafford House after they'd married. He'd been insistent on that, although he'd never said why. It had been easy to agree. Her romantic mind had reasoned that he didn't want to be separated from her. Taylor frowned deeply as she stared out the lounge window. How was it the reasoning hadn't worked when applied to his frequent trips away? But by the time the mists of first love had cleared, Taylor had realized that her marriage to Michael Evans was not a real marriage at all. Very likely it had also been a costly mistake.

What Taylor remembered most about those seven months of knowing Michael Evans, three of which had been as his wife, was that she knew no more about him when he'd kissed her goodbye and left on his last trip than on the first day she met him.

When Michael never returned, never communicated again, when he had in essence disappeared, Taylor had been forced, rather hysterically at the time, to admit to a grave error in basic common sense. Yet she'd continued to wait, because after a while she'd had no choice. Life had become more complicated than she'd believed possible. Taylor sighed, and feeling suddenly very alone, made her way to a chair and sat down. In a way she wished that she hadn't decided to make the trip. She already missed her family and wanted the peace of love she was sure of. And she was afraid of what she might learn. She didn't want to consider the past, as she'd done endlessly and to no avail, but the present—and the future. This trip was important, because it would change her future. It had to.

In the meantime, she would sit through this minor interruption of her plans and wait—she was very good at waiting—again.

THE MAN with dark glasses stared thoughtfully at the door after it had closed. He silently slipped the leather ball into his trouser pocket and half sat on the edge of Roger Hillard's desk, a liberty virtually no one else would have been allowed. He found himself momentarily caught up in the little drama that had just been played out.

Dane Farrow had spent more years of his life than he cared to remember observing people, places and things; events, situations, dramas large and small. Being alert had become a business, and it had saved his life more than once. What he'd just observed, something thoroughly mundane by anyone else's standard, was a very scared young woman, and one who was also confused. It was a terrible combination. Fright and confusion invariably got people into trouble.

With a wry twist of his mouth he thought to himself that she was too little, too fragile to be of trouble to anyone, or even to get into trouble herself. But Dane knew, also from his learned experience, that looks were generally deceiving.

One thing he would agree on was looks. Taylor Ashe Evans had them. She was pretty, but in a way that came to you after a moment or two. It was subtle, low-key, understated. She had thick dark hair that was nearly as black as his own. If he had to guess, he'd say her eyes were probably gray. He'd had some experience with women, afterall.

Dane reached for the stack of unwrapped books as he returned to his review of Taylor, making a note of things about her that no one else would pay attention to, like the fact that her nose was a bit short and her chin dimpled when she talked. She was less than average in height and very lithe in her mauve sweater and dark slacks, feminine and soft. She'd be a feather in someone's arms. But other things struck him about Mrs. Evans. One was whether or not she *really* was Mrs. Evans. She wore no wedding ring, and she was decidedly nervous about any mention of her married state. It was clearly not something she wanted to talk about. He also found it odd to use a courier to deliver simple rare books. There were few things in the world so precious that they needed to be shipped with an escort.

A quick examination of the books showed nothing unusual in their appearance. Dane had no qualms about reaching then for the papers that Taylor Evans had given to Roger. There was a cover letter accompanied by a list of more rare book titles and a pink invoice with a duplicate. Dane read it carefully; it was an itemized list of the parcel with a complete description of the condition of each book, giving its history and the price that had been agreed upon. Dane carefully reached over the desk and placed the receipt under an ultraviolet lamp normally used to detect counterfeit money. He read the receipt again.

The door opened and Roger came in, closing it behind him.

"I'm going to go mental in this job. First thing in the morning, and I've got an invalid passport to deal with. Certainly not like the old days, eh, Hawk?"

Dane looked at his friend as Roger reseated himself heavily with a sigh. Dane arched a corner of his mouth.

"No, it isn't. But it's a lot safer job, and it probably makes Ann very happy to know where you are every day," Dane assured him. His voice was still low, with that rough rasp. An act of war had changed it years ago.

"Yes, marriage does put a damper on things."

Dane took one more look at the invoice and replaced it in its envelope. "I hope you're not complaining. You were ready to be changed. The world is changed. There's no place for people like us anymore."

"Oh, I know, I know. It's a damn shame, Hawk, but you know, I loved it. I loved being right in the middle of hell. But..."

Roger leaned back in his chair and patted a middle that was still tightly muscled from years of physical work. "I guess we're too soft now."

Dane grunted, hiding his warm affection behind the dark glasses. "Speak for yourself."

Roger shifted the papers on the desk indifferently. "Still, how the mighty have fallen. This is a far cry from freeing hostages and overturning corrupt Third World governments."

"For you it was good training for Her Majesty's work. And the pay is regular. That alone is a novelty," Dane said wryly.

Roger grew thoughtful. "I hope I haven't made a mistake getting involved with someone like Ann. She's so gentle. And I'm such a lout."

Dane regarded his friend. "That's true, you are a lout. But Ann doesn't think so, obviously."

"Then I hope *she* hasn't made a mistake," Roger growled at Dane.

For a peculiar moment Dane thought of Taylor's strange interview of just a moment ago. She was cautious—and frightened. He wondered what mistakes she'd made?

Roger suddenly sat forward, his thoughts apparently overlapping with Dane's. He looked at Taylor's passport and frowned. "Taylor. Unlikely name for a woman."

Dane pursed his lips. "We Americans are peculiar that way."

Roger shook his head and chuckled. "I can't believe she traveled with an expired passport. Why didn't she check first?"

Dane slowly got up from his perch on the edge of the desk and wandered to the window to look out.

"I think she has other things on her mind."

"Probably running from her husband. Maybe he used to beat her," Roger said flippantly.

Dane narrowed his eyes. He had a vision of Taylor's delicate body, her face with its large, appealing eyes turned to him in open curiosity and embarrassment just a while ago.

"I hope not," he said softly.

"Well, the consulate will get right on it. Probably have everything ready by this afternoon, late. Which reminds me, I have to get her signature on this form, and get it to Ellen Townsend. . . ." He pulled the form from a pile of other papers, then quickly rewrapped the parcel of books.

Dane idly walked back to the front of the desk.

"So. You haven't said whether you'll come for dinner tonight. Ann's expecting you. I think she wants to pry from you stories about my sordid past."

"The list is long and distinguished," Dane quipped. "Thank Ann for me. What time?"

The phone began to ring. "Eight would be good," Roger said, reaching for the phone.

Dane easily lifted the form and pack of books. "Can I lend a hand with this?" Already he was heading smoothly toward the door.

Roger nodded, his eyes curious but indicating consent, "Hillard here," he spoke into the phone.

THE DOOR TO THE LOUNGE opened after a soft knock. Taylor turned her head hopefully at the sound, and was utterly surprised to find the silent stranger in the doorway. He was carrying the rare books. She felt her stomach tighten in some sort of odd alarm. Taylor stood quickly, but found that the additional height gave her no advantage at all. They simply looked at each other for several seconds. Taylor could only feel rather small, and she wondered if her sense of intimidation was based on his hard face, which was not handsome, but strongly masculine, or on his silence. Confronted by his appraising silence, she could not gain any leverage, but she tried to stand taller.

"Are you . . . Mr. Hillard's assistant?" she asked in a calm, low voice.

"My name is Dane Farrow, and I'm only his friend."

"Oh," Taylor whispered absently, mesmerized by the strange texture of his voice; its tone had a near-caressing quality. Then Taylor became indignant. "You mean . . . then why did you—?"

"Sit and listen to the personal details in your interview? I'm discreet," Dane said calmly, with a hint of amusement in his voice. "I won't tell anyone."

Taylor was so surprised by his answer that she could only stare foolishly. Then she blinked and gently took the books from his large hand.

"I'm Taylor—"

"I know. Ashe or Evans."

She looked to see if he was making fun of her, but couldn't tell again because his gaze was hidden. She smiled uncertainly, turning away to hide her confusion.

"You needn't be embarrassed with me. My opinion doesn't count, you know."

"But you do have one, don't you?" she inquired. Dane merely slid his hands into his pockets and didn't reply.

Taylor absently ran her hands through her hair and sighed. "Never mind. I'm sure I must have seemed very foolish."

"I've felt that way once or twice," Dane offered, his eyes following her nervous motions.

Taylor quirked her mouth wryly. "Somehow I don't believe that."

Dane was struck by how quickly she'd adjusted to the circumstances. No tantrums, insults or threats. No sighs or grimaces of suffering or inconvenience. He found himself paying more attention to her, and decided that she had clear features and a beautiful mouth.

Feeling his scrutiny, Taylor fiddled with the package and walked to place it on the table.

"Thank you for returning the books."

Dane merely inclined his head. He slowly pulled the form from his pocket.

"I believe Mr. Hillard needs your signature on this form."

"Oh . . . yes," Taylor said, hurrying to her purse for a pen. Dane handed her the paper and watched her bend her head as she scanned the form. Her hair, swept back off her forehead, fell forward on one side, to the left, and when Taylor lifted her head, dark locks framed her face in a suddenly alluring sexy fashion. The momentary change drew Dane's attention as Taylor absently swept the hair back in place.

"I can have someone bring you fresh coffee," he began.

Taylor shook her head. "That's all right. I've caused enough trouble. I can make coffee myself here."

"Would you like a sweet bun or something?" Dane inquired politely.

Taylor laughed softly. "All right. I *am* hungry." She fingered the form and Dane watched her frown, knowing why she hesitated.

"What's it to be?" he asked smoothly. "Ashe or Evans?"

Taylor's frown deepened, and she blinked at him in indecision. Finally she crossed to the table and bent to quickly sign her name. She turned and retraced her steps to Dane and handed him the form.

"Ashe," she said with finality.

## Chapter Two

"Darling, are you sure you're okay? We don't have to make a fuss for Hawk. He's practically family, you know."

Dane stood at the window again. Not because there was anything to see in the twilight, but because old habits were hard to break. He liked to know what was going on around him. He was also listening to the quiet, intimate exchange taking place between Roger and his wife, Ann. Dane's jaw muscle flexed tightly, and he slid his right hand into his pocket to close around the leather ball.

"Don't worry. He's going to hang around a few more days. You'll have lots of time to charm him." Roger chuckled softly at his wife's response.

Dane worked his fingers around the leather object. His hand still had a tendency to stiffen and the drawn skin along his forearm to tighten stubbornly.

"Of course I worry about you, love."

The endearment made Dane restless and he silently moved from the window to the wall left of Roger's desk. There were three photographs hanging there. One was of a monarch being greeted by the British prime minister, after the Asian leader had been saved from a bloody coup. In the background stood Roger and Dane among the military brass. People often wondered why that particular picture hung in Roger's office. He and Dane were physically different men then and now, and their presence went undetected.

A second picture showed Roger and Ann on their wedding day a mere eighteen months ago. She was an ethereal blonde, over whom Roger protectively towered as rice was being thrown by well-wishers, just as he'd actually had to protect her when she'd been kidnapped two years earlier. Dane hadn't been involved in that adventure, having been off on one of his own in South America, but it had been Roger's last. He'd found in Ann a more sensible reason not to risk his life for adventure or money.

Dane knew that Roger had fought long and hard against becoming involved with Ann. But Roger was to find out, as Dane had many years before, that the heart has its reasons, which reason cannot know. Ann's father, a wealthy banker, although grateful for the safe return of his only daughter, had been nonetheless reluctant to then turn her over to a man of Roger's ilk. A man for hire, a vagabond. Intelligent and shrewd, yes, but also with a violent past. But true love had won out.

"I should be leaving here shortly. Can I bring you anything?" There was a pause, then Roger answered caressingly, "Just me, eh? Would you turn away flowers?"

Dane allowed himself a small private smile that held both envy and sadness. And amusement. He couldn't visualize Roger buying a bouquet of flowers. But this was what love did to people and what love probably sounded like. Talk of flowers, low, whispering voices—promises to come home.

The third picture showed a parade of marchers celebrating after a civil revolution had ended. Weary fighters were being mobbed by allies and grateful citizens. Dane and Roger were again almost unnoticeable. That had been the year they'd first met and playfully fought over a French hellion named Madeleine, daughter of a local diplomat who thought being in a war zone was exciting. In the photo Dane had an arm around the shoulders of the tall redhead. She was trying to keep the overexuberant crowd from bumping into Dane's wounded shoulder, which was swathed in a bloodied cloth.

Dane stared hard at the picture. He didn't have a copy of it himself. In any case Madeleine, not being the least bit sentimental, would have said it was silly to keep things from the past, while fighting so hard to change things for the future. But Dane realized with an arching of his dark brow that he had no image of the girl who'd been his wife, other than the ones he carried in his memories. They were the only ones he wanted. It had been reckless to marry in the middle of a war, in the middle of a country he didn't know. But then, war made people reckless. Dane recalled that Maddy hadn't wanted to get married at all. She'd argued very persuasively that they could all be dead in a week. But Dane had believed in the tradition of marriage, because marriage meant hope and a future. The issue had grown cloudy, her argument weak during a month-long cease-fire somewhere in North Africa, and they'd been married. It had been a drunken, wild affair with the bride and groom dressed in fatigues and holding their guns, surrounded by strangers they barely understood.

But they'd understood each other, had believed fervently in the same causes, had been fearless, idealistic— so young and invincible. They'd loved as hard as they fought, and had it not been for the loneliness of war and the sense of urgency, of living from moment to moment, they might never have come together at all. Still, the commitment of marriage had played havoc with Dane Farrow in the most unexpected ways. First of all, he'd lost his edge. Not that he was any less astute—just more cautious. But being cautious required thinking, and thinking cut into one's response time. A moment to think could be a moment in which someone died.

Dane had wanted to send Madeleine back to France and to her family, who would watch out for her until he himself could return to her. Maddy had refused to obey. He knew it was selfish to have her follow him from town to town, to live under hideous conditions. But there had been a youthful exhilaration, a joie de vivre that had been spontaneous and wonderful between them.

Then things got worse before they began to get better, and tragedy struck. Their little band of rebellious guerrilla fighters was living in an abandoned prison. It had been checked for booby traps, but not carefully enough. Not before Dane, forcing a stubborn door to open, had inadvertently tripped one, killing four comrades, including Maddy. He had suffered extensive burns on one arm, belatedly raised to protect his face; he'd suffered temporary blindness, and received a gaping wound in his throat from fragments and debris. It would be almost five months before he'd recovered sufficiently to leave a crude, makeshift hospital and be transported to a real one for better medical care.

Dane looked at the picture once more, then turned away. He recalled that upon reaching Tunisia after the explosion, he should have been enjoying the first two months of parenthood. Madeleine had been six months pregnant when she'd died.

"Nonetheless, you have Mrs. Hamilton move that chair for you. I don't want you lifting anything, do you hear?" Another pause, and then Roger chuckled deep in his throat. "I love you, too. See you soon."

Roger hung up and looked half over his shoulder at his friend. He knew the history of each of the pictures on the wall as well as Dane. Much of it had happened a long time ago, and they never talked about it, in any case. But Roger remembered Maddy. He cleared his throat.

"Sorry, Hawk. Did I sound like a complete fool?" he asked with no sense of embarrassment.

Dane turned to face him, his expression smooth and masked.

"You sound like a man in love with his wife. Why don't you go home?"

Roger looked at his watch. "Yes, it's about that time. But there's still Mrs. Evans, isn't there? Mustn't forget about her." He picked up his phone, pressed a button, and spoke with authority to someone on the other end.

Dane hadn't forgotten her. After getting her signature on the new passport application, he'd returned twenty minutes later with a bag of muffins he'd secured from the terminal commissary. He had enjoyed studying her quiet pleasure at having something to eat, offering to share it with him. Dane had declined, leaving her again, wondering with amazement why he'd never met anyone like her before—someone young, attractive and apparently uncynical—someone who was normal and who lived at ease with the world.

After hanging up for a second time, Roger turned once more to Dane.

"Pretty boring day for you. You didn't need to hang around, just because I couldn't get away."

Dane ambled around to the front of the desk. The fringes of his mind were still somewhere in the past, but he smiled slightly at his friend, raising his brows over the frames of the tinted lenses. "I missed your wedding and I haven't seen you in eighteen months. Today was time well spent. Was I in the way?"

"Not at all. I just thought you might have had business to see to."

Dane put his hands into his pockets, pinning his leather jacket open.

"It can wait."

A young woman walked quietly into the office and briskly approached Roger's desk with an envelope.

"Here are the papers, Mr. Hillard. Everything seems to be in order."

"Thank you," he murmured absently as she left. Roger frowned over the crisp new passport. "You know there's more here than meets the eye, Hawk. I wonder what Taylor Evans, or whatever her name is, is up to? She's an awfully nervous woman."

Dane slowly leaned over until his hands were braced on the desk in front of Roger. He gave him a lopsided grin. "And I was worried that you'd lost your touch."

Roger gave him a look of disgust. "I'm only in love, Hawk, not dead from the neck up. I still know a tall tale when I hear one."

Dane lifted the envelope from Roger's hand.

"That's good. Do you mind?"

"I don't know. What do *you* have in mind?"

Dane stood straight. "I'm not sure," he said.

"I don't think it's worth the time. I still think Taylor Evans is an unhappy wife with domestic problems. That's none of our business. I admit I'm curious about the courier thing, but...I'll just have a routine check run on

her and her company on Monday morning. In the meantime, I'm letting her go."

"I think she's in trouble, Roger. But I don't think she
knows it."

Roger frowned. "Hell, Dane. *You* don't know what it
is, either. Why get involved?"

Dane shrugged negligently. "I'm just curious. I think
I'll drive her into London."

"Dammit, Hawk. Those days of intuitive guesswork
and sniffing out trouble are over. We're getting too old
for this." Dane didn't respond, and didn't seem moved
by Roger's sudden statement. Roger looked at Dane and
sighed. "Okay, okay... She's not bad. A little young and
a little small. But she's not your type."

Dane's shadowed gaze fell to the envelope in his hand.
His jaw worked, and he swiftly put the memory of
Madeleine aside.

"I don't have a type," he said in his rough voice. "I'll
see you at eight."

Dane turned toward the door and Roger, who trusted
him implicitly and knew him better than almost anyone,
suddenly sat forward over his desk.

"Hawk?"

Dane stopped at the door and looked at Roger. Very
slowly a knowing smile covered Roger's mouth.

"Her eyes are gray. Like smoke."

Dane nodded. "I know."

Roger grimaced. "I might have guessed you would."

THERE WAS no answer when Dane knocked once again on
the lounge door and slowly entered. He spotted Taylor
fast asleep huddled in a corner of the slightly dilapidated sofa, her winter coat used as covering. Her head

was tilted back against the cushions, exposing the smooth skin under her chin. Her long, thick lashes lay feathered against her upper cheek and her mouth, full and well shaped, was sensually relaxed, not tight and nervous as it had been this afternoon.

Dane came quietly into the room and stood looking down at Taylor. He knew Roger was right. Something highly personal and domestic was happening in her life that was beyond his business or understanding. But his instincts, honed over years of being able to detect trouble, told him that Taylor was in the midst of confusion, anger and hurt, all of which she'd tried to keep to herself this afternoon. She had not been successful, at least as far as Dane was concerned, because her eyes were a dead giveaway. She didn't know how to control their expression, and they were a virtual mirror of her mind and heart. She didn't have much experience in the world—and it showed.

Dane was just as interested, however, in her business reasons for being in London. Roger had said he was a little suspicious, too, but he had not been as careful in looking over Taylor's papers. For that Roger could be forgiven.

The "normal" job he'd angled for after having married Ann *was* routine and boring, and it *was* a far cry from the dangerous excitement he and Roger had known together for some fifteen years. But at least Her Majesty had recognized Roger's many years of service and taken proper care of one of her own. And even if Roger had noticed that the pink sales invoice contained some sort of code, he would have turned over the case to some indifferent, heavy-handed assistant who wouldn't believe, as Dane believed, that Taylor knew nothing about it—that in some peculiar way she was being used.

Dane stood watching her, thinking that she was probably the kind of woman a man would have to be careful
with. Gentle. Alert to her feelings, so as not to hurt her.
Dane himself admitted he didn't know much about
gentleness. It didn't fit into his prerequisites for sur-
vival. His relationship to Madeleine had never been
gentle.

Dane quietly removed his dark glasses and accepted the
momentary painful adjustment to the fluorescent lamp-
light. He'd been right about Taylor's hair being so dark
that it was almost black, like the finely arched lines of her
brows. There was still something very youthful about the
way she slept, a kind of careless abandon in the bend of
her head. Dane's eyes roamed freely over her features.

Sometimes he regretted his ability to so thoroughly
analyze a situation or a person. He was usually fright-
eningly accurate. It was a trait that had long ago led Roger and others to nickname him Hawk. It also meant that
he'd sometimes find himself knowingly pursuing some
circumstance he would have been well-advised to stay
away from. Dane sensed it now so strongly that it made
him tighten the hard line of his mouth even more grimly
and thoughtfully narrow his deep-set eyes. Taylor Ashe
Evans was going to need someone to help her. But she
was a married woman and that helper should be her husband, Dane reflected, whoever and wherever he was. And
assuming he wasn't the problem.

Dane crouched in front of Taylor as she slept. There
was a feminine delicacy about her, but also a sense of
determination as strong as that streak of independence
she'd shown in Roger's office. Dane liked that. He
looked down at the slender left hand that lay exposed and
limp over her lap. There was not even a hint that she'd
worn a wedding ring; no telltale band of pale flesh. He

lifted his gaze once more to her face. Slowly, with a kind of unconscious but natural curiosity, Dane put out his scarred hand and used the backs of two fingers to gently stroke along Taylor's chin, her jaw, along the short distance of her exposed neck to the top of her soft sweater. Before his movement was finished, Taylor was slowly turning her head toward the hand and its silky touch.

Dane saw her lashes flutter and saw the hint of a smile change her mouth. In one graceful, fluid motion he stood straight and replaced the glasses. Taylor opened her eyes.

It felt eerie, but not threatening to open her eyes and find Dane quietly watching her. They stared at each other for a moment, and Taylor felt an instant attraction that was so brief, she suspected the feeling was the languishing tail end of her dream. Still, she sensed that something was different and wondered how long Dane Farrow had been standing over her—and why. She sat up quickly, scrambling from under her now-crushed winter coat.

She began blushing as she swung her feet to the floor and pushed her dark hair from her face with a sweep of her hands.

"I . . . guess I fell asleep," she murmured.

Dane lightly tapped the papers he held against his leg. "You probably needed the rest. Especially if you had someone snoring next to you on the flight," he said easily.

Taylor bit her lip and nodded, stifling a yawn. Then halfway through it she gasped, her eyes flying open in obvious mortification.

"I wasn't snoring . . . was I?" she asked quietly. Dane watched her expression for a moment, and a slight smile lifted a corner of his mouth. He refrained from telling her that in sleep she was charming. "No. You didn't snore."

She noticeably relaxed and glanced quickly at Dane as she searched for her shoes. "What time is it?"

Dane slowly bent, retrieved her low-heeled pumps from the floor at the end of the sofa, and silently handed them to her.

"A little after five," he answered, watching openly as she attempted to put herself to rights.

Taylor looked up at him in consternation, then quickly to the darkened window behind Dane.

"It's so late. It's already dark."

Dane walked to her and handed her an envelope of papers. Taylor gave him a quick look before accepting them.

"You'll be in London in time for dinner."

After hesitating for a moment, Taylor opened the new passport that had been issued to Taylor Ashe. She felt a quiver in her stomach. Step by step she was making decisions that were giving her back control of her life.

"Thank you," she whispered, but there was a despondency to it that surprised Dane. She moved to the table to place the documents in her purse.

As she walked past Dane, he realized that she barely reached his shoulder. He also caught a faint whiff of her perfume. His nostrils flared at the gentle scent. He turned slowly toward the door.

"I'll give you a few moments to get ready. I'll come back for your bag," Dane said in a tone of command.

Taylor faced him, her eyes widening with surprise. "Why?"

Dane looked at her. He would like to see her eyes without his dark lenses, he thought to himself. "I'll be driving you into London to your hotel."

"Why?" Taylor challenged again, softly this time.

Dane tilted his head. "Would you rather I didn't?"

Taylor blinked and pursed her lips. "What I meant was, why are *you* taking me?"

Dane's eyes were still well protected from her. "It's the least we can do for keeping you here so long," he answered somewhat evasively.

Taylor hugged her arms around her waist. "We? You said you weren't Mr. Hillard's assistant."

"That's right."

"Then you don't work with this office."

"I never said that," he replied carefully.

Taylor only frowned in confusion as Dane opened the door.

"Are you always so accommodating to delayed travelers?" Taylor asked lightly, feeling the need to keep talking.

Dane looked down at the floor for a moment, then slowly back to Taylor. "I'm never accommodating," he said quietly, the rough texture of his voice hinting at another meaning that for the moment completely escaped Taylor. But before she could think of an appropriate response, he'd left again.

After that Taylor realized that she'd never met anyone quite like Dane Farrow before. He was worldly, mysterious, had an aura of authority and control. And he was probably dangerous. Not evil—Taylor believed that at once—but capable of the decisions and leadership one imagined high-ranking military men as making and demonstrating. He didn't fit any mold and very likely didn't follow many rules. In that he was much like Michael. The differences, however, were glaring, even in the scant time Taylor had been in Dane's presence, she could tell. Michael was a consummate flirt. He flirted with life, responsibility, truth. He was boyishly cavalier, getting by on the strength of his charm and personality, his easy wit and fast talk. Michael was fun and extremely likable, but—as Taylor had already found—he had as much substance as a puff of smoke.

Dane, on the other hand, seemed strong, mature and a force that would have to be reckoned with. He was not likely to back down from anything, nor would he foolishly look for trouble. In comparison Michael seemed like a boy. Dane Farrow was very clearly a man fully grown and grounded.

Easily carrying her one suitcase, Dane silently passed every security checkpoint in the immigration section without being stopped or questioned once, again making Taylor wonder about his role here. But she suspected he had none. It was sheer force of personality that commanded such acceptance, and it made her feel protected.

Dane responded to a playful salute from someone at the exit, and the door opened automatically. Taylor and Dane passed through into the chilly February night.

Dane silently placed her case near a column. "Just wait here. I'll get my car."

Taylor nodded and pulled up the collar of her coat. The nap she'd managed to catch had done more harm than good. She was now only aware of numbing exhaustion, and she was hungry. In a moment a car pulled up in front of her. Nothing fancy, and nothing new.

Dane stepped from the car and for a moment watched her against the dreary backdrop of the terminal. Her coat of winter white made her stand out rather distinctively. She'd had a long, trying day, but she smiled slightly at him and waited patiently for whatever was going to happen next. Dane was impressed. Taylor Ashe was a lot stronger and self-possessed than she looked. He liked that, too.

It took less than a minute to store her case in the back of the car and get started on the road to London.

"I think I'm going to miss that room," Taylor quipped with a sigh. "It was beginning to feel comfortable."

Dane allowed himself a private smile at her sense of humor, but it didn't show on his face.

Taylor didn't expect an answer. She'd already guessed that Dane was a private man. A quiet one. One not often given to smiles and laughter. She suddenly smothered a yawn, wondering sleepily if Dane Farrow *ever* smiled?

They were riding through a London suburb of quaint, small houses and more contemporary attempts at high-rise apartment buildings.

"Do you live in London?" she asked in the quiet darkness. The silence was making her drowsy.

"Sometimes," Dane answered cryptically.

"You don't sound British."

"I'm not," came the reply. "I'm American." He glanced briefly at Taylor. "I know. I don't sound American, either, I suppose."

"Why not?" Taylor asked, looking at him in the dark interior of the car.

Dane shrugged. He couldn't explain his life of the last twenty years in a sentence. "It's been a long time since I've been back in the States."

Taylor half turned toward him. "Why not?" She watched him purse his mouth, but he didn't answer. She turned her gaze out the window. "I'm sorry. I didn't mean to be so personal."

"It's not personal," Dane replied quietly. "Just not important."

Taylor hazarded a quick look at his hard, chiseled profile. Her curiosity about him was growing by the minute, but it was obvious that Dane was going to give nothing away. There was one pressing question on her mind, but she frowned over how best to proceed.

"Is . . . your family with you?" she asked. For a long moment Dane didn't answer. But again, when he answered, it was confusing for her.

"I always travel alone."

It really didn't answer her question.

"Why don't you tell me what hotel you're booked into?" Dane suggested smoothly, forestalling any more questions.

Taylor felt foolish. He wasn't interested in chitchat. She gave him the name of a hotel near Green Park.

"That's not a very good area," Dane commented.

"I know. It's central to where I need to be. And it's not expensive. I'm on a budget," she said lightly.

"You've been to London before and you aren't familiar with the city?"

"Well, it's always business. I've never stayed more than two days," she added wryly. "Time is money, my boss keeps telling me. But this time I'm taking a few more days of my own time."

There was a slight hard edge to her answer, but Dane didn't pursue it, and the conversation died.

After that Taylor watched his hand on the steering wheel, as he drove with easy assurance through the crazy rush-hour traffic. He drove with his left hand, keeping the right free.

Even though it was fully night, Dane still wore the dark glasses, and of course Taylor wondered why. He didn't strike her as the kind of person to sport an affectation. Yet the tinted lenses did not seem to impair his ability to judge distance, depth, shadows or directions. She began to feel perfectly safe with him.

It was out of sheer habit that Dane kept his right hand free. In his dark past it had been the hand that held his gun or machete, the hand capable of the most powerful blow. Now it was the hand that he still worked to coax back to full strength since his injury.

And it wasn't so much that he didn't want to talk with Taylor; it had struck him that he might not have much to say. His experience with polite society was limited, and he was more often than not an observer, rather than a participant.

He was not the kind of man that women found attractive enough at first to want to begin the dalliance of romance. His affairs had always been quick, clear, physical and uncomplicated. The closest he'd ever come to anything else had been with Maddy.

In a funny way he was both fascinated by and fearful of Taylor, and he'd felt the same way the first time he'd met Roger's wife, Ann. Taylor and Ann were so far beyond the realm of his experience that it was like being witness to a rare species of the human race—women who were soft, gentle, normal.

Madeleine had been a woman fully capable of taking care of herself. She fired a gun as well as he or Roger and never complained about the appalling living conditions they'd found themselves in. Their relationship had been stormy, even their lovemaking a mixture of fiery passion and physical battle, often ending with them both drenched in sweat and completely breathless.

Dane knew he could not do that with Taylor. He wouldn't. He would take his time. The thought of intimacy with her might seem inappropriate under the circumstances. But it didn't surprise him. And he liked the idea.

A car suddenly cut sharply in front of them, missing Dane's front fender by inches. Uttering an oath, he was forced to brake short. The sudden jerk threw Taylor forward, but Dane's reflexes were doubly quick; a long arm shot out across her chest, and the hard muscles of his arm held her safely in place.

Dane stopped the car and turned to face her. "Are you all right?" he asked.

Even though the wind had been knocked out of her, Taylor couldn't help smiling. He was obviously used to giving orders, too.

"I'm fine!" she gasped.

He continued to look in her direction; his eyes trying to read her true response. Then Dane reached out a hand to touch her hair, but stopped and turned to face forward again.

"I'm sorry," Dane apologized brusquely, already concentrating again on the road.

Taylor laughed softly, catching her breath. "That's okay. I feel right at home now. New York is filled with bad drivers."

But the jolting of her body made her suddenly ache for a quiet room and a bed with a firm mattress. In another moment they were pulling up in front of a small, unpretentious hotel on a busy London street. Taylor climbed out as Dane retrieved her case and they headed inside.

Taylor gave her confirmation slip to the clerk and waited, while Dane stood unobtrusively to one side, but he was so silent and watchful that the skinny, middle-aged clerk became nervous and intimidated, shooting him furtive looks. The clerk glanced quickly at the form and promptly handed it back to Taylor.

"I'm sorry, but we no longer have a room available for you."

Taylor just stared blankly at him. "What . . . what did you say?"

The clerk shrugged, pushing his wire-framed glasses up his long nose.

"There's no room. When you didn't phone in this afternoon, we let the room again."

"But I didn't know I had to," Taylor said, shaking her head in confusion.

"It's right here on the slip." The clerk, smirking in self-righteousness, pointed to a line that was nearly invisible at the bottom of Taylor's form. "It states that if you're going to be later than four o'clock you must notify us, or the room becomes available again. I'm afraid we gave it to a young couple. Honeymooners, actually."

Taylor took the now-useless form and stared helplessly at it. Her eyes were beginning to burn again, and she couldn't seem to think clearly.

"Well...at least it went to a good cause. But what am I going to do? Are you sure you have nothing else? Even for one night? I'm sure I can make other arrangements tomorrow."

The clerk shook his head. "I'm sorry. We really are fully booked."

"Might I use your phone?" came the low rasp behind Taylor. For a moment she'd forgotten about Dane, and now turned bewildered eyes to him.

"I—I'm afraid I can't," the clerk began weakly, stepping back as Dane quietly approached the counter.

"I'll just be a moment," Dane added, essentially ignoring the clerk who, after Dane reached in front of him for the telephone, made no move to stop him.

Dane half turned away and dialed a number.

Taylor redirected her attention to the problem at hand. She looked pleadingly at the clerk. "Can you at least—? Is there another hotel that perhaps—?"

"Madam, there are many. But I don't think you'll have any luck. Valentine's Day weekend, you know."

Taylor couldn't mentally make the connection; she was beginning to see the day ending in a nightmare of inconvenience. "Can't you help at all?"

"Never mind," Dane said smoothly, turning back to Taylor. "I've found something for you."

The clerk looked so relieved that he cheerfully wished them a happy weekend as they left his hotel and climbed back into Dane's car.

The ride took less than ten minutes, but it might as well have been hours. Taylor had no idea where Dane was taking her and she no longer cared. She felt a sudden urge to burst into tears of utter frustration, but fought silently against it. She didn't think that Dane was the kind of man to suffer hysterical women, and she wasn't going to embarrass herself.

Yet she was grateful when they finally parked again in what appeared to be a residential neighborhood of two-story row houses, all exactly alike. The door to one opened, and an older woman emerged to wait for the two people in the car. But Taylor sat still, unable, it seemed in that instant, to move even an inch. She was giddily beginning to think she'd be very happy to curl up where she was and sleep the rest of the night.

Taylor was surprised when Dane pulled open her door and reached in, to grab her small hand in his and help her from the car. He led her up to the door where the woman, no taller than Taylor but a great deal stouter, waited with fists on her hips. Taylor was thinking how much she liked the incredible strength and warmth she felt in Dane's hand, calluses, rough palm and all.

The woman gasped as Taylor and Dane stood under the entrance lamp. "Good heavens! She's about to drop. Poor thing."

Dane placed Taylor's suitcase inside the foyer, while Taylor allowed the milk and honey voice to wrap itself around her with soothing, maternal sounds.

"Trudy, this is Taylor Ashe. Roger had to detain her at immigration this morning."

"Taylor?" the older woman questioned at the odd first name, grimacing in apparent disapproval.

"Make her one of your tea things, Trudy, and just get her to bed," Dane ordered quietly. He turned to Taylor, took her package of rare books, passed them to Trudy and began to unbutton her coat.

Taylor stared dazedly into his face and stood unresisting, like a child, as he slid off the coat and hung it on a peg.

"What about you?" the woman was asking Dane.

He looked down at Taylor. "Don't worry about me."

Taylor blinked tiredly. "I—I'm sorry," she whispered to him.

"Come along, dearie. I have just the thing for you. Then a bit of sleep, and you'll feel more the thing in the morning."

Dane was already turning away to leave, and the woman Trudy had Taylor by the arm.

"Wait a moment. Please..." Taylor said, finally making Dane stop; he turned back to her.

"I'll go get the water started," Trudy said and quietly padded away.

Dane stood in such a way that he was silhouetted against the light from a street lamp. His body loomed large, silent and imposing. But Taylor felt no threat from him, and knew that she never would.

"You'll have to show me how you do this," she whispered in a voice laced with fatigue.

"Do what?" Dane asked.

She gestured absently with her hands. "Get things done. Make people listen. Move mountains."

"Moving mountains is beyond me, I'm afraid."

Taylor grinned slowly, her large eyes drowsy. "That's okay. Two out of three isn't bad. How do I repay you?"

Dane looked at her silently for a moment. A number of possibilities came quickly to mind. "By being careful," was his answer. Taylor could only stare in confusion. "Good night."

"Good night, Dane Farrow. And thank you."

Taylor waited as he silently faded into the dark. She heard his car start, and then pull away down the street like a quiet ghost.


DANE QUIETLY WATCHED as Ann left the room with a tray and glanced with a warm and private smile toward Roger. The empty cups and saucers she carried rattled gently, until the sound finally faded in her wake. Dane's eyes dropped to the brandy snifter in his hand and he gently sloshed the golden liquid in the glass. Ann was a very beautiful woman. And a very gentle and sweet one. Roger was a very lucky man. But he would guess that Roger already knew that.

"Come on, Hawk," Roger yawned from his prone position on a floral sofa much too delicate looking for a man of his size. "Ease up, will you? You've been miles away for the last hour or so. Are we old married couple boring you?"

Dane merely gave a slight grin and took a sip of the brandy, enjoying the burning jolt that trailed down his insides.

Roger grunted. "For God's sake," he growled in disgust. "Don't tell me you're thinking about that Evans woman. Or is it Ashe?"

Dane slouched in his chair. "All right, I won't," he murmured, his tone at once rough and affectionate.

Roger sighed and closed his eyes. "Whatever happened to Isabelle?"

"Isabelle was almost two years ago. She decided to get married. To someone else."

Roger paused. "Why not to you?" He asked the question as a matter of course. He knew Dane, and knew that he took commitments of any kind very seriously. Maddy had been proof of that under ridiculous circumstances, and Maddy had been fifteen years ago.

"I wasn't in love with her," Dane answered easily. "And I doubt she was in love with me."

Roger chuckled. "Yes, but you certainly had a good time."

Dane looked at the warm brown liquid and took another sip. "I suppose I did."

"But?" Roger prompted.

Dane raised his veiled eyes to his friend. Sometimes it was on the tip of his tongue to say more, to admit to feelings and needs that ran deep, but which he kept down. And maybe Roger understood without him having to say anything at all. But he wasn't going to talk about things that were never going to happen. What was the point?

"But I had work to do. I had two contracts to fill for materials to West Africa, and another to Ecuador."

"Yes, well... People still work and run businesses and fall in love."

Dane grinned. "Trying to convert me?"

"Hell, yes!" Roger said fervently, but that was as far as he would go. Even he, Dane's best friend, would not presume to tell him how to live his life. He sat up quickly. "But that doesn't mean you should get involved with Taylor what's-her-name."

"Ashe," Dane supplied calmly. "What have you got against her?"

"Nothing, except that her story's fishy, her business is suspect and she looks like the sort of helpless female who gets into trouble without even trying!"

Dane considered all of that, but Ann reappeared before he could respond to Roger's observations. Both men stood as Ann leaned against the door frame, her loose, flowing lounge dress lending her an air of effervescence and bright warmth.

"Can I get you two anything else?" She spoke to Roger, and Dane took the cue.

"I think I'll call it a night. I thank you, Ann, for letting me stay over with no advance warning."

Roger joined Ann at the door and took her hand in his. "It was no problem at all. I'm so glad that you could stay." Ann smiled.

Dane watched the two of them standing in the doorway together and felt that he was intruding on their privacy—and their happiness. It was almost a tangible thing.

"I'll be off early in the morning."

"Oh, please don't. Roger is enjoying purely male talk for a change. You can keep each other company while I run some errands."

"You mean you and Mrs. Hamilton," Roger corrected sternly.

Ann beamed up at her husband and squeezed his hand. "Yes, of course I do." She turned to look hopefully at Dane.

He thought of Taylor as he'd left her in Trudy's hallway, with her large eyes and soft smile, her hair a gentle tumble around her small face. He wanted to get back early to find out what her plans were, where she would go, whom she would see. Dane slid his right hand into his pocket and closed it around the leather ball. He really wanted to see *her*. But it could wait.

"I'll baby-sit with Roger," Dane joked with a straight face.

Ann laughed, and Roger grimaced as they waved briefly and headed toward their bedroom.

Dane stood silently in the middle of the living room, listening to the murmur of their voices as they walked away; and there was a sudden, soft giggle from Ann. In a moment he heard the closing of their door, locking them away into a world of supreme togetherness and privacy. The apartment grew very quiet. Instead of heading to his room, Dane sat down once more and picked up the brandy glass. For a long moment he reflected upon his life and that of Roger, the obvious ways in which they were the same—and the ways they weren't.

When he was much younger, even after Madeleine, after recovering from the explosion, Dane had always maintained the sense that his life was going to be different from that of ordinary men—a life of the unexpected and often the very dangerous. He couldn't even remember now how such a life had ever got started. His father, a career officer, had retired a lieutenant colonel from the U.S. air force. He'd been stationed in Frankfurt, Germany, at the time and had decided to return to Colorado and live there, but Dane had been reluctant to accom-

pany him. He didn't know what he'd be returning to.
There was no home there, no other family, no friends.
Years of changing locations and never establishing roots
had made him into a restless spirit. Dane knew it wasn't
because he necessarily wanted it that way, but because he
*knew* no other way.

Living the way he had all over the world had given him
a good working knowledge of several languages. That
had led him through his father's military connections and
friends of friends to meet all kinds of people. Soon Dane
found himself being asked to work on small diplomatic
concerns as a civilian, and later as a more established
contact for the U.S. State Department. He grew to like
the work, although it still kept him moving from place to
place. But that was okay. He had no place to go home to.

His relationship with his father had never been close,
and there was an irony in that. Dane had always wished
his father could have been stationed in one place, so that
they could have done more together. Instead his father's
first commitment had been to the military. But the life
that Dane had led as an adult—unsettled and constantly
moving around—had not been so different from his
teenage days with his father. And he somehow couldn't
seem to find the way home.

He and Roger had done things, been places, seen
things that most people only dreamed about. Their existence had made them worldly, respected, sometimes
feared. Dane's private work for two world governments,
the U.S. and Britain, had paid well. It had allowed him
to start his own contracting business, which built pre-
fabricated housing units for poor countries, and to buy
land in Colorado, his home state, where he hoped to settle someday. He had never decided on when "someday"
would be, but he'd recently begun to think about it more

and more. Maybe it was because Roger had met Ann and got married.

Dane finished the drink and, withdrawing the leather ball from his pocket, absently began to exercise his hand and arm. With his free hand he rubbed the stubble on his chin and thought about what factors had made the difference. One was that Roger had given up his life of the past, had put it into a proper perspective and made other plans and decisions for his future. They included loving someone, and together planning a family. Another factor was that they were both getting older. Roger was already forty-two and cognizant of the fact that Ann was almost thirteen years younger. Ann was all the family Roger Hillard had in the world. Dane himself was just shy of his fortieth birthday, and for all he'd done in his life, often asked himself what it was all for. What did he have to show for it—except enough money and means to make him comfortable the rest of his life, a battered and scarred body—and a tenuous relationship to his father? He missed him. But how did one return home after so many years away?

Perhaps if Maddy had lived and their baby had been born, there would be some sense of accomplishment instead of this gnawing, growing sense of emptiness. He could never say for sure what it was about Ann that might have been the vital turning point for Roger, something that made it easy for him to change his way of life, be gentle, make a commitment. But Dane knew that for some reason, when he looked at Taylor, he could imagine what it might be. Softness, vulnerability, inner strength. They combined to force one's need to protect, comfort, to even love, maybe in the hope of receiving the same in return.

Dane got up smoothly from his chair, restless and tired all at once, impatient with thoughts of a woman he'd met only fifteen hours ago. But somehow she'd managed to touch him and make him completely aware of her—and she belonged to someone else.

Dane himself was feeling vulnerable. He was not so much of a man that he couldn't admit it. He, too, got tired of being alone.

## Chapter Three

On Saturday Taylor woke to the gentle hissing of steam coming up through a radiator. For a moment she speculated that it was rather noisy for a hotel, until she remembered she wasn't at a hotel, but had been deposited with an older woman named Trudy. Dane had brought her here. Taylor further guessed, rolling onto her back, that in some way Trudy and Dane were well-known to each other, since she had been welcomed with no questions asked.

Slowly Taylor opened her eyes. She stared at the ceiling and suddenly knew she was in Dane's bed. She moved her head, and her eyes roamed the small room with its delicate floral wallpaper and functional fiberglass curtains, which covered the one narrow window. There was one bureau, an old-fashioned wardrobe closet, a chair and the bed she lay in. It was not a room used by someone who lived here on a day-to-day basis—it had nothing personal by which to identify the occupant. But it was reasonably comfortable, even if it had an air of being temporary. It was Dane's temporary space, the place where he stayed when he was "sometimes" in London.

An odd feeling washed over Taylor. It was a combination of giddiness and awe. She had not been in bed with a man since Michael. In most ways she'd lost that sense of intimacy that is created in the space between a mattress and warm bed linen. But a peculiar touch of sensuality made her feel that she was not alone. For a second it was frightening to suddenly yearn for the physical closeness of another person, and became aware that the image that materialized was that of a mysterious stranger. She had not awakened with thoughts of Michael, of whom she generally didn't think much anymore, but of Dane Farrow.

It was nearly noon when Taylor finally ventured from the charming room and went in search of Trudy. She remembered nothing of the layout of the house and made a few false turns, before discovering the kitchen on the first floor in the back of the narrow structure. The hallway continued into the kitchen, but off to the left was an entrance to a small parlor. It was here that Taylor peeked in and found Trudy in an overstuffed chair, her feet in scuffy slippers propped on an ottoman, reading the newspapers with the aid of a magnifying glass. A radio was playing quietly in the background. Trudy suddenly looked up and spotted Taylor standing hesitantly in the doorway. She broke into a genuinely sunny smile, her cheeks spotted a natural rouge red.

"So you're up, then," Trudy said, thrusting the papers carelessly into the cushions and coming to her feet. "Did you sleep well?"

"Yes, thank you," Taylor murmured as Trudy, with more agility and energy than one would have imagined, bustled past Taylor and into the kitchen. "You must be starved. Couldn't get you to take a thing last night. You were fast asleep before I brought the tea up!" She chuckled and quickly put plates and cups and saucers onto the small Formica table in the kitchen. Then she straightened to look more thoroughly at Taylor, squinting through pale blue eyes.

"Now let me have a look at you. Ahh..." she sighed with a twinkle. "You're a bright one, you are. No bigger than that."

"I... beg your pardon?" Taylor asked, confused.

"Never you mind. You just sit down and I'll put the tea on and make you some breakfast." She glanced at the kitchen clock. "Well, maybe it should be lunch."

"Please don't go to any trouble. Tea and toast is fine."

Trudy frowned and shook her head. "You're just a wisp of a thing. You young American women and your diets. Dane said you hadn't eaten yesterday, but you look as if you never do!"

At the mention of Dane's name Taylor was alert, but Trudy was off and running with a steady stream of inconsequential chatter as she placed several muffins in a toaster oven and poured hot tea.

"Was... he here this morning?" Taylor interrupted casually when she had the chance.

Trudy gingerly placed the steaming muffins on another plate and sat at the table with Taylor.

"No, but he phoned. Wanted to make sure you were settled. Told him you were sleeping peaceful like. He said you were put through the bureaucratic wringer yesterday at Heathrow. It's enough to do anybody in."

Taylor smiled privately and took a sip of the strong tea. She felt pleased that Dane has asked after her. "I'm sorry I took his room last night. I'm sure I can find something today."

Trudy impatiently waved that aside. "I'll hear nothing of that. You'll stay with me as long as you and Dane wish."

"He left nothing upstairs. Did you have to move all his things because of me? I'm sorry."

"Oh, well . . . there wasn't much to move. Dane travels light. It's his way."

Taylor stared into her cup and then back at Trudy. "What can you tell me about Dane? How long have you known him?"

Trudy seemed to consider both questions as she put generous amounts of sugar into her tea and broke a muffin to spread jam on both halves. She frowned. "Not many people ever ask about him. He's not one to make himself noticed, if you know what I mean. Most people . . . they don't want to know about a man like Dane. He's not like most men."

Taylor thought about that. She could believe he wasn't like other men, but then what kind of man was he? What did Trudy mean, "men like Dane"?

Trudy shook her head and sighed. "I met him when he was fifteen years old, trailing around the world after his father. His dad was a career officer in the military. Dane was a bit sullen and wild then. Oh . . . not really, I suppose. His mother had just died and he was missing her. He badly needed a little maternal care and love at the time. He was lonely. His father was all brass and order, and I think Dane sometimes needed something softer."

"And his father?"

"Well, his father is retired," Trudy answered, but Taylor could see she was carefully considering each reply. She waited for Trudy to continue, but she did so in an evasive way. "I worked at the base where Dane's father was stationed. Took him under my wing. He and my son, Nicholas, became real good friends. And later, after my Nicholas—" She stopped and cleared her throat, then smiled briefly at Taylor. "A long time, I've known Dane. He's a fine man."

For no reason other than that she was inclined to agree, though she still knew nothing of the man, Taylor smiled. "I met him at immigration yesterday. He said he didn't work there, but he seemed to command a certain authority."

Trudy nodded. "More tea, love?" she murmured, starting to rise.

"No, thank you. This is fine. What does he do?"

Trudy shrugged. "Oh, a bit of this and that. He keeps himself busy."

Taylor waited. "Where?" she asked, trying to coax out the information.

"He has his own business. And he does consulting type things. You know. He's been everywhere. Done just about everything." Trudy finished with a sigh.

It was all very unsatisfactory, but Taylor didn't even consider just then that Dane was none of her business and for the moment shouldn't be. Not when there was still Michael, although he was very far away from her in more ways than one.

Another question came to mind, one that was now sparked by the memory of the room upstairs.

"Is...Dane married?" Taylor asked softly and lowered her gaze when Trudy looked sharply at her. Taylor expected her to say what she herself knew—it was none of her business. But Trudy surprised her in quite a different way.

"Are *you* married?" she asked Taylor instead. It was not at all rudely done, but nonetheless Taylor felt herself burning with embarrassment.

"Yes," Taylor answered in a barely audible voice, afraid to admit it, her eyes wide but suddenly dull. Trudy noticed and inwardly questioned her guest's response.

But she smiled kindly at the young woman before her. "Then my answer doesn't matter, does it?"

Taylor lowered her gaze again to her now-empty cup. "No, I—I suppose it doesn't," she replied softly. Trudy stood, and in passing Taylor on her way to the sink, she lightly patted the young woman's shoulder. It was almost as if she understood. And because she might very well have, Taylor turned to speak to the older woman over her shoulder.

"Trudy?"

"Yes, dear?"

"I'd really appreciate it . . . could you please not tell Dane that I—I asked about him?"

Trudy raised her brows. "Now, why ever not?"

Taylor shrugged vaguely. "I don't know. I just don't want him to think . . ."

She stopped; it was on the tip of her tongue to admit to being both interested in and intrigued by Dane Farrow. Strangely, it didn't bother Taylor that she was. It only troubled her that she was not free to do so.

Trudy chuckled. "Of course, I'll say nothing. Men are peculiar, anyway. He'd want to know why you asked."

Taylor shifted in her chair and suddenly felt short of breath, anxious. She couldn't be interested in Dane Farrow. She couldn't be interested in anyone.

Trudy came back to stand by her chair. When she spoke it made Taylor jump.

"Well, now Ms. Ashe. What are you up to this afternoon?"

The subject of Dane was closed. Taylor smiled at Trudy. "Please call me Taylor." She stood up and also carried her dishes to the sink, feeling restless. All her work and inquiries had to be done by Wednesday. because she was going home. Dane Farrow had only touched her life under the queerest of circumstances, and only for a moment, and she was never going to see him again.

"I'm here on business, but I can't do much until Monday. I thought I'd just go exploring today."

Taylor washed her hands at the sink and dried them on a towel, not looking at Trudy. "I . . . ah . . . I thought I'd visit a few places downtown. . . ."

"Shopping?" Trudy asked cheerfully.

Taylor laughed. "I'm afraid not. I didn't come with a lot of money. And I still have to pay for my room and board."

"You'll do no such thing," Trudy said firmly, crossing her arms and looking at Taylor. "Dane brought you to me, and he has his own reasons for doing things. You're my guest."

"But . . ." Taylor made to protest, but Trudy turned away, moving out of the kitchen and down the hall. "If you don't hurry, everything will be closed before you get all your errands done. Now here's my address and phone, just in case you get lost."

Taylor gave up the argument after that and went to get her coat and bag. Trudy was waiting by the door to send her off.

"Now, you stay warm."

"I will," Taylor promised, smiling at Trudy's maternal fussing. A plump hand touched her arm. Taylor looked hesitantly at the other woman, who was frowning slightly.

"I have got one more question I'd like to ask you."

"Sure." Taylor waited.

"Well...just what kind of name is Taylor for a female?"

Taylor laughed lightly at Trudy's perplexed expression.

"I have two brothers that are a bit older than me. When I was born, they were allowed to come up with a name between them. Taylor was it."

Trudy rolled her eyes to heaven. "What a lark," she mumbled, no doubt referring to the strange habits of American families.

Outside Taylor found the day raw and gray. Cold seemed to seep into her clothing and linger. For a moment, she considered taking a taxi downtown, but instead walked until she found a tube station. She would take it to the National Gallery stop, the one nearest Trafalgar Square. During her subway ride Taylor considered the task at hand. It had nothing to do with books or bookstores, but with Michael. If she was going to make one last effort to find out what had happened to him, it had to begin here in London, the city with which he'd seemed so familiar and comfortable—where they'd first met.

She had such scant clues about his life here, but it was better than nothing at all, which was what she'd dealt with in New York for over three years. There had been no records with either Social Security or Internal Revenue—nothing that verified Michael Evans's existence.

Taylor pulled out the envelope she carried, which she always guarded carefully. Its contents would have been confusing to anyone else. A book of matches from a café, a receipt from a shirtmaker. There was part of a torn business envelope, the printed return address belonging to an import-export company. That was it. And she remembered the name of a small hotel where he'd stayed the year they met. Taylor recalled the building and street as being dingy and unappealing. An unlikely place for a businessman to stay. But someone there, or at any of the other locations, might remember him.

Her hands shook as she put away the envelope with its cryptic contents. There were many other things to deal with besides finding out why he'd disappeared. There was the question, for instance, of whether or not she wanted Michael back in her life. Assuming she found him at all.

Taylor's train came to her stop and she slowly made her way out of the station. The square was a colorful and eccentric mix of people and events—a continual happening, rich in opportunities to participate, photograph, gape. But today Taylor paid no attention as she walked several blocks off the square and turned a corner toward the Strand. In the middle of the block was a hotel. Taylor's stomach tightened at seeing the marquee, tightened even more as she approached, almost as if she expected to go inside and find that Michael was checked in, after all.

At the desk there was a middle-aged woman, overweight, over made-up and overdressed in a fire-engine-red dress—in the way of someone who simply knew no better. The woman's hair was dyed a brassy blond, bordering on orange, and it clashed horribly with the color of the dress.

There were two foot-high cardboard cupids placed on the counter. One was holding a sign that said Happy Valentine's Day. The other one read Have a Heart. The woman looked curiously at Taylor, and Taylor could guess that they were both thinking the same thing. She didn't belong here.

"Help you, dearie?" the woman squeaked nasally, her accent broad and cockney.

"I hope so." Taylor smiled tentatively. "I'm trying to find a man—"

The woman blinked and gave a raucous laugh, slapping her fat hand on the counter. "Ain't we all, luv!" She looked Taylor up and down. "You ain't going to find the kind of man you need. Leastways, not here."

Taylor shook her head, ignoring the comments and observations.

"No. But I know who I'm looking for. You see, he used to stay here maybe three years ago."

The woman flipped a wrist at Taylor in disbelief. "Go on. Your man wouldn't stay here. There's nothing but riffraff and fly-by-nights here, and even the ones that look decent always seem shifty to me!" Again she laughed at her own joke.

Taylor took a furtive look around the lobby. It was not by any stretch of the imagination grand, but it was orderly and clean, if a little threadbare. There was one rail-thin bellman, who, from the looks of his face, spent as much time drinking as he might working in this hotel of questionable reputation. He sat on an old Queen Anne chair near the door, staring dazedly into space.

Taylor looked back at the woman, who was adjusting the neckline of her fancy dress. "Is it possible to check the records?"

The woman didn't look at her, giving her attention instead to a tabloid newspaper with sensational headlines. "Sorry. Can't do that. Rules, you know."

"It's very important. I just want to see if the—this person I'm looking for—has been here in the last three years."

The woman gaped. "Three years! D'ya have any idea how many books I'd have to pull out?"

"Please," Taylor asked quietly, her voice holding an urgency that caught the woman's attention.

"Are you in trouble? Who is this fella?"

Taylor stiffened at the personal question, but knew that unless she had this woman's sympathy, she wasn't going to get anywhere. She told her the truth. "He—he's my husband. I haven't seen him in...more than a year," Taylor tempered, "and I have to find him."

The woman sighed and clucked her tongue. "The crumb," she murmured scathingly. But shaking her head, she got off her stool and headed for an office behind her. "You wait here."

Taylor let out the breath she was holding tightly in her lungs. "Thank you, very much," she said sincerely. While she waited, a phone rang in the back office. Taylor could only half hear the conversation and only paid half attention. Then the woman's voice rose in a strident, argumentative tone, and after a short exchange, she could be heard slamming the phone down. In another moment she reappeared under the weight of three heavy ledgers. She plopped them onto one end of the counter and gestured to Taylor.

"I shouldn't be doing this, but here you are. Three years' worth. What name you looking for?" She opened the first book.

"Michael Evans," Taylor answered. She stared at the books in some fascination and some hope. Somewhere in these books might be some important information. A date when Michael was last here.

"Michael Evans..." the clerk repeated as she began scanning the names. "Are you sure that's the name he was using?" she asked, frowning over the book.

Taylor's head jerked up sharply. It had never once occurred to her that Michael might have used another name. She froze as the additional implications began to hit her one by one. What if he had used another name? Why would he want to?

Taylor squeezed her eyes shut as another sweeping, fearful possibility attacked her. What if Michael Evans wasn't his real name? She drew in a sharp breath and pressed a shaky hand to her mouth.

The clerk looked up at her. "You feeling all right?"

Taylor gave her a weak smile. "Fine... fine."

"You'd better get started. You could be here for hours," the clerk went on.

Taylor was there exactly two hours, and when she had finished, she had nothing to show for it but a headache and burning eyes. She'd come to the hotel with so much expectation. She might have known it wasn't going to be so easy. Taylor slowly closed the last of the ledgers. No Michael Evans. The clerk, who'd grown bored with the task of looking after ten minutes, looked up from her paper.

"No luck, eh?" She didn't seem surprised.

"No. None." Taylor sighed. "But I thank you, anyway."

The woman shrugged. "Forget the creep. You're pretty and young. Find yourself another man."

Taylor smiled. That suggestion was hardly the answer to her problem, but she had not discarded the possibility of another relationship. Someday. When all of this was behind her.

"Thank you," Taylor murmured, and turned to leave.

As she opened the door, two men were coming in. She didn't pay too much attention, other than to note one was well dressed, middle-aged with iron-gray hair, and the other man was tall with red hair and a beard, and he wore a small gold loop earring in his left earlobe.

The gray-haired man held the door and nodded politely as Taylor passed. She gave an absent smile, and turning up the collar of her coat, she moved down the street.

Taylor stopped at the corner and looked at her watch. It was a little after four. There was not going to be enough time to check out her other sources. Maybe one more. She knew the café was not so far away and decided to walk the distance.

Taylor turned twice to try to get her bearings. She briefly noticed that the tall, redheaded man was standing against the entrance to the hotel. That was not the direction she wanted, and she turned to walk the opposite way.

The café was about a quarter of a mile away, near Charing Cross. It was already beginning to get dark, and the overcast day became colder and even drearier to Taylor; the tips of her fingers grew numb, despite her red leather gloves. As she approached the café with its unpretentious front—easy to miss, if you weren't looking for it—Taylor again felt her hopes rise at the prospect of possibilities. She was also anxious, and it was an anxiety tinged with a good deal of private anger. She hated Michael for putting her through this.

The glass in the café doors was fogged and wet from condensation, and as she opened the door, a swish of heat met her from the warm interior.

Only a few people looked up at her entrance, as she slowly made her way into the room. It was small, and noisy with conversation and laughter from the full complement of customers. They were almost exclusively male.

Taylor approached a waitress who was writing a bill for a customer. "Excuse me. I'd like to see the manager if he's here," Taylor said.

The waitress looked at her indifferently. "He ain't hiring, ducks."

"I'm not looking for work. I want to talk to him about . . . something else."

"American, right?" the waitress asked, giving the bill to her waiting customer. From her pocket she took out a small, brightly enameled pin in the shape of a heart. She put it onto his coat.

"Happy Valentine's Day," she said sweetly with a smile. It disappeared when she turned back to Taylor. "I'll see if the manager is interested." She disappeared through a door near the kitchen.

Taylor waited and looked around. The place was busy, although it hadn't been the one time Michael had brought her here. Then there had been just the two of them during that one afternoon—and the cook, who seemed to know Michael as a frequent customer. It was an odd café. It no longer had the interesting charm she remembered. There was nothing attractive about it, and the atmosphere had something covert and uneasy about it. These people were all of a kind, and probably knew each other. It would be very hard for a stranger to just walk in and be comfortable, and she felt very uncomfortable.

A short, heavyset man came out of a doorway. He stood and openly examined her, his expression closed and unfriendly. He came over to her.

"Yes?" he asked by way of opening. "Who are you?"

Taylor tried not to wrinkle her nose at the overwhelming smell of onions and ale that surrounded the man. "My name's Taylor Evans. I want to know if maybe you know a Michael Evans. Or maybe some of your staff might remember him as a customer.''

The man's eyes narrowed. Taylor thought he'd stiffened for an instant, but then the indifferent look returned. He spoke, showing poorly cared-for teeth.

''Never heard of him,'' he said, and abruptly turned to walk away.

Taylor's mouth dropped open; the conversation seemed to be ending very quickly. She struggled for a way to stop him.

''But maybe someone else has,'' she said hurriedly.

''My staff don't know anybody I don't know.''

''What about your cook? Michael seemed very friendly with the cook.''

The man hesitated. ''I took on a new cook last year.''

Taylor bit her lip. It didn't seem as if that was the truth, but if it wasn't, this man would soon make it so. He was that kind. She only wondered why he might lie.

Taylor fingered the clasp on her bag. ''It's just—very important that I find him. He used to come here. Three years ago.''

The manager shrugged. ''Things change in three years, lady. Perhaps you came to the wrong place.'' He started to turn away again, spotted something behind Taylor and began to walk toward her. He passed to go to the cash register and reached behind it. When he turned around, he held out his hand.

Taylor automatically reached out to take what he was offering. It was a pin, just like the one the waitress had given her customer, and a box wrapped in pink tissue paper.

''It's Valentine's Day,'' he said gruffly.

''Yes, I know,'' Taylor said in confusion, eyeing the gifts suspiciously. She put the candy into her bag and pinned the heart to her blouse. "Thank you," she mumbled to the man, not knowing what else to say. The pin and candy were a poor substitute for the answers she sought. She began to leave, not being able to think of anything else to say or ask.

"What do you want this Michael for?" the manager asked.

Feeling tired, hungry and dejected, Taylor opened the door of the café. She looked with distaste at the little man. "I'm his wife."

The man stared hard at her, but not a muscle moved in his face or body to tell her what he might be thinking.

"At least... I think I am," she said, confused. Taylor blinked at his continual staring, and feeling strange and suddenly on guard, she quickly left the café.

It seemed much colder now, but Taylor didn't even bother trying to huddle inside her coat for warmth. She was too busy feeling disappointment and frustration. She'd expected it to take a while to get on the right track to Michael's whereabouts, but she hadn't counted on an obstacle course and roadblocks, like the manager of the café. Taylor had a strong sense that it wasn't so much that he didn't know anything, but rather that he wasn't *willing* to give her information.

It was dark now, and she wasn't comfortable being alone in this seedy area. A tall man passed behind her and quickly entered the café as Taylor walked away slowly, wondering what to do next, and she only caught a glimpse of him. With no particular goal in mind, Taylor began wandering. A sense of futility was beginning to settle on her.

Of course, she'd thought of the possibility of not finding Michael, and she'd already considered proceeding with a divorce if no other alternative appeared. Taylor raised her chin stubbornly into an unexpected gust of biting wind. She'd tried her best to wait, to hope that sooner or later she would hear from Michael, but she was no longer sure about what she was waiting for. She had her own life to live, and she wanted the freedom to do so.

Whatever love she might have had for him had died an agonizing death during the years of silence, neglect and unanswered questions. Thank goodness, her family had been loving and supportive and had refrained from telling her the obvious—that they'd tried to warn her to wait and be sure.

Taylor absently window-shopped, yet was acutely aware of the evidence of Valentine's Day, the red, the hearts, the angels with wings, the many couples around her, paired off and holding hands, openly displaying their affection for one another. Many of the women carried small bouquets or even a single flower. Suddenly she felt terribly left out and unwanted . . . and unloved.

Taylor's steps slowed as her sadness deepened. This was a bad idea, coming to London, believing she could settle in just a few days everything that had gone on for years. And it was the wrong time to come. She had no idea that one single day could make such a difference. She missed her family.

Taylor looked up as a foursome of teens crossed her path on their way to some Saturday night event. Two of them wore dark glasses, obviously a cool thing to do, she thought wryly. But it evoked an image of Dane with his dark, foreboding looks, his aura of danger, which didn't go with how he'd treated her yesterday and last night.

She wondered where he was. Did he have family, or a lover to curl himself around? Taylor felt a melting warmth flow through her at the idea of Dane as a lover. With a shaky hand she brushed her hair from her face, trying to free her imagination of the idea that came to her then, of the two of them together. Ridiculous. He would never be interested in someone like her.

Taylor shivered. She was cold and it was getting late. She'd go back to Trudy's and perhaps start on her rounds again tomorrow. *Oh, wait.* Taylor hesitated in her steps. Tomorrow was Sunday. She sighed. She had no idea what she'd do by herself in London on a Sunday.

She stopped and looked around, grateful that a tube entrance was a block to her left. As she turned to cross the street, a movement caught her eye over her left shoulder. There was a man several yards behind her. He bent his head to drop a cigarette butt onto the sidewalk, and crushed it with his feet, then quickly turned a corner away from her. Taylor frowned and felt apprehension grab at her. Of course, she had no idea who he was…just someone on the street. But there was something about him….

She quickly crossed the street and headed for the subway, resisting the urge to turn around again.

TRUDY CAME into the living room with a cup of coffee and handed it to Dane. He was not one for tea. But then, he wasn't British. She believed the two factors to be intrinsically connected.

Dane was slowly walking the room, the little leather ball being tossed lightly into the air and caught again. He put it down onto a side table as he took the cup from Trudy. She shook her head and sighed.

"You're like a caged tiger, Dane Farrow. What's on your mind now?"

"Nothing's on my mind," Dane said easily, although it irked him that both Trudy and Roger knew him so well that he had no secrets. Was he becoming transparent?

"All right," Trudy said, sitting down heavily and propping up her feet. "Then who?"

Dane didn't answer, but sat down to drink his coffee.

"Never mind. It's that pretty little lady, isn't it?"

Dane gave Trudy a sharp look through his dark lenses. She chuckled.

"Don't you scowl at me, young man. What makes you think I wouldn't notice?"

"I'm just trying to see that she's not in any trouble."

"Why do you care? You're not in that line of work anymore. There are lots of people she could go to, if she needs help." Trudy knew she was baiting him. And Dane knew it as well.

Again Dane had no answer and began to flex his right hand, rhythmically opening and closing again.

"Right now you're wondering where she is."

"She doesn't know anyone in London. She said she didn't know London."

"You want to believe her, I can see that. But you're not sure, is that it?"

Dane looked briefly at Trudy. "I think you missed your calling in life," he teased.

Trudy sighed. "Well, this is the first time you've ever brought a young lady home for me to watch over. Do you suppose that means something?"

Dane got up restlessly, pushing his hands into his trouser pockets. "I don't know, Trudy," he admitted softly. He could be honest with her. She was the closest he'd come to a mother since his own had died. And Trudy herself had always treated him like a son, a wayward one to be sure, but with love and understanding. Just as she had her real son, Nicholas, who'd died a soldier fighting a war in the north.

"Do you know the young lady's married?" she asked very softly.

Dane didn't face her. "She said she was. She also said that she and her husband were not together. There's some sort of separation."

"Ahh," Trudy said, nodding her head. Perhaps Taylor's interest in Dane just that morning was not so inappropriate, after all.

There was a soft knocking on the front door, and then the ringing of the bell.

"That must be her."

"Stay still. I'll get the door," Dane said, and walked into the hall.

When Dane opened the door, Taylor's back was toward him. She turned abruptly to step inside, almost in a rush, and collided with Dane. He put out a hand to steady her, but holding her arm, could feel her stiffen.

Dane frowned, tightening his hand almost unconsciously. "What's wrong?" he said alertly.

"Dane!" Taylor said in surprise. "I—I didn't think you'd be here. I—"

Dane looked over her shoulder into the dark street. Immediately he pulled her inside and closed the door.

Dane released her, but stood looking down at her. Her eyes were overly bright. "I want to know what's wrong," he told her again.

Taylor tried to smile and failed. She felt safe now, but she could barely catch her breath. "Nothing's wrong. I...it's just that...I thought I was being followed." She looked up at Dane, and when he only stared and didn't answer, Taylor laughed lightly, relaxing again. "I'm sorry. I must sound like a lunatic. And I'm being silly, but..."

"But still you're shaking," Dane observed.

Taylor took a deep breath and began to unbutton her coat. Dane came to her assistance, sliding it off her shoulders.

"Thanks," she murmured, embarrassed by the way she'd practically fallen into the house. She turned to face him once more and did feel very glad that he was here. Her imagination had run wild for the last hour or so. Now she felt safe again.

This time when she smiled at Dane it was genuine. She lightly put out a small hand and grabbed his right wrist. She could feel the tight rough skin there, but her eyes never wavered from trying to find his through the dark glasses.

"I'm fine, really," she said easily.

As she made to release him, Dane's hand turned over to grab hers. Taylor felt her eyes widen at his firm grip, and her gaze returned quickly to his face. But in the same amount of time he let her go.

"Trudy is in the living room," was all he said.

Although she tried to understand what had happened, Taylor just couldn't. His touch had merely been reassuring, but again something between them changed. She felt a connection—but in that moment, it frightened her with its implications and potential for something more.

When Taylor continued to look at him in confusion, Dane put his large hand on the small of her back to urge her forward. Trudy met them in the doorway.

"Did you have a good day, love?" she asked cheerfully.

"It . . . was fine" Taylor replied evasively.

Trudy looked at Dane with a silent question, and somehow he silently communicated. She nodded once. "Well, then, you can tell Dane all about it while I do dinner."

In the living room Taylor sat nervously in a chair, and was made even more uncomfortable when Dane pulled up a chair just facing her. He sat down and slowly leaned forward to brace his arms on his knees.

"Tell me about being followed."

Taylor blinked. She'd already forgotten about that. "But I wasn't, really. I mean, there were always lots of people around me...."

"But there was someone you saw more than once?"

She spread her hands and smoothed them down her thighs. "I don't know. For a moment before coming back, I thought there was someone...." She chuckled. "Dane, this is foolish. I'm sure I overreacted, and—"

"Can you describe him?" he pressed, and Taylor could see he was serious about wanting to know.

"He was tall. And I think he wore very dark clothing. Slender." She felt helpless. "That's it."

Dane slowly sat back, but didn't comment anymore on her description. "Where did you go this afternoon?"

Taylor felt her stomach sink with nervous tension. She couldn't tell him. "I...just wandered around central London."

Dane looked down at his clasped hands. "It was very cold for wandering around."

Taylor shrugged. "I know, but I'm not a hothouse flower, and I won't melt."

Dane got up, knowing she was being evasive. She was hiding something, and he couldn't tell what the truth was.

She laughed lightly behind him, getting up to stand tentatively next to Dane as he glanced carefully out the window.

"You don't have to be concerned. I can take care of myself."

Dane looked down at her for a moment. Her hair was shiny and fluffed around her face. She was slender and very feminine in a white silk blouse and black slacks. Her eyes were earnestly appealing as she gazed at him. He wasn't so sure she could take care of herself, but there was nothing to be gained by making her defensive.

"Beautiful women always need to be careful. That's probably why you were followed," he said softly.

For a moment, Taylor couldn't tell if he was teasing or not, and she smiled uncertainly. "I'm not so special," she murmured. "People don't usually notice me."

Dane quirked a brow. "That's a matter of opinion," he answered dryly.

Dane suddenly reached out a hand, his fingers carefully lifted the lapel of her blouse, where she'd pinned the red heart. She bowed her head to watch his hands, feeling again an odd sensation, almost an urge to have him touch her.

"What's the red heart for?" Dane asked and dropped his hand again.

"Valentine's Day," she said, watching him.

"Valentine's Day?" he repeated, so blankly that Taylor found herself laughing.

"Don't tell me you've never heard of it? Or celebrated it?"

Dane put his hands into his pockets. "Of course I've heard of it. I guess I'm out of step with the rest of the world. I haven't had a valentine since I was a very young man."

Taylor grinned, her eyes bright with merriment. "You're not a very old one. Just out of practice."

"Thank you," he said dryly. "How did you celebrate?"

Taylor walked to her bag and pulled out the tissue-wrapped box from the café. "I didn't. You're supposed to celebrate *with* someone, remember?"

Dane walked to her. "Do you celebrate with your husband?"

The question brought her up short, and brought all of the past swinging to the surface. The smile faded from her face, and her eyes and mouth became not so much sad as resigned.

"No, we never did," she said quietly.

"Then how do you celebrate?" Dane asked curiously, observing her wistful sadness.

"I don't," she said, fingering the box. "This is for Trudy. To thank her for letting me stay here."

"And if I were giving a woman a gift, what would I give?" Dane asked, watching her carefully. The question was much more personal than the way he was asking it.

She looked up into his face; it was masculine and so much stronger than Michael's. "Usually flowers . . . or candy."

"What would I get in return?" His voice was gravelly, the sound rasping sensually along her spine, making Taylor feel breathless.

"Your valentine would give you love . . . and kisses."

"It seems like a fair exchange to me."

He suddenly stepped closer, and Taylor found herself bending back her head to see his features. He reached to unclip the small red pin from her blouse. Dane boldly slipped the tips of his fingers just inside the blouse, and the puckered back of his hand brushed against her skin as he manipulated the clasp. Taylor held her breath.

"For now, what I'll give is a tour around London. We'll spend tomorrow doing it. And I'll take this—" he tossed the pin lightly in his hand "—in return."

Taylor tried to treat it lightly, her skin still feeling his touch. Unconsciously she put up a hand over the opening of her blouse.

"It's only a pin. I think I'm getting the better bargain."

Dane lifted his head as he heard Trudy calling out to them for dinner. He turned back to Taylor and stood aside to let her precede him. His eyebrows arched above the rim of his glasses.

"That's what you think," he said quietly.

But after her surprise faded, Taylor smiled to herself.

## Chapter Four

Taylor finished her tea and sat back with a sigh of reple-
tion. She looked up into Dane's closed but watchful
scrutiny and laughed lightly. Her hair, gathered into a
loose ponytail, swung gently with her merriment.

"What's so amusing?" Dane asked quietly, pushing
his half-finished coffee away.

Taylor's eyes were bright and cheerful, and Dane
rather relished the fact that she was having a good time.
So was he, but that was a revelation he was keeping to
himself.

"Oh, I'm just thinking how much I'm enjoying this
English habit of having tea and dessert hours before dinner. It can ruin your appetite."

"Apparently not yours," Dane commented, nodding
toward the collection of empty plates on the table.

She shrugged somewhat shyly. "I hope I didn't make
a spectacle of myself."

"Trudy will be gratified. She's convinced you survive
on toast and air."

Taylor giggled. Then she sighed again and leaned back
in her chair to watch the people around her, the odd as-
sortment of young and old enjoying a Sunday high tea,
just as she'd always read about it. Dane had the better

view of people coming and going, since he faced the entrance. She didn't want to look directly at Dane, trying very hard to keep her curiosity about him in its proper place. But it confused her that he was willing to spend a Sunday afternoon with her, pursuing the most inane tourist activities known.

She hadn't believed his offer of the previous night, although the idea of spending time with Dane had been instantly appealing. So when he'd called Trudy's that morning to remind her of their "date" and to say he'd be around for her in half an hour, Taylor's anticipation had grown. She hadn't had a real date since Michael, but she was only mildly concerned about accepting one from Dane. She reasoned that it was harmless, and she deserved to enjoy herself whenever she could.

Perhaps she'd convinced herself that he was merely being nice because she knew so little of London—except that it struck her that Dane was not the type of man to do things to be nice. Taylor did speculate as to what his motives were, but not too closely. She really was having fun. And Dane was an unlikely escort, which made the occasion so much more exciting. Taylor allowed herself a smile. It was the best day she'd had in a while.

Dane wondered what Taylor was thinking, wondered what the smile was for. He'd never met anyone who smiled so often. She was easy to please, but he found that a novelty, just as he found the day with her more than agreeable.

It was only after he'd started from Roger and Ann's that morning, on his way to get her, that he'd asked himself impatiently what he thought he was doing. Roger had warned him that he was becoming too involved, had also reminded him that Taylor Ashe was ostensibly married and, therefore, beyond his reach. Technically

Dane agreed with Roger, but his instincts told him otherwise—about Taylor's marriage and husband—and he'd learned to trust his instincts.

Taylor had answered the door when he'd arrived, standing dressed in a long-sleeved black knit dress, belted at her small waist. The stark color emphasized the pale delicacy of her face and her large eyes, with their very direct gaze. With her hair pulled back from her face she seemed refreshingly uncomplicated. Her appearance had been directly at odds with her nervous state just thirty-six hours earlier, when she'd arrived in London.

Despite Roger's wry warnings, Dane had not forgotten that in some ways, Taylor Ashe was suspect. But at the moment, sitting opposite her, he was unconcerned.

Taylor looked at him out of the corner of her eye, and was disconcerted to find he was watching her steadily. She nervously fingered the pearl necklace she wore.

"I really appreciate the guided tour. I couldn't have seen nearly as much on my own."

Dane reached into his pocket, but not finding the leather ball, easily withdrew his hand again. Taylor watched his actions.

"It's a big city, and not laid out with any logic. You could end up walking in circles here just to cross the street."

Taylor reached for her purse, which lay on a chair next to her, and reached in blindly to search around its contents.

"I think I've seen a London most tourists don't get to see."

"Don't think of yourself as a tourist. That allows you to adjust to any city quicker."

Taylor withdrew her hand, holding the small leather ball. She held it out to Dane, watching his face. "Is this what you're looking for?"

Dane looked silently at the object for a moment, then slowly reached out to take it from her palm.

"You left it at Trudy's."

"Thank you," Dane said, quickly putting it away.

Taylor hesitated. Her heart began to beat a little faster. She was about to take a chance that would either tell her more about who Dane Farrow was, or let her continue on a level of uncertainty and speculation. They could either come closer, or stay where they were . . . polite and curious strangers.

"Can I ask you a question?"

Dane looked away for a moment, considering her request and what she was likely to ask. There were things he wasn't comfortable talking about. He looked at Taylor again. "If I can ask one of you, as well."

Taylor blinked. "I guess so. It seems only fair, doesn't it?"

Dane lifted his shoulders slightly. "Okay. Go ahead."

Taylor felt her eyes grow wider as she allowed herself to get personal with a man for a moment. She also suspected that Dane had granted her a privilege given to very few others. That, too, made her nervous. She unconsciously bit her bottom lip. "What happened to your hand?"

The question was spoken very softly, but what caught Dane's attention was the amount of genuine concern, a sort of empathy for the fact that he'd been, in some way, injured.

Dane didn't move the hand that rested on the table, and Taylor didn't drop her gaze from his face to look at it. "I was badly burned in a grenade explosion. An accident." Now he seemed to hesitate himself—memories pulled reluctantly from his past. "It was a long time ago."

"Don't they use grenades...in wars?" she asked, puzzled.

"That's right."

"Was it Vietnam?"

He shook his head. "Vietnam is not the only place in the world where people fought. Or continue to fight."

Taylor frowned. "Where in the world?"

Dane hesitated for another moment. "North Africa," he answered.

Taylor only looked at Dane, at the lines and angles of his face, sharpened and set in place by what he must have seen and experienced. She didn't know about wars, but she could guess what it did to people—to the ones that survived. It was such a little bit of information, but it made Taylor curious for more. What had sent him to fight a strange war, and when it was over, whom had he come home to?

"Does your hand still bother you?"

Dane spread the fingers, expanding his hand to its full width. He examined both sides dispassionately. "Probably less than I imagine. The scar tissue doesn't concern me. I use the leather ball to keep my hand strong."

Taylor frowned. "Strong for what?"

Dane pursed his wide mouth. "In case I have to use it."

There was a shadowy other meaning to his words that sent a chill through Taylor. She wondered what he'd used it for in the past; to what purpose.

An explosion, Taylor thought in bewilderment. So deadly and extreme. She already knew that Dane was given to wearing black or gray turtleneck sweaters. She could guess that the burns went beyond his hands and arm, and that the dark clothing hid much of the damage. Taylor looked into his face and slowly smiled. "I don't think you have to worry about appearing weak," she said quietly.

"Thank you. I'm reassured," Dane said wryly, signaling the waiter for the check.

Taylor raised her brows in surprise and grinned at him. She believed that he'd actually teased her. She was about to struggle into her coat when Dane reached across the table and grabbed her hand. Taylor stopped immediately and raised her eyes to his.

"Can I ask my question now?" His rough-textured voice reached only her ears.

Taylor nodded trustingly.

Dane's hand was rough and warm around her own. He tensed his jaw and tilted his head toward her.

"When did you last see your husband?"

At first Taylor blinked in surprise. She didn't think he'd remember. That first day at the airport, information had seemed insignificant because they didn't know each other. But now it seemed suddenly important that Dane should understand that she was not in control of the circumstances.

The question also held a dozen implications—and the answer even more. She found herself blushing.

"Three years," Taylor whispered, watching his face for reaction. "A little longer, perhaps."

Dane frowned. He hadn't expected that. It had to be more than a lovers' quarrel to have lasted so long. He also realized that until that passport snafu a few days ago, Taylor had been known to the world by what he presumed was her married name, but had taken that opportunity to change it. Three years was a long time to be married but separated; it was a long time to wait. A long time without...

"What's his name?" Dane asked, to have something to say and not to think about her being alone...but not free.

"Michael. Michael Evans." Taylor didn't mention that for all she knew, that might not be his real name. She looked at Dane. "He left on a business trip to Europe, and I never saw or heard from him again."

"Surely you tried to trace him, follow his itinerary?"

She nodded again. "I tried, but...I didn't have a lot of information. I didn't know him very long before we married."

"You mean to tell me that for three years you've just been waiting?"

Taylor felt silly. She slowly withdrew her hand from Dane's. "Maybe I was fooling myself. Maybe I imagined that he cared so much, he would come back, or at least try to reach me if he could. I mean, people don't just disappear. In the end there is some explanation."

But there wasn't much conviction behind her words. More than anything Dane could detect not only the embarrassment of a marriage gone wrong, but complete confusion as to why. Three years... "Do you love him so much that you want him back?" he asked with a sort of detached curiosity, but the answer was suddenly important to him.

Taylor made a helpless little gesture that was neither yes nor no. She wanted to be careful how she answered. It was still too soon for confessions.

"I want to find out what happened. Three years is longer than we've known each other or were together. But I'd made a commitment. I felt I had to try to..." She shook her head helplessly in confusion.

Taylor's hand smoothed absently over the damask table cloth. She no longer remembered the loneliness. Other considerations had taken Michael's place. She didn't look at Dane as she spoke, and her voice was a bare whisper.

"I no longer feel love for him. I don't feel much of anything except a need to know." Finally her gaze reached his face again. "It's really important that I know what happened to him for sure."

"How will you find out?" Dane asked reasonably. And when Taylor stiffened, he became curious once again as to what she knew about Michael Evans and his whereabouts.

"I'm not sure yet," she answered hastily and reached for her coat.

Dane stood and came around to pull her chair out of the way. Taylor smiled over her shoulder to thank him and felt the reassuring pressure of his hand as he pushed up her collar to protect her neck from the cold outside.

Dane kept his hand there and used a little more pressure to turn her toward him. Taylor looked into his face, feeling as though she'd known this man for more than two days; she liked him. But she remembered clearly that she'd felt close to Michael at the beginning, too, and look where that had left her!

When she glanced at him again, her eyes were hesitant and her emotions guarded. Dane understood; it was reassuring to him that she was cautious. She was not a flirt, and she was not going to compromise herself or play Michael Evans false, no matter what he might have done or where he was.

"What will you do if you never find him?" Dane asked her.

She had considered that. There was no hesitation now. "It takes two people to have a marriage. If I have to, I'll get a divorce and go on with my life."

Clear eyes met his gaze, and Dane felt an overwhelming dislike of Michael Evans. He didn't deserve Taylor's loyalty, and yet Dane felt a jealousy that Michael Evans, who'd been out of her life for so long, could still command it. Dane squeezed her shoulder.

"Let's get out of here."

Dane's closeness abruptly made Taylor aware of her loneliness, aware that she was growing attracted to Dane each moment she was with him. Perhaps it was all out of proportion because she hadn't allowed herself to notice other men in so long; perhaps because she was away from home and the rules were all different. Perhaps because Dane himself was a mysterious, unique individual who had his own past and his own secrets and, as she was coming to sense, his own loneliness.

This new instant awareness threw her off balance; Taylor hoped the brisk outdoor air would quickly restore her equilibrium, but it only made her feel oddly heady, and very exposed before Dane. She somehow felt as if he could see into the very center of her soul. And she was afraid he'd discover more truths about her than she wanted him to know.

Taylor turned her face up to him, the wind blowing the feathering of loose hair at her temple and forehead against the delicate curves of her face. She tried to smooth the tendrils into place with one hand, her eyes squinting against the cold.

"I want to thank you for today. It seems I'm always thanking you for something. I'm not really so helpless, you know."

Dane's leather coat was open to the elements, but he seemed totally unaffected by either wind or cold, which only made Taylor feel colder.

"I'm not convinced," Dane said smoothly, briefly glancing around the street before bringing his gaze back to Taylor. "I still want you to be careful."

Taylor shook her head ruefully. "Are you still thinking about last night? I wasn't followed. Today I'm sure of it. Why would anyone want to follow me, for heaven's sake?"

Dane looked into her pretty face, at her sensually molded mouth with her ready smile. "Why, indeed?" he whispered.

Taylor was confused and looked away. "Look, I don't want to take up all of your time. It was a wonderful afternoon...."

"Do you have somewhere else to go this evening? Someone else to meet?"

She frowned. "You know I don't."

He wasn't sure, but didn't say so. "Then we still have this evening."

"I suppose. It's just that—"

"Just what?"

She looked awkward and unsure. "I don't know. I'm sure you have better things to do than baby-sit me."

He didn't. Dane suddenly realized that he had almost no one except Roger and Trudy and certainly nothing pressing to do. And certainly the prospect of spending the evening alone was unappealing. The very idea of a solitary evening made him a bit impatient.

"I hope you don't see yourself as someone who needs a sitter, because I don't. If you're fishing for a compliment, I'm not very good at them." Taylor blushed and looked at the ground. Dane immediately softened his tone. He really wasn't any good at subtleties—at being tender.

"I have nothing pressing to do this evening. I thought perhaps we'd finish our tour. Would you like that?"

Taylor squeezed her gloved hands together. She was afraid to answer, afraid of how it might seem. She kept reminding herself, as she'd always felt obligated to do, that she was married and as such, was not free to act as if she weren't. But perhaps she really wasn't married. She'd spent so much time considering Michael, and considering what was the right thing to do. Dane Farrow knew she was married. She'd been honest. So what was he up to?

"Yes, I'd like that," she answered softly; her insides fluttered, and she felt she'd be taking another irrevocable step away from Michael.

"Good." Dane nodded, leading her up a street. "We have just enough time to see the Tate Gallery. Do you like Turner?"

Taylor discovered she liked everything. She wasn't familiar with Turner's work at all, but Dane proved to be an interesting guide through the exhibition, holding Taylor's attention with anecdotes, drawing questions from her, and answering others easily. And yet there were just as many moments of contemplative silence, during which Taylor felt comfortable enough not to talk, listen or ask questions. They both seemed to know when it was appropriate and when it was not.

They left the museum and walked along Millbank. It was dark now. Taylor let out a sigh of contentment and looked at the tall man next to her. He never smiled, and still said very little, for the most part. But she felt his strength, presence and honesty, and he made her feel real—and alive.

Dane looked at her. "Are you tired?"

"Just a little."

"Are you ready to go back to Trudy's?" he asked carefully.

She looked across the river, watching the rippling of lights on the water. Couples were strolling together along the Embankment, whispering intimately, closed off in private little worlds. Everyone was with someone.

"No. Not yet," she answered, and then was concerned as to how it would sound.

But she needn't have been, for it was probably very akin to what Dane was feeling. In that moment, he found himself caught between doing the prudent, sensible thing, as he'd done most of his life, and wanting to let things happen naturally. He couldn't quite convince himself that he simply wanted to assess her behavior, see what Taylor might do, hear what she might say that would logically connect all the puzzle pieces so far: an absent husband, a trip of seeming insignificance to deliver even less significant rare books—a receipt that hid some sort of code.

And yet there was also just a young woman who was sensually attractive, though Dane doubted she knew it, who was bright and quick and open with her feelings. There had been no evidence all day of the Taylor surrounded by intrigue, and for the moment, it was the other Taylor that held his interest.

"I suggest we have dinner, then."

Taylor agreed readily enough. She liked the fact that he was decisive and took charge. She gave up trying to justify her actions, trying to be sensible. This was only dinner, after all.

But Dane did not take her to a café, restaurant or pub. Instead Taylor found herself being driven out of the downtown area of London and to a quiet residential block in Parsons Green. She kept her curiosity to herself until they'd parked and walked to a turn-of-the-century carriage house, which had obviously been converted to living quarters.

If she was surprised at the idea of being taken to visit with friends, Taylor was even more surprised to find that the friend was Roger Hillard. When the door was opened and Taylor found herself facing Roger, her eyes focused apprehensively on Dane's face. But Dane was busy dealing with his friend's surprise, although he calmly put his hand on the small of Taylor's back in a familiar way.

"Dane, I—" She tried to whisper quietly, but her words were lost in the exchange between the two men.

"I see you made it back for dinner," Roger said, although he was looking at Taylor and frowning. When he glanced at Dane again, it was clearly with an expression of mild disapproval.

"You remember Taylor Ashe," Dane said smoothly.

"Good evening...Mr. Hillard," Taylor said quietly, feeling very awkward.

"Roger, please. I didn't expect to see you again," he said forthrightly.

Taylor shook her head. "I am sorry. I really didn't expect that Dane...that Mr. Farrow would...I really think it's better if I leave and—"

"Of course you'll stay for dinner. It's just that—"

"Roger is only trying to say that he is surprised to see you. He's not very subtle, and he often puts his foot in his mouth. Isn't that right?" Dane said as Roger stepped aside to allow them to enter the house.

"Unfortunately Hawk is right," Roger said easily, leading the way into a living room that actually had a working fireplace, now cheerfully emitting a cozy, woodsy warmth into the room. Taylor took a quick look

around. The room was small, but very comfortably outfitted, and not at all what she would have expected of
Roger Hillard.

"Here, let me take your coat.... I'll tell Ann you're
here," Roger said, waiting for Taylor to remove it. Then
he waved them to chairs while he went to hang it up.

In the following silence Taylor stood, still feeling out
of place and uncomfortable.

"Ann?" she questioned softly.

"Ann is his wife," Dane answered, watching her. Dane
came to stand in front of her, saying nothing until she
raised her eyes to his face.

"You should have told me," she said earnestly.

"Would you have come if I had?"

"No, of course not."

"That's why I said nothing."

Taylor turned away, looking once more around the
room. She could sense that Dane was approaching her,
could feel the natural heat from his body. And when she
suddenly felt the touch of his hand on her nape, brushing aside the ponytail to lightly stroke the skin, Taylor
quivered with an overwhelming urge and need. She
turned again, to look up into Dane's closed expression,
pleading with her eyes.

"What's wrong?" he asked in a voice that though low
and raspy, expressed concern.

Taylor closed her eyes momentarily in response to the
soothing sound. She didn't know how to answer. Now
Dane's fingers were warm around her slender neck, his
thumb, with its broad, callused tip was stroking under the
edge of her jaw.

"You're thinking that this is not right. You don't belong here, and you shouldn't be here with me. You're
feeling very guilty right at this moment. And you don't

know if it's because you feel you should leave . . . or because you might want to stay."

Taylor's eyes opened and gradually widened at Dane's quiet assessment. The touch of his hand, the careless movement of his thumb were also bringing to mind what she'd been missing. A closeness of spirit and heart that made one person feel as one with another. She didn't have to answer, because somehow Dane understood. Dane could read her very well. But Taylor didn't want him to know or understand; it made her too vulnerable.

Dane must have felt something from her, or sensed something in Taylor's expression. His hand slid down on her skin until the thumb was near the base of her throat.

"It's okay," he almost whispered. "Everything's going to be okay."

Taylor blinked. At once her body began to relax. She believed him.

There was a sound of voices approaching from the hall. Dane removed his hand from Taylor's neck, although they exchanged looks before he took several steps away from her and stood with his hands in his pockets.

Roger came into the room, leading a younger woman by the hand. She was quite beautiful with very pale blond hair, worn twisted into a loose topknot. She was several inches taller than Taylor, slender—and about seven months pregnant.

Taylor smiled tentatively, but the lovely blonde was not the least hesitant as she was led to meet her guest.

"This is Taylor Ashe," Roger said. "This is my wife, Ann."

Ann reached out a hand to Taylor, which Taylor accepted; she felt the other woman's cool, soft hand squeeze hers.

"Oh, I'm so glad to meet you, Taylor. What an unusual name!" She released Taylor's hand and went to receive a kiss on her cheek from Dane.

Roger cleared his throat and Taylor continued to feel somewhat intimidated by being in the British immigration officer's home.

"Ms. Ashe arrived in London a few days ago, darling. I'm afraid she ended up in my office with a passport problem. But we took care of it."

Ann linked her arm familiarly through Dane's. She scowled prettily at both men. "I hope these two didn't treat you badly."

Taylor smiled at Ann, liking her and envying her poise and ease with these two men.

"Not at all. As a matter of fact Mr. Hillard was very understanding. I'm sure he could have put me on the next flight back to the States."

Roger rocked on his heels and grinned sheepishly. "Well, after spending one night with a passenger who apparently snored, I couldn't put you through that again."

They laughed easily—all except Dane. Ann looked into his hard, mysterious face.

"And what about Dane?"

There was an instant of silence as Taylor looked at him, too. Slowly a smile curved her mouth. "He's been very accommodating. He's been showing me central London," she said softly, remembering that Dane had said he never was. He tilted his head, acknowledging the gentle barb.

"I'm glad," Ann said. "Dane knows more about London than most of us who were born here. Now, why don't you all just sit and talk and I'll go back to dinner?"

Taylor took a small step forward. "Can I help you?" she asked shyly.

Ann looked at her, seeing the uncertainty—and something more—an appeal. She smiled and reached for Taylor's hand again. "How nice of you to ask. Yes, there's still loads to be done!" she exaggerated with a laugh, and led Taylor off to the kitchen.

Taylor took one quick look back over her shoulder, and found both Roger and Dane watching Ann and herself depart.

Ann was very easy to talk to and Taylor liked her at once. She clearly had a bubbly temperament, and immediately settled on a few mindless, and probably wholly unnecessary tasks for Taylor to perform. For a long time, the two women spoke of nothing but the dinner at hand and what Taylor and Dane had done around town. Then Ann wanted to know about her trip to London, and Taylor became reticent, hating more and more the circumstances that had obliged her to be secretive.

"I'm here on business."

"How exciting! Do you come here often?"

"No. As a matter of fact, I haven't been in three years."

"Oh. Well, maybe you'll come more often in the future. I'd love to have Dane bring you round again."

"I—I don't know."

Ann frowned. "Don't you like London?"

"Oh, I love London. And I'd love to spend time here, but..."

"Is it Dane? I hope you haven't let him frighten you," Ann said as she pulled serving platters from a cupboard. "When I first met him, I thought he was so hard and cold." She stopped to look at Taylor with eyes that were warm and reflective and rested a hand on her rounded belly. "Of course, I felt the same way when I met Roger. They're not easy men. But Roger is . . . is truly a wonderful person. Dane is, too. He just doesn't show it as much."

"Have they known each other very long?" Taylor asked, encouraged by Ann's openness.

Ann chuckled. "Oh, yes. Ages. When they were both young and foolish, they got into the most unbelievable adventures." She sobered and looked thoughtfully at Taylor. "Some of it quite dangerous. But they've worked for good causes—always." She sighed and turned. "And Dane has known his tragedies."

"Yes, I know," Taylor said softly. "The explosion, and getting burned."

"And nearly losing his eyesight. And, of course, losing Madeleine and the baby."

Taylor stopped her hands in their motion of slicing a loaf of French bread. She felt her eyes widen in surprise, but Ann, whose back was to her, saw nothing. And when Ann turned again, Taylor was thoughtfully arranging the bread in a basket.

"I haven't known Dane that long myself. But he's a very special man," Ann said softly. "I want to see him happy. He spends too much time with his contracting business, and . . . he's like a man without a country. He owns land in your state of Colorado, but I think he's afraid to go back there."

Taylor finished with the bread and got up to help Ann take a casserole from the oven. "Why would he be afraid?" She couldn't imagine Dane being afraid of anything.

Ann straightened, putting a hand to her back to ease an ache. "Oh . . . what would he be going back to? No house, no home, no family. Well, there is his father, but they've never been close.

"Roger says he hasn't been serious about a woman for years." Ann looked thoughtfully at Taylor and smiled quietly. "And I think you're the first woman he's brought to Roger for ever so long."

Taylor blushed and bit her lip. Ann raised her brows upon seeing the nervous reaction. She again placed her hand on her stomach, smoothing it over the bulge.

Taylor looked at her hostess. "When are you due?" she asked softly.

Ann smiled dreamily, looking at her stomach. "Just another six weeks. Sometime in early April. It's a boy."

Taylor grinned. "How do you know?"

"Roger wants a boy," Ann said wryly. "I wouldn't dare have anything else! Anyway, I had some tests. It's amazing what doctors can find out while you're pregnant."

"Everything from how much weight you should expect to gain, to when the fetus has the hiccups," Taylor said with a giggle.

Ann laughed, and took a salad dressing from the refrigerator. "And you can expect to deliver late. They say the first one is always late."

"And, of course, you'll go into labor in the middle of the night."

"You sound as if you know a lot about this," Ann remarked wryly.

Taylor blushed and shrugged her shoulders. "Only a little."

ROGER POKED at a log in the fireplace, and little sparks flew into the air and settled into the ashes. He turned his head to look toward the kitchen, listening once again to the soft burst of laughter. Shaking his head, he picked up his drink. Dane was sprawled comfortably in a corner of the sofa, his right hand slowly squeezing the leather ball. Roger took a sip from his own drink.

"What do you suppose they found to talk about that's so damned funny?" Roger asked, sitting down in a leather lounger.

"Us, no doubt," Dane said thoughtfully. Roger grunted.

"Well, I'm glad they're getting on. I'd rather have Ann laughing and smiling than not."

Dane looked at his friend.

"Is everything all right?"

"I suppose. Ann's near the end of her time and I'm nervous as a cat!" Roger grumbled, watching the flickering reflection of the burning logs in Dane's dark glasses.

Dane quirked a corner of his mouth. "Reactions of a first-time father. Don't forget women have babies all the time."

"Yes, but not *my* baby!" Roger said firmly.

Dane slowly sat up and looked at his friend. "It's going to be fine."

Roger frowned. "I think I'm too old for this, Hawk," he said with feeling.

Dane tightened his jaw and looked at the hand that was squeezing the ball. He heard Taylor's muffled voice. "You're never too old to want to love someone and to want to have a family."

Roger looked sharply at Dane, wondering if he would ever again seek out love and a family for himself. Roger thoughtfully sipped his drink. "So what did you find out today?"

Dane didn't have to ask what Roger meant, but he found himself hesitating. What he'd found out, Roger would not want to know. What Dane had found out had been enlightening, surprising, exciting and important only to himself.

"Not much. The books or her contacts here weren't mentioned at all."

"You still think there's something going on?"

Dane restlessly ran his hand through his hair. "Yes, I do. I'm just not sure what part Taylor plays in it all."

Roger frowned. "You sound as though it might matter. Is that correct?"

Dane was silent. He was remembering Taylor's revelation about her marriage—or lack of one. He was remembering the sense of contentment and ease he'd felt all day in her company. Maybe he was losing all objectivity. That was dangerous, and he didn't particularly like it . . . but it was happening, because his feelings were becoming engaged.

"I don't know," Dane answered honestly.

Roger looked into his drink.

"Did she mention her husband at all?"

Dane turned to look at Roger. "She says she hasn't seen him or heard from him in over three years. Nothing."

Roger raised his brows and whistled softly. "The plot thickens," he said dryly. "What do you think, Hawk?"

"I think she's here trying to find out something about him. I suspect he had business dealings here. But she says she wasn't sure what he did."

Now Roger frowned in earnest and leaned forward; the two men continued talking quietly over the width of the coffee table.

"A lot of things are adding up to a shady character, who may have been dealing less than straight, particularly with Taylor."

"And?" Roger prompted. His own domestic considerations aside, he could feel his adrenaline pumping with the whiff of mystery and trouble that surrounded Taylor Ashe.

"I don't think Taylor is going to find him, Roger. If I were to guess, I'd say Michael Evans is history."

"That's pretty strong, Hawk...."

"I know. But otherwise it doesn't make sense, does it? Do you believe that Taylor could have done anything to send him off, never to return?"

"Well, no. But you've only known her a day or so."

"But I know enough."

Roger chuckled silently. "I know you. The rest you'll soon work out."

"I intend to."

"Did you tell Taylor that?" Roger asked, surprised.

"Of course not. I'm not sure she's not more involved, too, but I don't think the possibility that Michael Evans could be dead has even occurred to her."

"She's such a little thing. It's hard to believe she might..."

"We don't know that," Dane said firmly, his textured voice showing a defensive edge that made Roger glance quickly at his friend. "Have you checked her story?"

"She's only worked for the company for six months. She worked for them three years ago, and then quit. The company is a legitimate auction house, but some of the employees seem to be of dubious character. I'm still working on it. So what happens next?"

"Tomorrow she'll probably deliver those rare books and the receipt. I want to see what happens when she does."

"You're planning to go with her?" Roger asked, confused.

"No. But I do plan on being there." Roger nodded, understanding.

Dane looked at his friend. "Is any of the network still in place?"

Roger nodded. "Some of it. It's been pretty much inactive the last few years, but I can reach it if I have to. Why?"

"I don't know yet. I may need them to do some work. Can you check and see who's around? And for the time being, Roger, this is just between you and me."

"I'll see what I can do." Roger nodded again.

They heard the women's voices again. At once Roger was alert to Ann's soft, musical tones, and turned his head slightly to hear her. He was very much in love with her, and it scared him silly to love that much. He didn't know if he could survive if anything happened to his wife now. He wondered absently if Dane had felt this way about Maddy. It was hard to say. When you were young, you could survive anything—even the loss of someone you loved. It changed when you were older. There wasn't as much time to recover and start all over again. Roger wondered if Dane ever thought of starting all over again. He somehow thought that his friend should. He was sure that he needed to.

Dane was also tuned in to the soft, feminine voices. It had been such a long time since such sounds meant anything to him. He and Roger looked silently at each other, understanding each other perfectly.

"What if she's involved, Hawk?" Roger asked pointedly.

Dane's jaw muscles tightened sharply, and behind the darkened glasses his eyes narrowed.

"You know me better than that. If Taylor's involved, then that's that. I'll do what I have to do."

He had no time to say more; the two women appeared from the kitchen to indicate that dinner was ready. Dane could tell from their bright faces that they'd gotten on well together. He wasn't surprised. It wasn't hard to warm to either one of them.

Ann went to Roger, who gave her a quick, warm peck of affection on the mouth, and whispered something into her ear. Taylor twisted her hands together, and tried not to notice, looking furtively at Dane. There was no one to whisper love words into her ear.

Dane frowned as he watched her smile, making her mouth a sweet curve. He felt his insides kick over at too many possibilities. He hoped to God she was everything she seemed.

THEY DIDN'T SEEM to have much to say during the car ride back to Trudy's. It was very late, and Taylor was feeling content, but puzzled and pensive.

Dinner had been a merry affair, made more so by Ann's bright personality and her affectionate bantering with her husband. Taylor found herself laughing and smiling a lot. Dane contributed as well, of course, but he tended to be much quieter, thoughtfully observant, as was his way.

When Taylor stood to light the dinner-table candles, her height didn't quite permit her to reach to the middle of the table. Dane had gotten to his feet, standing a little behind her to reach over her shoulder and finish the chore. The innocent pressing of his chest and hips against her back had caused Taylor to drop a lighted match, but Roger had quickly moved to put it out.

Later, when she'd offered to clear the table, Dane had taken a heavy platter laden with leftover meat out of her hand and into the kitchen, as Roger would not let Ann even think of lifting anything.

The mellow evening around such agreeable people had only made Taylor more aware of her uncertain status and of Dane, with his quiet, solicitous behavior and virile strength. But she wasn't in a position to do anything about it, not even to enjoy it at will.

And of course she'd been thinking off and on all evening about someone named Madeleine...and a baby. Each time she looked at Dane, she wondered, with a burning curiosity that touched her heart—who was Madeleine? And what was she to Dane?

Taylor sighed and leaned back against the headrest. It was foolish to even consider any possibilities. Tomorrow she would complete her business. On Wednesday she was going home. End of story. End of fantasy.

Dane had been thinking of Taylor going home since the night before, when he and Trudy had waited for her to return from a day on her own in London. He'd been thinking how gray things were going to seem without her.

She'd fitted right in with Roger and Ann, and after the initial awkwardness, Roger had been flippant and amusing with her all evening. She was very interested in the Hillards' expected baby, and Roger and Ann seemed to enjoy talking of their anticipation. And she had generated a lot of laughter when she'd asked Roger if he planned on being in the delivery room with his wife.

Roger had been speechless, and comically, his mouth had dropped open, because this had apparently not occurred to him. The blood had drained from his face, and Ann had giggled to see him so uncomfortable.

"I have a vision of him behaving rather badly. I know he'd want to try to help me, but I think if I suddenly cried out in pain, he'd either kill the poor doctor or faint!"

Roger had growled, but hadn't denied his wife's assessment. And Dane remembered thinking that if it were his child, he'd want to be there. For all he knew, it might have become necessary for him to help Madeleine in labor all those years ago. With bleak eyes that were fortunately well hidden, Dane had looked at Taylor across the dinner table...and she had stared back at him.

"I hope he decides to," Taylor had said, turning to look at Ann. "It's not every day you get to witness a miracle."

They entered Trudy's house quietly, knowing that she'd long ago retired to bed. But the fact that they were now alone, just the two of them for the first time all day, suddenly struck Taylor. This was different from the night he'd brought her to Trudy's from the airport; then they had been strangers. But they had passed that stage sometime earlier in the day—and this evening something else had taken its place.

Dane closed the door quietly behind them, and they stood shadowed in the dimly lighted foyer. Taylor unbuttoned her coat, but let it hang open. Now she felt awkward facing Dane, because of another awareness of him.

"They're lovely people. I'm glad you took me there, after all. You're lucky to have such friends."

Dane slid his left hand into his pocket and moved slowly to stand right in front of her. Taylor stared up into his face, her eyes wide, searching his dark features.

"I—I know what you're thinking, Dane," she said in a bare whisper. She didn't feel shy with him, only an apprehension that settled with butterfly movements in her stomach muscles. "Perhaps if things were different, if I . . ." She stopped, because he didn't say anything.

Dane reached with his right hand, the one he'd said he kept strong, and tunneled it inside Taylor's coat, closing it around her waist with a sensual gentleness. She just stood with no resistance, but also with no move of acquiescence.

"If things were different, you wouldn't be here at all, and this wouldn't be just a question—but an answer," the deep voice growled softly.

Then he bent his head, and Taylor found her eyes trained on his glasses, trying to see his eyes through the lenses, feeling there was still a barrier between them that wasn't of her making.

She stood until he pressed his firm lips to hers; her eyes slowly drifted closed. She didn't even pretend not to be curious as to what it would feel like to be kissed after so long. She was glad it was Dane.

Dane's hand at her waist pulled her gently, but they did not draw closer. His mouth slowly opened over hers, his intent unmistakable. Taylor felt mindless as she cooperated and enjoyed the gentle manipulation of her mouth, the rough stroking of his tongue against her own as it darted into her mouth with its tantalizingly slow seduction. The edges of his glasses touched her on one eyebrow and the other cheek, and she felt impatient for a moment at the space between them.

His breath was warm against her face; there was nothing tentative or unschooled about Dane. He knew exactly what he was doing, what he wanted, and Taylor knew that a man like him was not to be thwarted or denied. But then, she hadn't even thought to. His kiss was every bit as bold as she'd imagined it would be. He would not waste time with beginnings.

Just as quickly she came to her senses. She balled her hands into fists to resist the urge to reach them around his neck. She let her heels come back to the floor, where they'd been before she stretched up to reach him. And she lowered her head to break the contact of their lips. Her heart thudded in her chest. Dane released her waist, but didn't step back. Taylor was afraid to look at him. She shook her head, shame and guilt overtaking her all at once.

"Dane...I..."

"I know. That probably wasn't a smart thing for me to do."

She bowed her head. "No," Taylor whispered poignantly. But she knew he didn't understand all the reasons.

Dane tilted his head nearer, and she never moved. She couldn't.

"Did you mind?" he asked softly.

Taylor finally lifted her puzzled gaze to his shadowed face—his wide, perfect mouth. "It...complicates things."

He used his right hand to cup her chin and lift her face so he could see her eyes. "But you don't mind," he stated rather than asked, with a kind of assurance that made Taylor feel weak and small. He let her chin go and turned toward the door.

"Tomorrow you have business. But I want you to have dinner with me tomorrow night. I'll pick you up here."

"Do you think we should?" she asked, bewildered.

"I think we need to. Yes or no?"

She took a deep breath. "All right. Yes," she said clearly.

Dane opened the door to leave. "I wanted to kiss you while it was just you and I. You may find Michael yet. But I want you to consider this.... You may not."

After a long moment, Taylor blinked and took a deep breath. "I know," she said.

Dane nodded once, quietly slipped out the door and closed it.

# Chapter Five

Trudy closed the door behind Taylor, and through the leaded glass window next to the entrance watched her walk away. Her white-coated figure was half-hidden under the covering of an umbrella.

Trudy shook her head and turned. Then she walked down the hall to the parlor to phone Dane, who was waiting for her call. For the first time that she could remember, Trudy questioned the wisdom of what Dane had in mind. She no more believed that Taylor was involved in covert activities than she believed that Dane was a cold, hard man, as some thought him. She never asked him what gave him his suspicions about Taylor or why he felt she should be followed.

Nor did Dane volunteer that rather than being suspicious, he was concerned for Taylor and what she might unknowingly be headed into. He also realized, after kissing her the night before, that he now had another reason to believe that Taylor was innocent of duplicity...she'd been taken completely by surprise.

Nonetheless Dane's mouth was set with determination when he finished talking to Trudy. He wished he could believe that he was just overreacting, but he remembered the pink receipt Taylor had shown Roger upon arriving in London. He remembered what he'd seen when he'd held it under an ultraviolet light. The information had nothing to do with rare books.

When Dane left the Hillard apartment, he was also thinking it had been a mistake to kiss Taylor Ashe. He'd been a little too cavalier about it, perhaps, thinking she was just a pretty woman whom he found attractive. He'd started thinking about it while sitting opposite her at dinner. Her mouth was expressive and mobile, and her dimpled chin when she spoke held a simple, sensual allure. When he'd actually kissed her later, however, he'd been surprised to feel the restraint behind her response, a reluctance that belied the warmth of her mouth, and he knew he'd touched a need that hadn't been fulfilled in a long time. Her vulnerability confused Dane. He'd meant the kiss to satisfy his male curiosity, perhaps to shake a little the fascination he felt for her, to let him know that Taylor was no different from other women he'd been momentarily interested in and had pursued. But what he'd found instead was a woman who wasn't sure either of herself or her appeal with the opposite sex, a woman of limited experience in the ways of love. Whatever Michael Evans had been to Taylor, he hadn't been much of a husband.

And, Dane thought, as he headed to his car, carefully parked several blocks from Roger and Ann's residence, it had been a mistake to kiss Taylor Ashe...because one kiss had not been enough.

TAYLOR HAD WON the fight not to think about Dane for the moment. He had been forcibly replaced by the need to deal with the dreary London rain. It was untimely and inconvenient. Her travel to Bolton's Book Store with her package of rare books was hampered by having to maneuver an umbrella and watch out for puddles of water in the street, since she wore no boots. Her emotions felt alive with tension—in part because of what had happened between Dane and herself the previous night—in part because what she was feeling about him was now so irrevocably tied into what she might or might not find out about Michael.

The ambivalence Taylor had about finding Michael and dealing with the missing three years of their relationship was now becoming clear in the light of what she was feeling for Dane Farrow. She wondered if she had only imagined last night, or if something painfully real had happened to her. It had been a very long night; most of it had been spent in fantasies about Dane and their impossible situation.

Taylor reached the bookstore a little after the opening hour of ten o'clock. No matter what the outcome, the sooner she got this over with, the better.

Bolton's was a small, charming, dark hovel that smelled of leather and paper. Known only to a select clientele for its collection of out of print and often rare books, it was poorly lighted. Taylor had always been surprised that Strafford House had dealings with such an unlikely source. It didn't seem the sort of place to inspire big collectors of old books. But then it had also been surprising that of all the employees in the antiquarian book department, Taylor had been chosen to act as courier.

The bell over the door tinkled, and after several long minutes alone at the overcrowded counter, a middle-aged man with thinning, uncombed hair and thick reading glasses came out of a back room.

"Yes, yes...may I help you?" he asked in a rather high-pitched voice as he peered at Taylor through the heavy lenses.

Taylor smiled. This was the dealer who'd been here three years ago. "Hello, Mr. Neery. I'm from Strafford House in New York. Do you remember me? Taylor Ashe?"

The man stood staring at Taylor for a minute. Slowly the smile faded from his thin mouth, and he adjusted his glasses as if to see her better. When he spoke again, his tone was thoughtful and vague. "The young lady with the funny name. Yes...I remember you." As if coming out of a trance, he smiled again and fumbled his way around the counter, still staring at her.

Taylor couldn't imagine what held his attention, and his blatant staring made her curious. She put the wrapped books onto the counter. "I have a delivery for you from Strafford. Some rare books for one of your British clients. They've been getting heavier by the day," she said with a grin.

Mr. Neery reached for the books, hastily untying the cord and paper and examining the first copy. He looked at Taylor. "And the receipt. Do you have the receipt?"

Taylor nodded and reached into her shoulder bag. She withdrew an envelope, from which she removed the receipt, handing it to the storekeeper. A smile broke out on his face.

"Ahh..." he sighed, carefully taking the paper from Taylor. Then he picked up the books and with the receipt headed for the back room.

"I'll just be a moment," he said over his shoulder. "I just want to...er...log this in...."

Taylor shrugged at his disappearing back and turned to look absently around the cluttered store. To the right of the door were four narrow stacks of shelved books. There was just enough room for a person to walk through sideways in order to look at the titles. Taylor stared; in one of those stacks, three years ago, she'd first seen Michael. He'd been leafing through an old book, and when she'd spotted him, he'd slowly broken into a devastatingly charming smile, his blue eyes bright with appreciation as he looked her up and down.

"You meet the most interesting people in bookstores," he'd drawled, and then had boldly approached her to introduce himself. Her first thought at the time had been that he was very good-looking, and didn't look at all the type to be interested in dusty old books.

Taylor jumped at the voice behind her and came out of her reverie.

"Well, everything seems in order." Mr. Neery beamed cheerfully, rubbing his hands together. "I'll just . . . er . . . countersign a copy of the receipt for you to take back." He seated himself at an antique escritoire. "Are you leaving for America tonight?"

Taylor leaned against the counter and took another envelope from her bag. "Not until Wednesday. I have some other things to see to today."

"Oh, well . . . a dreary day for seeing London, I'm afraid."

Taylor clutched the envelope and bit her lip. "It's not sight-seeing exactly. I'm trying to find some information. Mr. Neery . . . do you remember Michael Evans?"

Mr. Neery never moved from his hunched position at the desk, but he stopped writing. He slowly turned in his chair to peer at Taylor even more closely than before, and his mouth was an open circle of surprise. "Whom did you say?" he asked softly.

"Michael Evans. I met him here about three years ago. Said he came by often because he liked old books."

Mr. Neery continued to stare silently.

"He was about five feet, eleven inches, with brown hair...." Taylor felt uncertain under Mr. Neery's myopic, yet assessing stare. "I assumed you knew him. Don't you remember teasing him that he certainly had an eye for the girls?" Her voice trailed away as Mr. Neery stood and approached the counter again, his eyes fixed in fascination.

"Why would you go looking for Michael Evans? That—that first meeting was three years ago."

Taylor blushed. "I—I know, but...well, Michael and I were married in New York four months later."

Mr. Neery's eyes widened and he paled. "Married..." he breathed, as if in disbelief.

"Yes," she said, confused by his reaction.

"Married..." he repeated, apparently even more bewildered. "Then—" he began, but stopped, as if not sure what to say.

"Obviously you didn't know."

"Nobody knew," he said absently, shaking his head. Then it snapped up and his eyes suddenly narrowed. "What happened?"

Taylor blinked. "Happened? Well...I don't know." She shrugged helplessly. "You see...I haven't seen Michael in three years. He...just seems to have vanished."

After a long pause, Mr. Neery let out a sigh and sat down again in his chair. But Taylor couldn't help noticing how peculiar he looked and how strangely he was behaving.

"Mr. Neery, have you seen Michael? Have you heard anything at all about him?"

Mr. Neery started shaking his head vigorously. "No...no," he stammered. "I—I'm afraid not. Three years...long time ago."

Taylor looked dejected and stared at the envelope in her hand. Mr. Neery recovered himself and got up to approach the counter again.

"What do you want with him?" he questioned sharply.

Taylor stared. "I told you. We were married." Taylor felt foolish. "It probably was a mistake. We hadn't known each other long . . . or well. I don't know why Michael left, but I assume he thought it was a mistake, too. Anyway, I don't want to spend the rest of my life wondering."

Mr. Neery narrowed his eyes speculatively. "You don't sound as though you would mind."

"I wouldn't," she said softly.

"He left you no letters, no instructions . . . ?" he asked anxiously.

Taylor watched his expression. "No. Nothing," she said clearly.

Mr. Neery sighed and spread his hands in relief. "Very sorry, my dear. Can't help you. Unfortunate situation, I'm afraid."

Taylor felt another avenue close, but she was no longer surprised. A definite pattern was forming in her dead ends. She looked at the envelope. Opening it slowly, she dropped its contents onto the counter. She'd been holding on to these bits and pieces like a lifeline. But suddenly Taylor realized that they weren't. They weren't going to tell her anything, and they wouldn't lead her anywhere. For whatever reason, Michael really had gone out of her life—and she was never going to see him again. An image of Dane standing in Trudy's doorway, telling her just that, flashed through Taylor's mind. For the moment she was too numb to feel one way or the other about it. It just seemed strange to think that after three years of questions, her search would end in London, where her short relationship with Michael Evans had first begun.

"What have you got there?" Mr. Neery asked, bending over to examine the scraps of paper, and holding his glasses so that they wouldn't fall off.

Taylor shrugged. "Not much, I'm afraid." She watched as Mr. Neery used a bony index finger to poke through the book of matches, the envelope corner, the haberdasher's receipt. "I went to the hotel where Michael stayed...."

"Did you, now?" Mr. Neery queried in a curious, low tone. "And what did you find out there?"

"Nothing," Taylor said, watching as he scrutinized the receipt.

"This shop no longer exists," he said, giving Taylor the receipt. "There's an office building where that block of merchants used to be."

"What about the export company? Do you know of it?"

Mr. Neery hesitated, staring at the address. "I'm not sure...." He glanced furtively at Taylor. "I'll just check a list I have. Perhaps...won't be a moment," and he left her again.

Restless, Taylor turned away. She walked to the door and looked out onto the wet, gray streets of London, at the rain streaking the door glass like rivulets of tears. She bleakly realized that when this day was over, she'd know, for better or worse, what she should do about her marriage to Michael Evans. She no longer felt sad about that, but rather an overwhelming sense of relief that she'd tried in every way humanly possible to do the right thing.

Taylor hugged herself, remembering suddenly the little touches from Dane Farrow. Remembering with a dreamy blush the titillating pleasure of his brief kiss and

the way it had made her feel. With both fear and excitement, Taylor acknowledged that she was looking forward to being with him again, knowing she would be free
to...

Mr. Neery closed the office door partway and carefully lifted the phone to his ear. He dialed a number and
then waited, nervously cupping the mouthpiece.

"Ah...this is George. Look, there may be a problem. There's a young woman here from Strafford to deliver the books...yes, everything's in order, but she's also
asking about Michael Evans. You heard me right. And
you're not going to like this...she says she was married
to him!"

Mr. Neery looked over his shoulder and peeked around
the edge of the door. He saw Taylor standing pensively
at the window, and turned back to the phone.

"I'm not sure what she knows, but she says she hasn't
seen him for three years. She was? Did Bella tell her anything at the hotel?" Neery moaned. "That woman's a
blasted idiot. No, I haven't phoned him yet. You do it.
Look, this could be bad...really bad, I tell you. Well, she
knows about the warehouse. Are you serious? I should
send her there? All right, but that could be a mistake.
You can ask all the questions you want, just get her out
of there fast! I'll see if I can get her to go. A number
where she's staying? I'll try. No, she's not leaving till
Wednesday. I don't know, but she can cause a lot of
trouble by Wednesday. Very good, I'll see what I can do.
Bye."

Stepping back into the little shop, Mr. Neery put a
cheerful smile onto his face and cleared his throat.

"Well, aren't you in luck. That export company is still
there. Now, you realize that it's a long shot. I don't know
what they do myself, but good luck...." He returned the

envelope corner and handed Taylor another sheet with written directions.

She accepted it gratefully. "Thank you, Mr. Neery. I appreciate your help." Taylor began gathering her things. "You wouldn't by chance know what kind of work Michael was involved in, would you?"

"No, no, my dear. I only recall him as a young man who was...ah...fond of books."

"Well, thank you anyway."

"Er...where are you staying? Just in case I remember something."

Taylor hesitated. "I'm afraid it's...it's sort of a private boardinghouse. And I don't recall the phone number offhand."

Mr. Neery looked disappointed. "Well, no matter. I think I've told you everything I know." He came around the counter and was already ushering her to the door.

"Thanks again," Taylor said.

"Not at all." Mr. Neery grew almost effusive. "You know a young man's fancy is so subject to change. Who knows?... You might be better off without him!"

Taylor found the comment so odd that she looked at Mr. Neery to see if he was joking. But he wasn't. His expression was one of benign sympathy.

"Oh," Taylor said, stopping suddenly as Mr. Neery reached for the door. "I almost forgot the receipt for Strafford."

Mr. Neery hesitated, and Taylor misunderstood his reluctance. "I have to show proof of the delivery. After all, the books were expensive," she reassured him. Finally Mr. Neery shrugged.

"Of course," he murmured, and initialing a duplicate of the pink receipt, he slowly handed it to her.

"Thank you," Taylor said, accepting the paper and absently putting it away. "And thank you for the information." Taylor opened the door.

"Good luck," Mr. Neery said. "I think you're going to need it."

DANE WATCHED INTENTLY as Taylor exited the bookstore. She stopped for a moment in the doorway to open her umbrella and to scan a sheet of paper. Taylor then looked about her before turning to her right to continue down the block.

Dane muttered an oath under his breath as he started his car. She was walking down a one-way street that he couldn't enter from his present position. He reasoned, however, that she was headed for the main street, probably in the hope of finding a taxi. He hoped she didn't elect to take the tube, or he'd have to park his car in order to follow her. As Dane swung his car out of its spot, he noticed the Bolton's store manager place a sign at the door, indicating that the store was now closed.

As things would have it, however, the short run down a street parallel to the Strand was hampered by a double-parked delivery vehicle and an elderly man tottering slowly across the roadway. By the time Dane reached the corner and looked around, Taylor was collapsing her umbrella and settling into the back of a taxi. Dane thanked God for her distinctive winter-white coat, which made it so much easier to locate Taylor anywhere in a crowd. When the taxi pulled away, Dane was only three car lengths behind it.

It became clear to Dane that Taylor was headed very much away from central London. Leaving behind the Strand and Whitehall, the cab headed along the Thames, then crossed the Chelsea Bridge into the Queenstown

Road. They were not headed into the best area, and Dane was even more concerned when they drew near the docks and warehouses on the Thames in Babbersea. It was also more deserted here, and Dane realized he'd have to drop back or risk being spotted. There was only a handful of cars in the area. He stopped at the corner of a dilapidated building. Reflected in the rain puddle a few yards in front of him was Taylor's cab, pulling up around the corner in front of the building.

Dane waited until she'd gotten out, the taxi had pulled away, and Taylor hesitantly entered the building. Then Dane slowly backed up his car, turned in behind another building, and parked it where it couldn't easily be seen. He got out, circled the building next to the warehouse, and stood deeply shadowed in a recess across the street that gave him a clear, undetected view of the entrance through which Taylor had disappeared. Dane figured he'd give her twenty minutes before going in pursuit. If she was conducting a deal, he thought grimly, it would be done quickly. And if she were to get into some unexpected trouble, twenty minutes was long enough to wait for something to happen to her.

He turned up the collar of his leather coat. His hidden eyes alertly scanned the area. There were several dumpsters and a burned-out abandoned car beyond the entrance near the opposite corner of the building where Taylor was. Through the gentle fall of rain, Dane noticed just the front end of a late model Jaguar in hunter green parked along the side of the building. Behind one dumpster was parked a motorcycle. Dane carefully made note of everything around him, his jaw working in tension. He, too, became part of the silent gray world around him as he silently waited.

THE BUILDING was dank and cold and had an odor. Taylor stepped into the entrance and sensed that this venture was probably a mistake. She knew she had the right address, but it now looked as if it had been quite a while since any business had been conducted here.

Water dripped through cracks in the ceiling, and there was only one naked dangling light bulb, giving off weak illumination. She heard a scurrying in front of her and didn't even want to consider what might have made the noise.

Taylor huddled just inside the door, debating the wisdom of staying or leaving immediately, along with the hope that here at last might be word of Michael. Then she looked around and doubted that there was even anyone there. Her heart raced in fright when somewhere above her a door squeaked open. She looked up the dark stairwell, and suddenly a head appeared over a banister, looking down at her.

"Who's there?" came the muffled question, echoing gently in the stairwell.

"I—I'm trying to locate someone who might have worked for this company," Taylor called. There was a pause.

"Who are you?"

"My name is Taylor Ashe Evans. I'm looking for anyone who knew Michael Evans."

There was another, longer pause.

"Come up." The head disappeared.

Looking once behind her toward the door, Taylor swallowed her indecision and carefully started up the stairs.

On about the third-floor landing, a man was standing in the shadows near a door.

"In here," he said, indicating the door.

Taylor stood silent, suddenly realizing that it was absolutely foolish on her part to be here alone. She had no idea where in London she was, or even how she was going to get back to the city. She was in what appeared to be a deserted warehouse, which hadn't seen active business in years, with a man whose face she couldn't see and with whom she had no idea whether she was going to be safe. When Taylor didn't move, the man made a gesture of impatience.

"Look, no one's going to hurt you. You asked about Michael Evans, right?" Again he pointed to the door.

Slowly, clutching her purse and umbrella, Taylor walked into a room. It was huge and empty, like a garage space. The dingy frosted windows against the back wall only let in a minimum of dim outdoor light to go with the three fluorescent ceiling fixtures. The support columns along the front and back of the room created dark corners. The door behind Taylor closed, and she began to feel her throat go dry with apprehension.

"Good afternoon," said a softly cultured voice to one side. Taylor turned her head to find three men in the shadows. One tall man in dark clothing was standing behind the other two. A second was of medium height and heavy, and the third, next to him, leaning easily on a walking cane, appeared well dressed in a suit. Their bodies from the torso up couldn't be seen clearly in the bad lighting, and Taylor realized she was at a disadvantage, since she stood directly under the fluorescent light.

"How may we help you?" the well-dressed man asked reasonably. The room was so cold that as he spoke, his warm breath vaporized.

"I thought there was a company here. An exporting business."

"And how did you come to think that?"

Taylor looked at the man who'd led her into the room, but he didn't seem to be paying much attention, leaning against the wall and staring into space. But the other three men were watching her. It was like facing an inquisition.

"I have part of an envelope with this address. It was among my husband's things."

There was a pause.

"And who was your husband, if I may ask?" The voice was smooth and cultured. It had a polite quality, one that would instill trust. But Taylor began to have the strangest feeling about him. He was of class and good breeding, and she wondered what he was doing here. More than that, how could he possibly be linked to Michael?

"His name is Michael Evans." The heaviest of the three men turned his head to the one who was well-spoken. There was a low burst of guttural conversation. But the well-dressed man slowly raised a gloved hand, and the other fell silent.

"How very interesting," the cultured voice said pleasantly.

Taylor took a step forward, her eyes bright and questioning as she stared into the shadows. "Do you know Michael?"

Again there was a pause.

"I believe I've...ah...heard the name before. Can you tell me a little more about this Mr. Evans? What did he look like?"

Taylor took a deep breath. This man knew something, she was sure, and maybe he could help her. With growing anticipation, Taylor briefly described Michael, how they'd met and where.

"And what was his business?" the voice asked softly.

Taylor shrugged. "I—I don't really know. I thought it might be exports and imports. He traveled a lot...."

"Why are you here now, looking for him?"

"Well...he seems to have...vanished."

Again the heavier man turned to say something, but this time the gentleman impatiently told him to be quiet.

"When did this vanishing act take place?"

"Several years ago. I haven't heard from him since."

"Not at all?" the man asked sharply.

Taylor frowned at the change in his tone. "No."

"Are you absolutely sure?"

Her frown deepened. She wished she could see his face. She took another step forward, and the man near the door suddenly became alert. The one who'd so far done all the talking smoothly stepped farther into the shadows, thwarting Taylor's efforts to see him. That made her suspicious and uneasy.

"Why won't you let me see you?" she asked reasonably. "Who are you?"

After a moment the man laughed gently. "No one very important, I'm afraid. But my businesses do require a certain amount of, discretion, shall we say? It won't help you to know who I am, but I will say this. I knew a Michael Evans once."

The two men near him began to whisper and move nervously. The gentleman ignored them, talking over their seeming objections.

"The Michael Evans I knew, however, was not a nice man. Nor was he a very trustworthy one. We did some minor business together, but Michael was...difficult."

Taylor stood stone still. She could feel the color drain from her face, could feel the awful damp chill of the empty building wash over her, until her coat seemed useless and she trembled. "Knew. You...said you knew him? Where is he now? What happened?"

"Where is he?" The man became cautious, shifting the cane from one hand to the other as he carefully phrased his answer. "That I couldn't say. But it wouldn't surprise me if you never saw him again. As a matter of fact, if I were you, I wouldn't count on it. Three years, you say?"

Taylor only nodded, her eyes wide and staring in the direction of the voice. But wave after wave of horror was surging through her body. He hadn't said it exactly, but the truth was suddenly there, and Taylor realized that the search had ended. She swallowed and felt a terrible knot in her stomach and tightness in her throat. She knew now. Michael was dead.

"A lot can happen in three years. By the way..." The voice was smooth and pleasant again. "Perhaps he left you something that could tell you more...anything?"

Taylor unconsciously bit her lip, and her hand pushed deep into the pocket of her coat. Her hands and feet were freezing and starting to go numb. "He didn't," she said, her breath forming clouds.

There was a moment of silence. "A pity," the voice said softly.

"Is there nothing else you can tell me? Maybe the name of someone else..."

"I'm afraid we had no other mutual acquaintances. In any case, Michael Evans's associates would have been suspect," he said dryly.

"What about yourself?" she questioned alertly.

The man chuckled in appreciation. "As I said, I didn't know Mr. Evans very well. Apparently you didn't, either. I'm sorry."

Taylor felt disappointment overtake her. "Thank you," she mumbled absently.

This time the man took a step forward. Taylor looked up.

"If I may offer some advice, forget Michael Evans. Go home and try to forget you ever knew him."

"Why?"

The laugh this time was dry and cynical. "I remember Michael. He was destined to have a bad end."

While Taylor stood digesting this observation, her stomach turning somersaults and her blood running cold, the heavy man began talking in low, angry whispers. Taylor heard reference made to herself, but couldn't understand what the conversation was about.

"You can't let her..."

"Don't be a fool...knows nothing..."

"What if...authorities..."

"Not worth the risk..."

Taylor frowned, looking at the three men. The tall, darkly dressed man was staring at her, not involved in the low-voiced discussion in front of him. He made Taylor uncomfortable, and she raised her chin as if she were indifferent to him, although she was feeling threatened.

"I'm sorry, my dear. I know you were hoping for better news, but there just isn't any. I'd like to make up for your inconvenience."

Taylor felt a bubble of hysteria deep in her chest. She bit her lip again, afraid that she'd either start laughing or crying uncontrollably. Inconvenience was hardly the word—

"I'll have my man take you back into London," he said smoothly. He raised a hand and made a signal to the tall man.

"Please...it's not necessary..." Taylor said quickly. She tried to think. *You won't ever see him again,* he'd said, and in horror her mind began to conjure up all the reasons why. Taylor looked at the man. She knew he was right, but he couldn't be trusted, either. "I can get back to London on my own." But he was ignoring her. In fact, he was now moving smoothly, without haste toward the door. The heavier man was leaving, too.

Taylor stared at her would-be escort. He stared back. She made the decision that she definitely didn't want him to take her anywhere. But by the time she'd turned to hurry after the three men, they had walked through the door, passing momentarily under one little strip of light. In that moment there was something familiar about them. Where had she seen them before?

"Wait!" she called, but the door closed. She moved to hurry to the door—and felt her arm grabbed. She was abruptly pulled around.

Taylor found herself looking into the face of a man with a full red beard and a small earring in one ear.... As full recognition settled on her, she never had a chance to gasp before his hand reached up to cover her mouth.

"Don't..." he mouthed in warning. They stood silently, listening to the footsteps fade away down the stairs until there was absolutely no sound at all ... and the two of them stood all alone.

Taylor was breathing heavily, her heart racing. She'd seen him before. Again she wasn't sure where, but she knew it was recently, in London.

Slowly he loosened his hand on her mouth and Taylor let out a shaky, frightened breath.

"Don't scream," he said firmly. He looked toward the door, but seemed satisfied that they were alone.

"I'm ready to leave now," Taylor said, hoping her voice was calm and her panic didn't give her away. She was in a terrible spot and she knew it.

The man with the rough features and look of indifference slowly began to grin. "I'm not."

Taylor swallowed hard, fighting not to give in to total fear. She attempted to twist her arm free. "Then I'll leave on my own. Let me go."

But instead of letting her go, he wrapped one huge hand around her throat, making Taylor gasp. His thumb began to press into the base of her throat, and she could feel the air being cut off. She stopped struggling, and grabbed at his hand.

"I said, 'not yet.'"

"That man—" Taylor tried to speak clearly, but she knew her voice shook. "He said . . . you were to take me back. . . ."

The man shook his head, his eyes cold and calculating. "He won't know if we delayed a bit. And you'll never be able to tell him, will you, now?" He grinned without a trace of sympathy for her. "I want you to do something for me." Slowly he released her and grinned again, at the look of fright on her face. "Michael Evans was a bastard," he growled angrily, taking a step toward Taylor. She began backing up, still afraid to take her eyes from him. "But he sure had good taste in women."

Taylor felt her back hit the wall, and she bumped her head, jarring her whole body. "Please," she whispered against her will. She didn't want to beg.

"He deserved what happened to him. Someone was bound to do him in. He did me an injury once—" he stroked a scar on the side of his neck that Taylor hadn't detected before "—so I guess he owes me, right?"

Taylor closed her eyes; her breathing felt labored. "I don't know what Michael did to you. I'm sorry."

"That's not enough," he said roughly. "Take this off." He plucked at her coat.

She started to protest again, then the door to her left fleetingly caught her eye. She reasoned that if she could make him think she was going to obey him, he'd relax his guard. If she could take off her coat, maybe there'd be a second when she could run for the door. Taylor felt she'd have a better chance on the stairwell than she would in the room, alone with this man.

Taylor lowered her gaze. She dropped her bag and umbrella and began to unbutton her coat. She tried to think how quickly she could get to the door. When the coat was unbuttoned, she slowly pulled it off her shoulders. Her heart quickened when the man reached to take it from her. Taylor suddenly jerked her arms free of the sleeves and broke for the door.

The man had only an instant of stunned disbelief before he cursed violently, threw the coat aside and started after her. Taylor's height played to her disadvantage again. The man reached her in three great strides, grabbing her hair and yanking it. Taylor's movement was checked and she came to a painful halt, a small cry escaping her throat.

He pulled her back and, releasing her hair, roughly pushed her against the wall. The wind was knocked out of her. Tears began rolling down her face. She tried to think of home and family. They need never know about this. But how could she hide it from Trudy and Dane? If she got out of this, if she got back to London, would they know something had happened if she said nothing? She wasn't going to think about Dane. But she began to struggle in earnest.

"I thought we could make this easy, but—" he began. Suddenly he reached for the front of Taylor's silk blouse; grabbing it, he tore the fabric away from her body.

Her hands came up to her chest, now covered by only her underwear. When she felt his hands pulling on her skirt, the panic came to the surface and broke free. Taylor screamed helplessly, and only stopped in shock when she was abruptly slapped across the mouth.

DANE LOOKED at his watch. Fifteen minutes had elapsed since Taylor entered the building. There had been no other movement around him, and the rain showed no sign of letting up. Beginning to feel impatient, Dane took a step out of his sheltering niche. But then the door to the building he'd been watching began to open, and he smoothly drew back against the wall.

First a young man exited, looking quickly around before opening the door wider. Two more men came out, and Dane noted the obvious difference between the three. The first was young and dressed in black jeans and leather jacket. The second was upper-class, from his expensively tailored suit and overcoat to his fine leather shoes. And the third was somewhere in between. An odd grouping. He began to ask himself what they might have in common.

Dane watched the door, expecting it to open for Taylor to come out, as well. The muscles in his jaw were already tensing with speculation, and he was bleakly wondering how she was going to explain this place and these men. But the door didn't open, and just as quickly, Dane's mind switched gears for another possibility.

The youngest man ran to open the doors to the half-hidden Jaguar, the other two men met him there and quickly climbed in. In another moment the Jaguar was smoothly pulling away. The younger man then came to retrieve the helmet and motorcycle and after a moment of gunning the engine, followed the car.

Dane watched intently, his eyes sharp, his gaze direct as he followed their departure. As soon as they were out of sight, Dane walked across the puddled yard and cautiously opened the warehouse door.

Once inside the deserted building, a feeling of dread instantly overcame him, but he was too controlled and had too much experience to let his emotions override good sense and caution. His immediate concern was for Taylor. Where was she?

Dane felt the years of sharp skills and instincts take over his movements as he quickly assessed the first floor and its layout. He began to walk through a shadowed hallway, staying close to one wall, where he stopped, somehow realizing it would lead to nowhere. There was some small sound above him, and quickly Dane tilted his head toward the stairwell. Changing his direction, he began to move slowly up the stairs. He knew better than to call out Taylor's name.

Dane had almost reached the next floor's landing when he heard the scream. He set his mouth in a closed straight line of grim determination, effectively suppressing all other feelings. Accurately guessing the direction and distance of the sound, Dane quickly sprinted up the next flight.

There was only one logical door to try, the others being too far away. Standing against the wall next to it, he used his outstretched hand to slowly push the door open. From this angle the room looked empty. He stepped in and away from the door, and almost at once saw Taylor curled up on the floor, her clothes disheveled. An instant knot formed in Dane's gut, and his right hand closed into an iron fist of rage. He knew there was someone else in the room, but right now he was more concerned with Taylor.

Later Dane would not be able to say what had happened in the next few moments. First he felt anger and then overwhelming fear sweep through his body as he saw Taylor lying there. He quickly looked around into the shadows. He'd started toward Taylor when there was a rush of movement from behind the door. Dane glanced over his shoulder and caught sight of a man escaping into the hall. From the hall he heard the sudden heavy fall of footsteps down the stairwell. He didn't even bother to follow the fleeing man. He hurried to Taylor and dropped to one knee next to her.

Dane didn't realize his hands were shaking until he reached out to take hold of her shoulders and gently pull her up.

"No...please," Taylor moaned through her sobs. Her blouse was hanging in shreds from her shoulder. Her arms were locked tightly across her chest. Her skirt was askew and dirty from the floor. One shoe had come off, and her stockings were torn.

"Taylor..." Dane began in a voice that he didn't recognize. "Taylor," he said again, more firmly, his own dread making him sound angry—and he was. He could have prevented this.

Taylor's hair was in tangled disarray over her face; she still didn't look up at Dane.

"Taylor!" he shouted, shaking her. This time her head came up, and slowly she focused on his face. Her eyes were shimmering and awash with tears. One corner of her mouth was bloody and slightly swollen.

Dane's jaw muscles tensed. "Taylor, did he...do anything?" he asked, feeling raw and helpless.

She was dazed and only stared at him. She was so surprised and so grateful to see him that she thought she would faint. "He...hit me," she barely got out in a quivering whisper.

Dane lifted a hand to hold her jaw. There was a bruise on her neck, another on her shoulder. "Is that all?"

She looked bewildered. She didn't understand.

"Taylor, did he...?" Dane couldn't even ask. But she quickly squeezed her eyes tightly shut.

"No," she tried to say, but no sound came out. Just more heart-wrenching tears.

Dane dragged her into his arms and held her close to his chest. He could feel her entire body trembling. He felt strange and awkward holding her. He wasn't sure how to comfort her, what to give, what to whisper to her.

He'd spent so much of his life fighting or preparing to fight that he had no techniques, knew no ground rules, had no experience for this. Dane didn't want to think about what might have happened, had he not followed Taylor. And he had to admit that he was wrong; he did know what he would have liked to say to her in that moment. But there was still this mystery. And there was still Michael Evans. Dane had every intention of getting to the bottom of both. What he wanted to say to Taylor Ashe would wait until then.

## Chapter Six

Dane sat perfectly still in the quiet room. There was just one bedside lamp, which cast a gentle light over the sleeping Taylor, so he sat in the shadows and reflected upon the happenings of the day. It was a more useful exercise than giving full rein to his rage. His darkened gaze on Taylor assured him that she was okay, at least for the moment. But the purplish, swollen corner of her mouth made him clench his hands and tighten his jaw as he recalled that, but for his curiosity about her reasons for being in London, the day would have ended in tragedy.

The fact that his instincts had made him follow Taylor to the waterfront warehouse didn't help very much, however. Dane was still angry. But if asked what he was angry about, Dane would have been able to focus on only part of the answer. Angry, yes, that if he'd responded just five minutes sooner, the warehouse incident might not have happened. Angry, too, that he hadn't seen the entire meeting as a setup and had let Taylor walk right into it. But Dane also knew that his anger served to mask his own uncertainty—and the fact that finding Taylor on the warehouse floor had completely unnerved him. It had proven beyond a doubt that he had more feelings for her than he was willing to admit to or that he could handle.

It was only the second time in his adult life that he'd felt so vulnerable.

The first had been with Maddy. Yet the two circumstances were quite different. With Maddy the tragedy had been instantaneous and irrevocable. But with Taylor this afternoon it had been *almost*; it had been *what if?* When he'd seen her slender body lying so still on that warehouse floor, half-naked, her clothing torn and disheveled around her, Dane had felt his insides tighten and his heart pound with dread. It had been a great many years since he'd responded to anyone with such emotion that he felt personally—physically affected.

Right now he couldn't recall one thing he'd said to Taylor as he'd turned her into his arms, her entire body trembling, before he stood to carry her out of the warehouse. Stuff about her being okay and it was all over, and he wasn't going to let anything happen to her. But he was certain he was trying to convince himself as much as Taylor.

Dane felt a bewildering sense of defeat. He suddenly didn't feel as strong or as in control as he'd been for most of his life. He'd found out once again this afternoon with Taylor how it felt to really care for someone—and how it felt to—almost—lose them. Because of what had happened, it was also clear that those men had been complete strangers to her, deepening the mystery surrounding her. Dane thought briefly of the four men at the warehouse, and recalled everything about them in startling detail. He knew that it would be easy to trace them, and he had the means to do so. He knew that Roger had a whole network of sources and contacts at his disposal, which had nothing to do with Her Majesty's various agencies. As a matter of fact, the less Her Majesty knew about them, the better. Dane meant to make use of them.

Taylor shifted slightly on the bed, groaning softly. Dane slowly leaned forward, watching her with concern. There was more strength and determination in her than he would have given her credit for. His gaze drifted over the paleness of her face to the awful bruise, and he felt his eyes narrow. Someone was going to pay for that.

Taylor drew her brows together in a frown. She could feel herself emerging from a dark, dreamless sleep. She fought to stay in that netherworld, because she knew that once awake, the horror of the day would return. But it was hopeless, and she groaned again, her breathing quickening as she remembered.

Dane silently got up and moved to the bed. He sat down carefully on the side and watched as Taylor opened her eyes. There was fear there, both in the shimmering depths and in the wide-eyed stare. Instinctively her hand came up, as if to ward off a demon. But just as quickly, recognition replaced the startled look, as Dane took hold of her cold hand. And then—he wasn't sure if he pulled her gently or if Taylor came forward on her own—she was suddenly in his arms, cuddled against his chest. Her mouth pressed against his dark sweater, and Dane felt the sensual heat of her breath on his skin. He knew she wanted to be comforted, but he also knew that Taylor had no idea of the effect her innocent need was having on him; he couldn't decide whose need was greater.

"Dane," he heard her whisper as she clung to him openly. Slowly Dane's arms closed carefully around her. His large hands stroked her back through the cotton nightgown she wore. In fascination Dane felt the delicate line of her back and followed the gentle curve down to the indentation of her small waist. Her hips were narrow, and he stopped there as he held her tight, but Taylor merely wriggled closer to him, seeking his warmth and his strength.

Dane closed his eyes and just enjoyed the softness of her against himself. He felt an odd tightening in his throat and chest. He was afraid to admit even now how much he wanted to enjoy the ways in which Taylor touched and fitted his own body.

Taylor felt Dane's hands on her back. She sighed and relaxed completely against him. She felt safe again, as she had this afternoon when Dane had found her. In hysteria she'd pleaded over and over for him not to leave her, and he'd assured her in surprisingly gentle tones that he would not. Dane was a man of his word.

After taking a few moments to make sure she was not seriously hurt, Dane had retrieved her purse and bundled her in the soiled white coat, carrying her to the car. He'd driven the interminable distance back to Trudy's and carried her up to the guest room, shouting orders to the concerned older woman. Then, when Trudy had tried to take over the sensitive chore of getting Taylor out of her torn and filthy clothing, it had been Dane who'd said with a mixture of embarrassment and determination that he would see after Taylor, keeping both his promise not to leave her and his vow to protect her.

If Trudy was surprised, she didn't show it. If anything she rather complacently and discreetly went to run bathwater for Taylor, leaving the two to make a discovery that begged for privacy, and which she herself approved of.

Then Dane, feeling awkward and all at once inexperienced, set about being tender for the first time in his life. Taylor was quiet and unresisting as Dane removed her skirt and panty hose. Her whole body continued to tremble, and she kept one hand grasping his sweater, as though afraid to let him go. He was surprised when his own hands shook as he lowered the one intact bra strap and saw the bruises on her skin at the throat and shoulder.

Dane's anger grew as he examined her face, tear-ravaged and flushed, the cut on her mouth now swollen and dried with blood. He uttered an oath and touched Taylor's chin. She winced and looked into his face, her eyes still dazed and glistening with unshed tears.

"Why did you follow me?" Taylor asked, moving her lips awkwardly, her tone bewildered.

Dane was perfectly honest, although careful in his choice of words. "I was suspicious. We both know you haven't been absolutely honest about your visit to London."

Taylor quickly dropped her gaze. "No, I haven't been," she admitted.

"Why not?" Dane asked smoothly.

"It was very personal," Taylor said, her voice filled with emotion. "And it was something I couldn't really talk about." She looked at him once more. "I didn't mean to make you doubt me. But today I'm glad you did."

Dane shook his head. "It wasn't doubt. It was concern. I knew there was something going on, Taylor. I also know it's something way over your head. And it's dangerous."

"I—I guess it could have been worse," she croaked.

"It could have," he agreed tightly. "But that doesn't make you feel any better, does it?" She closed her eyes and wearily shook her head, her hair a tangle around her face.

Taylor released her death grip on Dane's sweater, and they were both abruptly aware that she had next to nothing on. Dane's eyes drifted openly to her pert, uplifted breasts, no longer concealed by the ruined bra. They were small, but perfect, with dusty-rose centers. Taylor's eyes sought his; for a moment she was glad she could read nothing through the dark lenses. His jaw tensed and he pulled the bed linen around her shoulders, covering her. Slowly he raised a hand to brush back her hair and examine her streaked face. Trudy had left a small washbowl and cloth, so Dane squeezed out the excess water and slowly began wiping her face.

"Dane? I'm sorry," she said softly, trying not to wince as he dabbed at her mouth.

He continued to stroke her face gently. "Why?"

"For not being careful...like you told me to be." Tentatively she reached out to touch the hand that was ministering to her. "Please don't be angry with me."

Dane was stunned. What in heaven's name made her think he was angry with her? She'd been assaulted and compromised; she'd obviously been deserted by a husband whose existence, let alone his reputation was questionable; she was being used yet again as a courier in a scheme that hinted at deep implications that were probably also connected to Michael Evans. She was in more trouble than she could possibly handle, and she was concerned that he was mad at her. Dane had no idea how to tell her that anger was the last thing he was feeling toward her. He'd realized that this afternoon, and it had been something of a shock.

"I'm not angry," was all he said; he abruptly got up from the bed, leaving Taylor feeling confused and exhausted. "Trudy ran a bath for you. I'll tell her you're ready." He dropped the cloth back into the bowl of water.

Taylor gasped and clutched the sheet to her chest. "You—you won't leave?" she pleaded.

He knew he should. There were things he had to see to at once. He had to talk with Roger. But Dane felt himself giving in to her.

"No. I'll be here."

Even though Taylor had been persuaded to rest after her bath, Dane had stayed. He was pleased that Taylor felt this need for him, because it was a beginning he wanted. While she slept, Dane began, with the efficiency he was known for, to set in motion the many people and mechanisms that would locate and identify the four men at the warehouse.

Dane called Roger to inform him of Taylor's mishap. Roger's reaction was swift and not unlike that of Dane. Roger had only to remember the perilous circumstances under which he'd met Ann to know how quickly a bad situation can turn worse.

"Is she all right?" was his first question.

"Just shaken."

"What do you know so far?"

"I have good descriptions of the men. Bolton's bookstore is involved, and there's a warehouse we have to check out."

"Good. I'm going to make some phone calls, and then I'll meet you at Trudy's."

"Roger, I can handle this."

Roger chuckled. "I know you can. But I can *smell* this whole thing goes really deep. I don't want to miss it."

"Ann will kill me—"

"She'll understand. It's for you... and Taylor," Roger said firmly, and Dane knew that Roger once again understood more than the obvious. "I'll pick up Ann on my way over. She'll want to help, too."

"Thanks," Dane said unnecessarily.

"I owe you a few. See you soon."

It was late in the afternoon, and while Trudy and Ann kept vigil over Taylor, Dane and Roger sat quietly talking over the information they'd quickly gathered. There had never been a doubt in the mind of either that the task would take a little time, but could be done. It took exactly five hours to begin getting answers.

It had been easiest to trace the Jaguar, and Dane was not surprised to find that it was registered to an international banking firm. A little further digging showed that one of the firm's partners was a Philip Mayhew Jones. Even Roger quickly remembered him as the purchaser of the rare books Taylor had carried from New York. The man on the motorcycle was just a local punk, who served as a gofer and lookout. He'd been traced through the license on his bike.

Dane and Roger had a good bit of luck while checking out the manager of the bookstore. One of Roger's sources had spotted the heavyset man and the tall bearded one covertly leaving the shop through an alley door. A tail on both men proved the heavier man to be the owner not only of a small neighborhood café, known to be frequented by petty criminals, but also a fleabag hotel in downtown London.

Then Roger put the word out on the street that he wanted the identity of the tall man with the neck scar, who had red hair and beard and sported a gold ring in his ear. A few names came back, and Roger ran them through the files at Scotland Yard. The name and description of a Bick Rafferty showed convictions for smuggling, grand larceny, suspicion of murder—and rape. The police were currently looking for him.

Roger sat back in his chair and stretched his great body, yawning.

"Good work, Roger," Dane said, putting down a sheet of paper with information.

Roger grunted. "So what shall we do with all of this? What does it prove?"

Dane got up and went to lean against the fireplace mantel. "Nothing yet, except they were the ones at the warehouse today. I don't think Taylor has the first clue as to who they are. But there's some connection."

"Do you want me to bring them in for questioning?"

Dane thought. He put one hand into his pocket and swept the other through his hair. "No, not yet. I don't want them to think there's anything wrong. Let them go on with business as usual. I want to know what the business is."

"But there was the fellow at the warehouse with Taylor. He must have seen you."

Dane's jaw tensed. "I know. *Him* I want."

"I can have him brought in. There's enough stuff on his record to hold him on suspicion for a couple of days."

"That'll do. I want to know when you get him, Roger."

"Hawk..." Roger began with a frown. Dane was a private man, not given to looking for trouble if he didn't have to. But Roger knew that Dane, like himself, was capable of great anger when justly provoked. What had happened with Taylor was just cause in both their minds.

Dane shook his head. "Don't worry. I won't do anything rash. And it will be completely aboveboard."

Roger continued to watch Dane. He could see his mind tenaciously working over each point of information. "Anything else?"

Dane casually reached for the leather ball on the mantelpiece, where he'd left it that morning. He squeezed it absently for a moment, then put it aside again. "I'll let you know," he rasped, turning away.

Both men turned to the door then as Ann quickly came in. Roger walked to meet her, taking her hand.

"Are you getting tired?" he asked anxiously, boldly resting a hand on her protruding stomach.

Ann shook her blond head and smiled warmly at her husband. Dane saw the obvious love and care that these two people shared and immediately thought of the feel of Taylor in his arms as she sat pliantly and let him ease her out of her clothes, his curiosity about her stirring his senses and increasing a need that was both physical and emotional. It made him feel strange.

"I *am* getting hungry!" Ann exclaimed and laughed cheerfully. "Trudy and I are putting together dinner...if you two have finished plotting and planning."

"We were doing no such thing," Roger said unconvincingly.

Ann took his hand and turned to walk back to the dining room. "Rubbish," she said sweetly. Then she looked at his silent companion. "Dane?" Ann questioned. But he didn't answer, merely cocking his head, as if listening to sounds from the upstairs guest room.

Ann smiled gently and walked to stand in front of him. She touched his arm. "It's at least half an hour till dinner. Why don't you go see how Taylor's doing?" she suggested with quiet understanding.

Dane nodded briefly and turned to the stairwell. He'd sat quietly, reflecting on Taylor Ashe and wondering with uncharacteristic wistfulness if he dared hope for a second chance—

Now fully awake, Dane let Taylor lie in his arms. But the day wasn't finished yet, and there were still questions that needed answering. Slowly Dane disengaged himself from her hold, sorry to have to lose the moment.

Puzzled, Taylor glanced into his face as he sat up and put distance between them. She settled back into the pillows.

"How are you feeling?" Dane asked, trying to keep his attitude impersonal. He knew he'd succeeded when Taylor blushed and dropped her gaze.

"Better...and foolish," she said quietly.

He watched her. "We have to talk, Taylor." Her eyes flew to his face and he corrected her assumption. "About what's going on."

"Yes. I suppose I—I owe you an explanation."

"I want to know why you came to London."

Taylor felt her insides quiver. "To deliver those books," she said flatly. "And...to try and find Michael," she finished.

Her eyes were downcast, so she didn't see the impatience and anger already tightening Dane's mouth. He sat perfectly still. It had been right in front of him for days and he'd never seen the obvious missing link. Michael Evans. All of the mystery and confusion had little to do with Taylor, after all. It was all about Michael.

"Your missing husband," Dane stated.

"Yes. Only...I don't think he's missing anymore." She looked away. "He's dead. He was involved in something—I don't know exactly what—and it got him killed."

"How do you know that?"

"Those men this afternoon." Her chin began to quiver as fresh tears threatened.

"Taylor, look at me." He took her hand and held it. Slowly she did as he asked. He watched as tears began to fall again. "I want you to tell me everything about you and Michael. *Everything*. Where you met and how. What he looked like. What his habits were. And I want to know exactly what happened the last time you actually saw him.''

She looked carefully at him for a moment. ''They're right, aren't they? About him being dead?''

''It's not hard to figure out. Quite honestly, everything points to it. The sudden disappearance, the long absence, no word, no trace of him—and no leads.'' Dane looked steadily at her. ''Michael Evans was very careful to cover himself. He never intended that you should know too much about him. He may be dead, but you still want to know why. I want to know also.''

In a subdued voice and almost by rote, Taylor told Dane about Michael and herself. It went on for nearly half an hour with Dane only interrupting to ask questions. When she finished talking, there was a long silence.

Whether or not Michael Evans had actually loved Taylor, Dane was sure they'd never know, although in a very naive, starry-eyed way, Taylor had clearly been in love with him. It had been the love of youth and inexperience, and although he believed she no longer had feelings for Michael, Taylor's quest to find him puzzled Dane.

''Why did you wait so long to do anything?'' he asked.

Taylor blushed; unknowingly her fingers squeezed his tightly.

''Because I didn't know what to do or how to start. I kept thinking that I'd hear from him.'' Her voice dropped to a whisper. ''And I was ashamed. Everything happened so—so fast between us. I didn't really know who Michael was or what he did. I didn't know who I was married to. Or even if—if I was really married at all. How do you pursue someone who may not even be real?'' she asked emotionally.

Dane watched as a tear rolled down her cheek; her voice grew even lower. "And there was another reason why I waited. Why now it's even more important to trace Michael if I can." Her hands squeezed even harder. "Michael was gone almost six weeks when I realized . . . I was pregnant."

For a long moment there was only silence. Taylor waited for some reaction. She thought Dane would pull his hand free, withdraw. He would have to view her differently now. And he did, but not in the manner she half expected.

Dane was surprised, but only because it had never occurred to him that there might be a child. For a moment he stared at Taylor, seeing her not as an attractive young women, for whom he was developing unexpected, deep feelings, but as a reminder of Maddy—together with their baby, they would have been a family. He would have belonged somewhere—and to someone. In Taylor he now saw someone with responsibility for another's life, someone who was totally dependent upon her.

And, too, with a sudden sadness, Dane realized that a child was the ultimate connection between a man and a woman, proving their love and commitment. He felt anger and jealousy for Michael Evans, who had proven neither, leaving not one innocent victim—but two.

Taylor's having a child cleared up more of the mystery. Her interest in Michael was more than personal, it was maternal and would necessarily supersede any other consideration.

Dane did indeed look at her with new insight. Even without Michael she was still not free, but irrevocably tied to the product of their union. Dane knew that this new development changed some things, but not the way he felt about her. And he wasn't sure that was so smart.

When there was no response, Taylor bravely lifted her face to look at Dane. But as always, he was so careful and closed with his feelings. She had no idea what he was thinking.

"Her name is Holly, and she's nearly three. Michael never knew—but I still have to figure out what I'm going to tell her someday about her father. That's why all of this is so important. I don't care about Michael. I care about my child—and her identity."

"Holly," Dane repeated with a gentle amusement, and Taylor was surprised when his mouth quirked slightly. Now he seemed to be studying her through the dark glasses. "At least she gets a girl's name," he teased with his gravelly voice.

Taylor was so thankful that he wasn't going to judge her that she missed the subtle tone of helplessness in his voice. She lifted her small hand to rest it against his firm chest.

"I'm sorry I didn't tell you sooner, Dane. Michael left me nothing but Holly, a few books and a lot of unanswered questions. I consider her the most precious of the three."

Dane waited a moment. "What kind of books?"

Taylor blinked in confusion at the abrupt change of subject. She shrugged. "Books of poetry. They're old but not important. The bindings are rather beautiful and hand-tooled." She frowned. "Does it seem important?"

Dane hesitated and shook his head. "Probably not. But I want whatever information you have that I can use."

Her eyes scanned his closed expression. She slowly shook her head. "You don't have to know. Perhaps if we'd met under different circumstances, or...if everything hadn't been so—complicated..."

"Then what?" Dane coaxed in curiosity. She gnawed her lip, and winced when the bruised skin protested.

She looked openly at him. "Then perhaps my meeting you would have been more than special, and we might have had a chance. But there's no need for you to be involved." She looked at the sharp lines of his face, the well-shaped but hard mouth, the glasses that kept him a mystery. When he finally spoke, the rough edge of his raspy voice was low and caressing.

"I'm already involved," he admitted.

Taylor stared, feeling her eyes widen at his words. He seemed to be looking carefully at her, studying her face. He slowly reached out a hand to hold her chin and tilted her face at an angle.

"Does it hurt?" he asked quietly, but there was a harshness that said he was still angry.

She nodded.

"You shouldn't have been there alone," he said, grinding out the words. "You should have told me."

"I thought I could handle it," she said.

"You have to be more careful who you trust."

"I can trust you."

"How do you know that?" Dane asked, slightly impatient.

She looked at the hand still holding hers. "I don't think I have anything you want." She shrugged lightly.

Was that what she thought? Did she think so little of herself, or too much of him?

Dane shook his head in amazement. "What I want, I can't have," he said ruefully.

Taylor fixed her gaze on his face. "What is it?"

Dane's thumb, so near the corner of her mouth, gently stroked next to and under the tender injury. When he began lowering his head, Taylor automatically lifted her face to meet him halfway. His lips carefully touched the hurt spot. The fingers on the side of her face wove their way into her hair. Dane's mouth shifted a hairbreadth to fully kiss her lips, but gently and so briefly that it was like a feather touch; a mere hint—a promise.

"It's you," he whispered against her mouth. "I want you."

TAYLOR SAT staring at the office wall. She'd never thought to find herself here again. It was where her London trip had first begun, where she'd met Dane Farrow, in Roger Hillard's office. She was once again at Heathrow Airport for a flight back to the States—and she hadn't seen nor heard from Dane in more than twenty-four hours. Not since her ill-advised adventure at the warehouse. Not since Dane's declaration, which had stunned and excited her—and finally made her smile. But Taylor had been confused when he stood up from the side of the bed and against her protests, moved some distance from her.

Taylor had been breathless at his confession, and was more sorry than ever that Michael still stood between them. She realized that this factor was on Dane's mind, as well. They both knew Michael had been a mistake. This time with Dane it wasn't another mistake. Yet it didn't seem that there would be a chance to convince him. Perhaps he thought it was happening too fast and that at least one of them had to consider their circumstances rationally. The task had fallen to Dane. She wished it didn't have to. She wished it was in him to go with the moment and his feelings.

Taylor's eyes were bright and filled with the recognition of what had to be. She nodded her head. "You're right," she whispered softly. "We do have a lot to talk about."

Dane shook his head, already knowing what he had to do. "No more tonight," he prevaricated. "Perhaps tomorrow, when you've rested." And she'd believed him.

But Dane had not returned to Trudy's the next day, and Taylor's hours of anticipation had soon turned to confused wondering as the day grew into night with no word from Dane; even Trudy couldn't enlighten her.

Then this morning the call had come in, but from Roger, instructing Trudy to have all of Taylor's bags packed, and for Taylor to be ready to leave for the airport by noon. No amount of questioning poor Trudy had gleaned any answers. She was just as confused and just as concerned as Taylor about what was happening, and what Dane had in mind.

Taylor had spent hours trying to figure out why Dane had so abruptly withdrawn from her. She thought it might still be Michael, or the sudden revelation about Holly. But he'd known all of that, and still he'd said he wanted her.

Taylor stood up impatiently from her chair and paced the room. Whatever had happened didn't change the fact that she was leaving. Suddenly the door opened behind her and when she turned, Dane stood in the doorway.

They just stared at each other, Dane taking in her lithe body, dressed for travel in gray slacks, with a red sweater pulled down over her hips and belted at the waist. Her hair was tied back in a ponytail with a bright red ribbon, and her cheerful appearance was in sharp contrast to the bewilderment in her eyes. The broken skin at the corner of her mouth was no longer raw and bruised, but none-theless a reminder.

To Taylor, Dane looked exactly as he had the first time she met him. And she noticed that he seemed as closed and formidable now as he had then. With quick insight she realized that his coming to her now, in Roger's of-fice at the airport, was deliberate. It was impersonal and cold and reminded Taylor that she didn't know Dane—or anything about him. She didn't know what made him who he was or what was important to him, whom he might have loved—or lost. She imagined she'd learned over the last several days what his strengths were, but she didn't know his weaknesses—or the things that might make him afraid. Taylor did know how she felt about him, and she believed she wasn't wrong to feel it.

"It's time to go," Dane said.

For a long moment Taylor just stared at him, her look pleading and hopeful, again demonstrating to Dane how easy she was to read. He wanted to believe what he saw in her eyes.

"Is that all you have to say?" Her tone was soft, and hurt.

Dane clenched his fist and put it into his pocket. "I don't think there's any more to say."

She blinked. "Dane, what happened?"

"You had a bad scare. You found out most of what you needed to know about your husband—" his blunt reminder of her status made Taylor blush "—and you can return home now. You can forget what happened and put it behind you."

Taylor was shaking her head. Slowly she walked to-ward Dane, her eyes riveted to his face. "There are some things I don't want to forget. The night before last, for instance."

Dane glanced away.

Her poise began to give way, to be replaced by sadness and a dread at having to leave this way. Taylor's voice quavered and became a thin whisper.

"What happened?"

Dane's jaw worked in tension, the hard muscle flexing rapidly. "What happened was I realized it was no good. It couldn't work. You have a daughter to think about, and yourself. I'm a different person, Taylor. And I don't have anything to give."

"I haven't asked for anything," she said in a small voice, her eyes filling with tears.

Dane shifted restlessly. He walked to lift the now-cleaned white coat from the back of a chair and let it drape open. "I'm not any different from Michael, you know. I think you deserve better than either of us." He held up the coat for her to put it on.

Taylor stood rooted to the spot. "Do you . . . still want me?" she asked.

Dane heard every nuance in her voice. "Yes, I do," he answered with a blunt honesty that surprised Taylor. "But it doesn't change anything. I want you to go home."

His words and tone were firm and clear, and Taylor knew he meant it. The spark of hope within her died. She listlessly struggled into her coat, gathered her things and left the room with Dane right behind her. She wasn't going to make things difficult or make a fool of herself by crying, but she felt a lump of emotion lodge in her throat, threatening to choke her.

As she walked the corridors of the terminal building, she kept her head high and her mouth firmly closed. When Dane lightly touched her elbow to steer her in the right direction, he could feel the trembling of her body.

She paid no attention to the man or two here and there, strategically placed by Roger, just to make sure everything went smoothly. Taylor was only aware of the man next to her and felt the cruel injustice of fate, which had so precipitously brought them together, now only to separate them, possibly forever. The thought drew a sharp intake of breath from Taylor, and her eyes flew open in alarm to gaze at Dane's hard countenance.

"When will I see you again?" she asked.

Dane didn't answer; just a few feet ahead of them stood Roger with two airline flight officials. The waiting area was completely empty except for the small gathering of silent men and Taylor.

"Your passport, please," one man asked, and she pulled it from her purse with shaking hands.

"I can guarantee it's in order," Roger said dryly, looking at Taylor with the same kind of stony facade that Dane used. She tried to smile, to let him know she realized he was doing a job, but failed miserably and lowered her head.

She missed the change in Roger's expression. He did not necessarily agree with what Dane was doing, but he understood the need. Ann had been furious with both Dane and himself, and while Dane couldn't be persuaded to change his mind and let Taylor stay longer, Roger had given in to his wife's entreaties to deliver an envelope to Taylor. He pulled it from his pocket now and ignoring his best friend's glare, gave it to Taylor.

"It's from Ann," he said in a low voice, so the officials could not hear.

Taylor mumbled a thank-you and clutched the envelope.

The official gave the passport back to her and signaled behind him for the departure gate door to be opened. He turned to Roger.

"She can board now, Mr. Hillard. We've secured all the other passengers. She's got—" he looked at his watch "—ten minutes."

"Thank you." Roger nodded a dismissal to the man.

Taylor felt her chest constrict, her stomach roll with tension. Only ten more minutes. She was perilously close to tears, and Dane stood coldly silent. She turned to him. "Dane?" she whispered, but his only response was a tightening of his mouth.

Taylor bit her bottom lip, and with a control she didn't know she possessed, turned to Roger and held out a small hand.

"You've been very kind and understanding. I'm truly sorry if I've caused anyone trouble."

"Not at all," Roger responded, taking her delicate hand and glancing briefly at the silent Dane. "I'm sorry your trip ended so poorly."

"Will you please tell Ann I'd love to know when the baby is born?"

Roger blushed. "We'll do that."

The official checked his watch for the third time. He cleared his throat. "Ah...Mr. Hillard?"

Roger put up a silencing hand, watching the painful struggle taking place between Dane and Taylor.

Once again Taylor turned to Dane. "Dane..." she tried again.

This time he looked down at her. He saw such anguish on her face that his insides twisted. He made an impatient gesture with his head, and uttered a profanity through clenched teeth. Then, taking an iron hold of

Taylor's arm, he turned abruptly and began walking with determination to the next waiting area.

"B-b-but sir!" the airline official called in agitation.

Roger again put up a hand, a slight smile on his mouth. "It's all right. This will only take a moment."

Dane's sudden movement took Taylor completely by surprise; she had to almost run to keep up with his long strides. Then they stood alone in the unused sector, and Dane stopped so abruptly that Taylor bumped into him. The moment seemed electrically charged.

Then, without warning, Dane abruptly removed his glasses; Taylor stared at him. She blinked when she saw his face fully, for the first time without the protective shades. Dane's expression was an odd combination of defiance and resignation. There was a vulnerability that was so apparent that Taylor's heart went out to him instantly. And completely.

Every muscle in Dane's face showed his ambivalence, the emotional war that was going on inside him. A lot of it had to do with a past heavily laced with conflict and violence, and some had to do with the last vestiges of his memory of Maddy.

Taylor didn't realize she'd been holding her breath until she sighed softly as she examined Dane's face, ravaged by war. His eyes were deep set under a brow ridge that was prominently defined and edged by arching, heavy black brows. The area around both eyes that is normally etched with laugh lines was a pale crisscrossing of delicate scar tissue and skin grafts. In contrast to his tanned face and near-black hair, his eyes were a shade of light green. His coloring bore testimony to a man who had spent a lot of time outdoors all around the world, good weather and bad. He did not have the smooth, comfortable good looks that Michael had possessed, but then Michael's had lacked the honesty and blatant masculinity of Dane's.

Dane carefully watched Taylor's reaction and found no censoring or rejection in her eyes, which were the sultry, smoky gray he'd imagined.

Taylor was viewing the lines and markings that mapped out the life he'd led, a life harder and tougher than most. It touched her deeply that he'd been battered and bruised, but she wanted him to realize there was no need for him to protect her from what he was or had been, any more than he needed protection from her.

"I'm afraid I won't meet your expectations," he said in his gravelly voice.

Taylor smiled tremulously, and lifted a hand to lay it caressingly against his cheek. "You're wrong. You already have." She sighed.

Dane frowned at her, his eyes scanning her face intently. As if against his will, Dane uttered her name and roughly gathered Taylor into his arms. He held her so close that Taylor could detect his heartbeat; and his breathing came hurried against her neck. His lips pressed to her sweet skin. He tangled his fingers in her hair, pulling her head back slowly as his mouth made the journey from her jaw to her mouth and captured it with an erotic intensity that made Taylor dig her hand into his shoulder and try to circle his neck.

Her mouth opened under his to feel the quick plunge of his tongue as he explored with a tantalizing slowness that made Taylor weak. It was like a salve to her raw nerves, and she melted happily against Dane's broad, hard chest as his lips manipulated and possessed hers with a poignant hunger.

One hand cupped the back of her head as his lips and tongue drove at her, kissing her with rising passion. The other hand found the opening of her coat and burrowed inside to circle Taylor's waist. She came up on tiptoe to accommodate his height, and his hand slid to her derriere and pressed her slowly to his thighs. The hard outline drew a gasp from Taylor, who tightened her arms around his neck.

Suddenly Dane ended the kiss, so abruptly, so angrily that Taylor felt dazed. He firmly pulled her arms loose, holding her away.

The tears welled up again.

"Dane...I think I love you."

He looked anguished and quickly replaced his dark glasses. "I'm sure you thought you loved Michael as well."

"Yes, I thought I did," she admitted. "The difference is, I never told him so."

"All right. You've told me." Dane released her and stood back. "Go home, Taylor," he whispered, but she thought she detected reluctance in the command.

"Am I ever going to see you again?"

He shook his head. "I don't know." Taking her hand, he led her like a small child, back to the frantic agent.

Dane pretended not to see the tears falling, and released Taylor's hand, pointing her toward the exit. She never turned around, and hesitated only a moment before walking bravely through the departure doors. She didn't mean to turn around again, but at the last moment, Taylor did. She and Dane stood in such a manner that each was the last thing the other saw as the door was fastened between them....

Dane stood still, wondering if he'd just made the biggest mistake of his life. He felt Roger's hand clamp down on his shoulder. "You should have told her, Hawk, that those hoodlums were trying to trace her here in London.''

Dane was slowly shaking his head. He put his hands into his pockets and turned from the closed doors. ''No. They obviously think she has something they want. But the less she knows the better. It made more sense to get her out of here. I wanted her safe. Besides, she has her daughter to think of.''

Roger pursed his lips and nodded as the two men headed back to the main terminal. Dane had told Roger after dinner two nights ago about Taylor's revelation. Given Dane's background and tragedy, Roger had half expected Dane to become remorseful and silently moody over his own loss. Well, he had, but in a surprisingly magnanimous way that Roger found self-defeating.

Dane cared about Taylor Ashe. Very possibly it was much more than that. It didn't matter that it had happened so quickly and so thoroughly. Roger knew that in matters of the heart time was an irrelevant issue. But in that case, rather than pushing Taylor away, Dane should be embracing and welcoming the feelings she was offering.

Taylor was strong and bright and even brave in a wholly innocent way. Roger could see that these were exactly the reasons why Dane was drawn to her. Of course, there were other reasons Dane hadn't even admitted to yet.

But Roger wasn't worried. When all the mystery was over, he had a feeling that it would be Taylor who finally brought Dane home again.

# Chapter Seven

It was almost three weeks later when Dane got the call. It might have happened sooner, except that Dane had left London shortly after Taylor.

Dane's leaving had been timely. And necessary. He had business to take care of, shipments of housing equipment to arrange, going to Greece, Turkey and Israel. The details of dates, shippers, delivery sites, even promises of dock strikes had been a welcome relief from the other thing on his mind—Taylor. He tried to reestablish his solitary routine and simple daily existence, but his life of austerity all at once seemed particularly odd and unappealing. The mental gymnastics of dealing with foreign countries and governments, of negotiating to construct inexpensive but efficient housing for the poor seemed ludicrous when he had no home of his own. The life he'd established had always been just fine. Now it no longer seemed so.

He felt rather bewildered and lost, and didn't like it one bit. He didn't like facing the fact that meeting Taylor Ashe had touched on him so profoundly that, having sent her back to the States, he felt as if something essential was missing from his life.

He was at least willing to admit that something very significant had happened between Taylor and himself. Had they become lovers, then sex and a satisfying gratification would have explained much of the attraction. But not having consummated their brief relationship, although he would have been deaf, blind and dumb not to have recognized the mutual attraction, meant that they had begun to connect on a much deeper level. It was a level that suggested need, companionship, peace, comfort, understanding, family. Simply put, Dane woke up one morning and knew that he was in love with a slip of a young woman who was sweet and honest, and who thought far better of him than he thought of himself.

So had he been crazy, as Roger had suggested, to send her home? Probably not. He couldn't risk anything happening to her by her husband's former associates. He especially couldn't risk something happening when she had a child to take care of. Nor could he risk blowing a chance to be with Taylor later, once Michael Evans's life and death were no longer a mystery. And he knew he wanted that chance.

The information that Taylor had a child of almost three had had another strange effect on Dane—an unexpected curiosity about children; after all, he'd never been around any. When Maddy had been pregnant, he'd not been that aware of the changes in her body. Being in a war zone had only produced worry in Dane about her condition, not curiosity. Maddy herself had never made an issue of it, never been sick or out of sorts. And she had been killed before the process could be completed.

But Dane had been watching Ann in the late stages of her pregnancy with fascination, and had been just as fascinated by Roger's display of extreme gentleness and concern for his wife. It was so private and so loving that

Dane realized just how much he lacked in his life. Now he imagined Taylor going through these same changes, her small body first accommodating a new life, then bringing it into the world, forever a part of her. He felt anger and helplessness that she might have done so all alone.

Dane and Roger's investigation of the now infamous warehouse incident had ground to a halt after the initial spurt of information on the four men. For one thing, the man they wanted most, Bick Rafferty, had simply disappeared. Roger wasn't surprised. He reasoned that when Dane had rescued Taylor from the assault, Rafferty couldn't be sure if he'd been seen, identified or followed. A disappearing act was the quickest way to force people to lose the scent. It was to Roger's credit that he'd simply staked out Rafferty's haunts and waited until he turned up again.

Dane had only been back in London two days when the call came. Carefully worded directions with more than one possible meaning took him one evening in mid-March to an address far off the beaten track, and frequented by Roger's contacts.

Knowing the whereabouts and movements of the warehouse group, as well as those of the myopic manager of Bolton's, Dane felt reasonably comfortable that Taylor had not been followed to the States. But he had nonetheless taken precautions with one phone call to New York. Rafferty had been the only one of the four that he and Roger had lost sight of, and Dane had very specific reasons for wanting to see Rafferty alone.

Dane parked his car three blocks from the location Roger had called him to, having driven the last quarter mile with no headlights. He looked around the streets and found one of Roger's men. With a brief nod, Dane pro-

ceeded into the building and to a room along a darkened
hallway. Roger was standing outside the room with yet
another man. They were dressed entirely in black, and
their faces seemed disembodied and ghostly. There was
no greeting.

Roger inclined his head. "He's in there."

"Has he said anything?" Dane asked.

"Just that he has nothing to say. He thinks we're from
the security sector of Customs. He has a history of illegal importing and exporting."

"Good," Dane said tightly. "Then this should be a
complete surprise."

With that Dane slowly entered the room. It was dark
except for the proverbial spotlight in the center, under
which Bick Rafferty was seated. He was sitting in such a
way that Dane could not be seen or identified from the
waist up. Rafferty cast a disinterested glance in Dane's
direction and then looked away.

"You're wasting your time. I got nothin' to say," he
said smugly.

"That's quite all right. I'll do the talking," Dane told
him, seeing a flicker of doubt in Rafferty's face at the
sound of Dane's intimidating, gravelly voice.

"And you can't keep me here, neither. I ain't done
nothin' wrong."

Dane slowly began to walk around the man, his footsteps completely silent, his movement eerie in the semi-
dark room. "We have no intention of keeping you."

Dane was now on Rafferty's other side, and could see
his curious glance. "As soon as I'm finished, you may
go."

"Hey—who are you? I don't know you." He started
to rise from the chair, but Dane easily pushed him back
into the seat.

"You might say I'm an avenging angel." Dane returned to his original position by the door. Deliberately he began to remove a black leather glove from his right hand. He could see Rafferty's eyes focus on the action. Dane began to circle the man once more.

"You're a coward and a thug. I don't like thugs." Dane stopped for a moment right behind Rafferty.

Rafferty laughed nervously. "You can't touch me. I can report you!" Dane finished his walk and this time stopped directly in front of Rafferty, towering menacingly over him. Now the spotlight completely prevented the man from seeing Dane's face.

"To whom? And for what?" Dane asked.

Rafferty began looking around for a way to escape. "Look, I don't know what this is about. Who the hell are you?"

Dane was silent for a moment, then slowly raised his right hand. "This is about the warehouse."

The other man stiffened and his eyes grew wary. "What did you say?"

"And someone you tried to hurt." With that, Dane took a swift, backhanded swing and felt his knuckles connect sharply with bone. The blow snapped Rafferty's head to the left, and he went tumbling out of the chair in a heap.

Dane gritted his teeth at the pain in his hand and replaced the glove. "Next time, as the saying goes, pick on someone your own size," he drawled dryly and turned to leave the room.

Roger saw the dark, dangerous expression on his friend's face. "You still want me to bring him in officially and hold him?"

Dane let out a deep sigh to release his tension. That hadn't felt as good as he thought it would. He flexed his hand, then shook his head. "No, let him go. I think we'll find out more if he's on the street. Besides, now he knows that at least *I* know about the warehouse. He's going to go to his friends with that news."

Dane and Roger further discussed the connection between Bolton's and the auction house in New York that Taylor worked for. They considered, for example, the fact that the pink receipt had contained a code that once broken, referred to dates and places that suggested future movement of rare books between the U.S. and Europe. But they couldn't figure out why the books were so important.

Dane knew Taylor had gone home with a copy of the receipt, presumably as proof for her superiors that she had delivered the books. But sooner or later someone in London was going to contact someone in New York with the news that Taylor Ashe had been married to Michael Evans, and that information was presumably going to be valuable. Dane began to wonder if Taylor was going to be any better protected with her family than she would have been with him.

Also unknown was the involvement of Philip Mayhew Johns. Since he'd not only been at the warehouse meeting but also had questionable connections to the likes of Bick Rafferty, Dane wanted to know everything about him. But unlike Bick Rafferty or the other two minor players in this game, Johns was well insulated by his social standing and professional position, both of which seemed unimpeachable.

Roger, who'd always tried to keep Ann shielded from his erstwhile covert activities, had been shocked to find that his wife not only knew what was going on, but wanted to help and was even willing to throw herself into the fray. Roger realized that he had been foolish to think he could hide anything from her, and had sadly under-estimated her strength and abilities. Being eight months pregnant didn't help, but in an unexpected way, it didn't hurt, either.

Ann was willing to indulge her husband's fussing over her because she recognized it for what it was—an expression of love and concern. But she had become very fond of Taylor Ashe and considered her as a friend in need.

Ann knew that her mother, Alice Kramer, was an acquaintance of Nancy Johns, Philip Mayhew Johns's wife. Ann made sure Mrs. Johns was invited to the baby shower being held for her, where Ann proposed to inquire, with great interest if necessary, after Mr. Johns's life as a banker.

Roger didn't relish the idea of his wife being involved, but he did concede that she had rather a good idea. Indeed, when Ann reported back later, Roger found that he was able to weed out from the chitchat some useful facts about Johns. But there ended Ann's brief career as a spy. She had two weeks to go in her pregnancy, and Roger wasn't willing to take chances. While she found it all high adventure, both Roger and Dane had come to the realization that it was anything but.

Dane had spent a good deal of his life fighting causes, settling disputes, saving lives. But it no longer had the same meaning it once did. He had had enough. And he wanted to go home, though he still wasn't sure where "home" would be.

But Trudy and Ann got Dane headed in the right direction. For one thing, Trudy was still furious with Dane for sending Taylor back to the States and berated him in no uncertain terms about it. "When you care

about someone, you don't send them far away. You keep
them as close to you as you can."

Dane was both surprised and amused by the outburst.
"How do you know I care?" he questioned in real curiosity.

Trudy confronted him with her hands planted on her
stout hips. "Because after taking her to her flight, you
said barely a word for two whole days. And then you left.
And since you've been back from God knows where,
you've been like a caged animal."

Dane didn't think he'd been so readable, but nonetheless he began pacing the room, proving Trudy's point.
"That doesn't sound like much evidence," he responded
dryly.

"I also know that you called the terminal in New York
to make sure she was met by her family."

Dane scowled at her. "Go on."

A sad, sympathetic look came into Trudy's pale eyes.
She shook her head. "Oh, Dane. How could I *not* know?
I've known you almost all of your life, and *I know*! You
behaved the same way after your mother died, and your
father was beside himself with how to handle you."
Trudy walked over to him and touched his arm. "And
you were exactly this way when they sent you to
me... after Maddy was killed."

Dane looked away. "Taylor Ashe is a married
woman."

Trudy smiled; Dane could see a twinkle in her eye.
"Don't look for excuses. Taylor *Evans* might have been
married. The young woman you sent home was not. I've
got two motherly pieces of advice for you, Dane Farrow. Get Taylor out of the mess she's in. And then don't
lose her."

That was the sentiment that kept coming back to Dane most often. *Don't lose her.* Even as information began to trickle back from all his sources on someone named Michael Evans, some from as far away as Hong Kong, he still wondered what kind of a chance he had. The information gathered was stacking up to prove that Taylor had made one hell of a mistake. Innocently, of course. Trustingly, because she'd probably not been raised to think or expect the worst of people. But Dane wondered if he himself was such a bargain.

It turned out that Michael Evans was only one of the names that he'd used. He'd used at least three other aliases, but no one had a definitive answer as to which one was really his. The authorities could only speculate that one of three male bodies that had been washed ashore in Spain three years earlier was the man who'd called himself Michael Evans. He'd last been seen in Spain, and there was no evidence that he'd ever left. The fat little proprietor of the hotel and café had been there, too, as had Rafferty. Johns had been in London.

Dane knew that that was it. All the information that Taylor would need to know, and even some she wouldn't want to know, had been gathered about her husband. He was dead, she was a widow, and there was a little girl who would never know the man who'd fathered her.

Dane looked at the information spread out over Trudy's kitchen table. It still didn't make sense. How did Taylor get so involved? And what did rare books have to do with a well-heeled London banker, a sleazy café operator, and a man whose sole occupation was to intimidate people—physically or otherwise?

ANN'S PART in Dane's transformation was not yet over, he discovered. On the evening of April 5, his calculations were interrupted by a strained call from Roger. Ann was in labor, and they were on their way to the hospital.

Dane had to smile wryly. He knew that Ann would have the best care and would come through fine. He wasn't so sure about his best friend.

At the hospital, Dane sat alone in a private waiting room. Occasionally a curious nurse would stick her head through the door, either to ask if he wanted anything or to give progress reports. The nurses, of course, wondered about the silent man in the dark glasses, who showed no inclination to hover outside the delivery room somewhere down the corridor along with Ann's nervous parents and Trudy. And he showed no inclination to know more than that all was going along quite normally.

Dane's calm, controlled demeanor, however, belied the turmoil that he was experiencing. He wasn't so much upset as suddenly, overwhelmingly sad. Roger was there to support and love Ann and witness the birth of their child—a child conceived in deep love. Dane envied his friend that. He realized that Roger and Ann would exist and develop and grow through their child in all the years ahead . . . and he envied them that, too. And he saw that Taylor Ashe had been right when she said witnessing a birth was like witnessing a miracle—and now he understood how she knew.

Even Taylor, for all she'd been through, all she'd doubted or questioned, had in the end had her own miracle of joy. And here he sat, alone, with nothing. Maddy had once said to him in her straightforward, clear way, that there was no such thing as history repeating itself, and when it was gone—one must let the past go—create new tomorrows.

Dane looked up quickly as Roger came in. He stood slowly and watched his friend, who'd been transformed in the last six hours and now stood there, a father. His graying hair was plastered to his forehead with sweat. His hospital gown hung from one shoulder and was completely ridiculous. His face was flushed with exhaustion, and emotion glistened in his eyes. He was clearly beside himself with happiness. Roger walked over to Dane and took his hand.

"We did it!" he exclaimed. "It's a boy!"

"Is Ann okay?" Dane asked, pursing his lips at Roger's elation.

"Yes, she's fine. Just fine. She's already decided to name him—Alexander."

Dane drew his brows together and tilted his head. "That's my middle name," he said hesitantly.

Roger beamed. "Yes. I know."

Dane glanced at the floor to hide his emotion. But Roger knew, and chuckling gently, slapped his friend on the shoulder.

Dane had lost a lot in his life. But Maddy had been right, after all. Suddenly the future loomed ahead of him—possible. And free.


THE CALL that came in for Taylor, quite a bit later than the one Dane had received, was not the one she'd been waiting for. She'd been hoping for two months that Dane would call, but he did not. He had remained depressingly silent across the Atlantic. Despite his confession to her as she boarded the plane to come back to the States, she was beginning to feel that he'd been serious when he told her that the fact that he wanted her didn't mean anything. But she had continued to hope.

The envelope from Ann that Roger had given her at the airport had helped. Its contents made it evident to Taylor that whatever feelings she'd been developing for Dane

had become apparent to Ann. Her note had been simple
and telling.

Dear Taylor:
Be patient. Dane needs time to realize what's important and what is not. He won't disappoint you.
   I'm sorry you had to leave so soon, but I know
you'll be back.
                                    Regards, Ann

Taylor had not slept any better on the plane ride home
than she had traveling to London. When her flight landed
she was exhausted, edgy and teary eyed. She didn't understand how her brothers, Quinn and Patrick, had
known to expect her, but when she saw them waiting at
the arrivals gate, she burst into tears.

They'd been concerned and curious, of course, and
although Taylor had managed to regain some control and
tried to laugh off her emotional state, Quinn had sarcastically remarked that she must be in love. Patrick had said
in disgust that if the next one was anything like Michael
Evans, he was dead meat—at which point Taylor had
started crying again. And Patrick had immediately been
curious about the fading, but still-apparent bruise on her
mouth; in response Taylor had quickly created a mythi-
cal allergy to a lipstick she'd purchased.

There had been several days of constant questioning,
but also the fussing and pampering of her family; the
latter led Taylor to see the wisdom of Dane's action. She
knew that her feelings toward him were unlikely to
change, and was not the least embarrassed that she'd
spontaneously confessed love. But being back in the
midst of people she was totally sure of felt wonderful.
And she'd missed Holly.

Her parents had baby-sat during the trip abroad and had Holly with them at their Putnam County home. Taylor had no desire to return even for a night to the Riverdale apartment, and after being met at JFK, looked forward to seeing her daughter and staying with her parents, until she could form a solid plan of action for their future.

The two decisions she'd already made concerned selling the Riverdale co-op and permanently quitting her job at Strafford House, since both had indirect ties to the late Michael Evans. Taylor had quickly accepted the suggestion that Michael was dead, and instead of experiencing any pain or remorse, she only felt enormous relief.

Taylor had, of course, been warmly welcomed home, and after hastily kissing everyone hello, had gone in search of her daughter. Holly was in the room her grandparents had outfitted just for her visits. She was startled by the night lamp going on, and by her mother's cooing and murmuring as she lifted the child from her bed.

The toddler had pulled her eyes open just far enough to recognize the intruder, then had snuggled against Taylor's chest. "Hi, Mommy," her childish voice had murmured, then she promptly fell asleep again.

When the call came for Taylor, she was in the middle of preparing breakfast for her mother and Holly, who were outside the Ashe home, enjoying a spring morning. When it was over, Taylor hung up the phone and stood pensively, staring out the window. The call had been from Mark Richards, a representative of the State Department. He wanted to know if she could come to his office to receive information and documents relating to Michael Evans. She'd told him she would be there by noon.

But as Taylor turned away from the window and sat down to think about what the phone call meant, her thoughts were not really of Michael Evans—but of Dane Farrow. And one of the first thoughts that crossed her mind was that there was no longer any reason for Dane not to want her, and she wondered how she could let him know.

The two months at home had not completely shut her off from London, and she'd heard from two very welcome sources. Taylor had been surprised when she'd gotten the first letter from Trudy—and also grateful. For Trudy had not only expressed her dismay that Dane had made Taylor return home; she'd gone on to express her own opinion that Dane had definite feelings for Taylor, and not only hadn't expected them, but didn't know how to deal with them. Over the next three letters, Trudy had also proceeded to tell Taylor about the Dane Farrow she'd known since he was a teen.

Taylor had hoped that Trudy would clear up the mystery of Maddy, but she hadn't. Taylor came to realize that, of course, she couldn't. If she was to find out, the information would have to come from Dane himself.

The second person to write had been Ann, and Taylor recognized with some wry amusement that in matters of the heart, women always seemed to know what was going on before men did. Taylor could only hope that sooner or later the facts would dawn on Dane, as well. Ann had informed her of all the activity that was going on to find "the answers," as Ann so carefully put it, and Taylor had laughed. She'd also been deeply moved that these people, whom she still didn't know very well, were as caring and open and protective of her as Michael had been closed and secretive. The irony was not lost on Taylor.

The second time Ann had written was to send a birth announcement for Alexander James, her new son.

While Taylor's parents and her older brothers knew that the trip had distinctly changed her, no one questioned her about it—except Quinn. He was the younger of her two brothers, and at thirty-five was seven years older than Taylor. Patrick was about Dane's age. Taylor, thanks to her age and size, had affectionately been known as the pip-squeak of the family. She was close to both her brothers, but it was Quinn who'd always been able to read her like a book, although he'd often kept his revelations to himself. So it was only when he quietly confronted his sister about her thoughtful dreaminess since returning home that Taylor felt relief at being able to talk about her unique adventure.

"I think in the future I'm going to be against you traveling overseas," he'd drawled into her ear one evening when the entire family, including Patrick's wife and two adolescent sons, had descended upon the senior Ashe household for dinner.

"Why?" Taylor asked, pulling out a handful of silverware from a kitchen drawer.

Quinn leaned closer. "Because I was right. You're in love. Every time you fly to London you come back in love."

"It's indigestion," Taylor had quipped, but she knew Quinn was not to be put off.

"You can tell me all about him after dinner," he'd said bluntly. And Taylor knew she would.

Oddly, Quinn was not unlike Dane; he could be very astute and clear-sighted. Like Dane he was a quiet, introspective man. Quinn had so far not married, and Taylor saw him more as a late bloomer who, sooner or later, would fall for a loving woman who understood him. Taylor had always lovingly referred to Patrick as the lawyer with the outward personality of a lumberjack, and Quinn, who was an architect and builder, as having the demeanor of a lawyer.

"He's a very unusual man," Taylor had admitted to Quinn much later. "He seems to have had a life on the move a lot, his work hard and probably dangerous. But I know he's also generous. And gentle."

Quinn had nodded absently. "Well, that's much more than you had to say about Michael Evans."

Taylor blushed. "What did I say about Michael?"

"Not much, I'm afraid. Just that he was handsome."

Taylor shrugged ruefully, looking down at her slender hands. "I was awfully young and silly, wasn't I?"

"Just young. You're allowed that, you know. I just have one question."

"What?"

"Do I get to meet Dane Farrow?"

Taylor attempted a weak smile. "I hope so."

And *everyone* had been curious about Taylor quitting her job at Strafford House. This was not as easily explained, and she was still struggling with her reasons herself. But she just had a feeling. It came to her only after she'd returned to New York and had time to think; Michael, Mr. Neery at Bolton's and Strafford House were linked. It was too much of a coincidence that she'd met Michael at Bolton's, that he professed a fondness for old books, that she'd worked for the rare book restoration department of the auction house. It was too convenient that Mr. Neery knew how to reach the warehouse in London, where men she now felt she'd seen or met before, seemed to know Michael. And she'd never adequately understood why *she* had been granted the singular, privileged task of being a courier. The more

Taylor thought about all those seemingly unrelated people, places and events, the more a pattern began to form—one she didn't like.

In the meantime she still had to earn a living. With a little ingenuity that surprised even herself, Taylor managed to secure some rebinding work on consignment from Sotheby's and the Pierpont Morgan Library. Her father had suggested perhaps teaching at one of the local colleges, but Taylor didn't want to be locked into anything long-term yet. Not until the loose ends of her life had been tied up.

When Taylor heard the back door open from the yard, the sound was immediately followed by the gentle, breathless voice of Taylor's mother and the high-pitched response of her daughter.

Taylor was just filling a bright plastic tumbler with milk and placing a basket with warm rolls in the center of the table.

"Be careful not to crush those, Holly," Mrs. Ashe instructed the pint-size dynamo moving around the kitchen table.

"I won't. Here, Mommy." Taylor smiled and looked down at the outstretched hand that was clutching several late daffodils.

"Thank you, sweetie. Those are beautiful."

"Grandma says to put them in water. I'll do it." And before Taylor could object, her daughter was attempting to drag one of the kitchen chairs to the sink.

Mrs. Ashe laughed. "She's *very* independent. Just like someone else I remember."

Taylor helped Holly move the chair and nodded at her mother's words as Holly struggled onto the seat, still holding the flowers. The little girl was clearly determined to do this herself, and thrust the daffodils at Taylor.

"Can you hold this?"

Taylor obediently took the flowers, but stood close and watched carefully as her daughter turned on the water, and taking a small ironstone pitcher that was on the window ledge over the sink, began to fill it with water. But the pitcher grew heavy and Taylor, seeing the impending disaster, quickly intervened, gently taking the pitcher from Holly's tiny hands.

"I think that's plenty of water, honey." Taylor put the flowers into the pitcher.

"Okay," Holly agreed, already losing interest, and carefully climbing down from the chair.

Taylor put the pitcher onto the breakfast table, and Holly ran from the kitchen into the living room.

"Come back, Holly. It's time to sit down to breakfast," Taylor called after her.

"I have to get Mickey," came back the insistent little voice.

Taylor sighed and saw the amusement on her mother's face. "Of course. She can't eat without Mickey."

Mrs. Ashe laughed as she poured coffee into cups for Taylor and herself, and sat down at the table. "At least she's given up on that ratty old pink blanket she used to drag everywhere."

"Yes, but I live in dread of what she's going to attach herself to next."

"I wouldn't worry. Holly demonstrates remarkably good sense for a three-year-old."

"Much more than her mother." Taylor grimaced, sipping her coffee.

"Don't be so hard on yourself, dear. It's more important that you consider the future for Holly and yourself." Taylor nodded, putting down her cup.

"But there's no rush. You know Dad and I love having you and Holly with us."

"Thanks, Mom. But it *is* temporary. By the way—would you mind watching her for a few hours today?"

"Of course not. Have a rush job to do?"

Taylor sighed, reaching for a roll. "No. Actually I just had a phone call. It was from a State Department official. He wants me to come in this afternoon."

Mrs. Ashe raised her brows and looked closely at her daughter. "Michael?"

"Yes, but I think this might be the last time."

"I certainly hope so. You've been through a lot over him. But I'm so glad you have Holly."

Taylor grinned. "Me, too."

Then they heard one of their topics of conversation returning to the kitchen, deep in conversation with someone. Holly came through the door, almost dragging a three-foot-tall Mickey Mouse doll, easily taller than herself. She put the doll onto one of the chairs.

"Now you sit there," she ordered in the perfectly imitated voice of an adult.

Taylor and her mother looked at each other and smiled patiently.

DURING THE LONG DRIVE to the Federal Building in lower Manhattan, Taylor could feel her tension mounting. This was the second time she'd been to Mark Richards's office. The first time had been when she'd first sought help in trying to find Michael. She knew that this time Mr. Richards had the answers.

Taylor walked down the corridor on the twelfth floor toward room 1209. She was surprised that her heart was pounding furiously in her chest in anticipation. But the funny thing was, she wasn't at all surprised to be escorted into Mr. Richards's office, only to find Dane Farrow sitting on a comfortable sofa against a side wall.

Taylor was sure she'd greeted Mark Richards courteously, had shaken his large hand and responded to his inquiries as to her well-being, but seeing Dane, silently watching her with the same kind of closed expression he'd maintained the first time she saw him in Roger Hillard's office, she was experiencing a sense of déjà vu. There was, however, a discernible difference, perhaps because she was looking for one. First of all Dane's jaw muscles were working reflexively. Secondly, his hand clenched tightly before slowly relaxing open again.

Taylor also took in other distinct details about Dane that only served to reinforce the jolting physical reaction that was going on inside her at seeing him again. Like the swept-back hair, still long enough to touch the collar of his jacket. The dark turtleneck sweater and dark glasses. Taylor allowed herself a small smile; now she knew that behind those lenses, Dane was watching her with equal intent. And with that knowledge she began to relax. Dane's being here was more significant than even he yet realized, and for once Taylor felt in charge.

Dane stood up slowly and gracefully by Mr. Richards's desk. He slid his right hand into his trouser pocket. Taylor inclined her head slightly and looked openly up at him. Her smile broadened a bit. Dane Farrow was nervous.

"Hello, Dane," Taylor said in her low, clear voice.

Dane also inclined his head, his face expressionless. "Taylor." Dane was struck almost at once by a subtle change in her. She seemed completely self-possessed and confident, and not as surprised to see him as he'd thought she would be. He was charmed all over again, however, by her delicate beauty, and felt as if a hammer had been pounded into his chest. His feelings had been real, after all, and he'd known for sure the minute she walked through the door.

Taylor turned back to Mark Richards, a tall, broad-shouldered black man who, it now occurred to her on this second meeting, reminded her of both Dane and Roger. Richards's eyes were careful and alert and Taylor knew, without any self-consciousness, that this man was aware of the dynamics between Dane and herself.

"Please, sit down," Mark Richards said to Taylor as he settled himself into his leather chair. "You don't seem surprised to find Mr. Farrow here."

"No," Taylor admitted. "I'm not even surprised to find he's a friend of yours."

Mark Richards arched a brow, cast a glance at Dane and leaned back in his chair. "Oh? And why not?"

"Because Mr. Farrow doesn't have insignificant friends. And he's highly selective."

Surprisingly, Mark Richards let out a healthy, full-bellied laugh, his perfect teeth flashing white in his dark face. His laugh faded, but there was an appreciative sparkle in his eyes.

Taylor looked briefly at Dane, who was still silent. "I hope he didn't trouble you with requests to keep an eye on me."

The dark brows went up again, but it was Dane who answered. "How did you know?" he asked, his raspy voice reminding Taylor just how much she'd missed its unique sound.

"I didn't. I was just guessing," Taylor confessed. What she didn't say was that two days after being home, she'd figured out that something had to have been wrong for Dane to have forced her to leave London so quickly; he obviously wanted her at a distance, where he needn't worry about her. And Mark Richards had also been very clear, more than a year ago, that there was probably little the government could do to locate Michael. It therefore stood to reason that if he had so much information now, it had to be because someone had contacted him. If it hadn't been Dane, her next guess would have been Roger Hillard. But Taylor felt a warm excitement to realize that Dane had reached far indeed to keep an eye on her.

Mark Richards chuckled again in amusement, and straightened in his chair to face Taylor. "I'll have to be careful. I can see you're a real threat to my job." Then he sobered. "Do you know why Dane is here?" he asked quietly.

Taylor swallowed, and her heart began to beat quickly again. "Yes," she murmured, and turned bright, calm and resigned eyes to Dane, in a way showing both thanks and relief. "You've found Michael."

Of course, that had been a figure of speech. No one had found him, but they were reasonably sure what had happened to him. The body would never be recovered, but there didn't seem to be any doubt that he was dead.

At one point Dane stood and in a sure, professional voice recited for Taylor how the investigation and evidence had piled up. Taylor felt nothing upon hearing the details recounted. It was very much like listening to the details of someone else's life, someone who was a stranger. Here was the evidence that Michael, or whatever his real name had been, was the stranger.

Mark Richards explained that although Evans was probably a false name, it could still hold up legally on a marriage certificate. But obviously Taylor needn't be concerned, since Michael's death made her a widow, and she could take her maiden name again, if she wished.

Taylor had nodded numbly. That was all fine and good, but what about Holly? What was to be *her* real name?

Dane passed an official-looking envelope to Taylor. Reluctantly she took it and looked up at him.

"That's a document that says Michael Evans has been declared dead." He watched her reaction. "It's all over, Taylor," he added in a low voice.

"Yes." She nodded absently. But when Taylor glanced again at Dane, there was another look in his eyes.

Another hour and she was through. Mark Richards got to his feet to shake hands with Dane.

"It was good seeing you again, ole buddy."

"Same here. And thanks for your help, Mark."

"Anytime. Where're you headed?" he asked as he escorted Taylor and Dane to the door.

Dane hesitated briefly before opening his mouth to answer, but Taylor, looking for an opportunity, spoke first. "Mr. Farrow and I still have business to discuss. I'm hoping I can persuade him to stay in New York a few days."

Her voice was a little breathless, but she looked at Dane and almost dared him to refuse. She also hoped he had no reason to.

Taylor had clearly pulled a quick one, and Dane had not been prepared. Quite honestly, he had no real idea at all what he was going to do now.

Mark helped him out, quickly aiding Taylor's cause, too. "Sounds good to me. Where are you staying?"

"With me," she hastily supplied, surprised by her own boldness. Both pairs of male eyes swiveled to stare at her.

"I—I mean my family. They'll want to meet the person who—" She stopped and lost the battle not to blush. Mark Richards got points for not noticing.

"Who what?" Dane asked quietly.

Taylor looked at him and slowly began to smile, her look personal.

"Makes things happen."

TRUDY HAD NOT been kidding when she'd first told Taylor that Dane traveled light. He had one sturdy black leather carryall that couldn't have kept him in clothing for more than a few days. Taylor was hoping that a few days were all they'd need.

They climbed into Taylor's car and just sat, both staring blankly ahead, and both clearly feeling awkward. Somehow the tables had been turned, and Dane felt oddly vulnerable. It had nothing to do with Taylor being in the driver's seat, although in *many* ways she was.

"I'm not sure this is a good idea," he said.

Taylor took a deep breath and turned to him with a bright smile. Not for the world would she let on how nervous she was, because she knew that whatever happened between Dane and herself now rested solely on her ability to put to use what she'd learned about him in London.

"I think it's a wonderful idea." Seeing his hard, stiffening profile, her brightness faded. "I knew you'd come," she whispered honestly.

"You were awfully sure of yourself."

Taylor shook her head. "No, no, I was just hopeful. Now I am sure." Dane turned his head to look at her. "Of you," she added.

"Are you?"

"You didn't have to come just to give me an envelope, Dane. You could have mailed it, expressed it or faxed it." She looked at him carefully, absorbing the details and all the little things that had first drawn her to him. She reached out tentatively to touch his arm.

"Why did you act as courier? Why did you come?"

Dane turned to look at her, to let his eyes feast on the dark hair framing her pale features and enormous dark eyes. His gaze settled on her beautifully shaped mouth. His internal nervousness seemed to have disappeared.

"Why do you think?" he finally answered.

## Chapter Eight

Taylor made a slow trip around the living room, picking up scattered toys, half-eaten, mutilated cookies, and a minuscule hand-knitted sweater with red hearts across the chest. She stopped at the entrance and leaned there, her arms and hands filled with evidence of Holly's after-dinner play. Taylor watched as her father and mother turned away from the window, while outside, Dane and Quinn drove away in Quinn's Jeep.

"Well? What do you think?" Taylor asked with uncertainty. It was the first opportunity she'd had to question her parents. Taylor had never been in doubt that they'd welcome him as a houseguest, and in fact Dane had been dumped unceremoniously right into the middle of the comings and goings of various Ashe family members, with not one awkward silence. Until now.

Just a little more than twenty-four hours ago, Taylor had been hoping that the Grand Central Station atmosphere of her family's home would keep Dane too off balance for even the two of them to talk alone. And it had certainly done that. But she'd known she'd been putting off the inevitable, and sooner or later there'd be a lot of questions to answer.

Taylor's father, a scholarly looking man, adjusted his glasses and ambled over to his lounge chair, which was off limits to everyone else in the family. Except Holly. He sat down and picked up the local newspaper.

"I think now it's quiet enough to read my paper." And he snapped it open to the financial pages.

Mrs. Ashe, a fine-boned woman no taller than her daughter, bent to retrieve one errant pink sock belonging to her granddaughter.

"I think I'll go check to see if Holly's covered." Mrs. Ashe said, leaving Taylor with her father.

"Is that all you have to say?" Taylor asked her father.

"What do you want me to say?" he asked absently from behind the paper.

In frustration, Taylor deposited herself upon the coffee table and pulled the paper away from her father's nose. "Just the truth. Do you like him?"

Mr. Ashe sighed patiently. "It's only important that *you* like him. And it's obvious to me that you do. Wasn't that the idea of bringing him home? To say 'Mom and Dad, this is a man I like and trust and think highly of, and I want him to meet my family'?"

Taylor grimaced at her father's old-fashioned, polite phrasing. He snatched back the paper.

"And he gets real high marks over the last one," he admitted dryly; Taylor blushed up to her roots.

"You never met Michael, and I know it's my fault. I should have insisted. But it's just that he was always traveling, or always had an excuse...."

"Exactly. That's why Dane gets such high marks. He didn't avoid us. Any man willing to subject himself with no warning to the complete inquisition of the Ashe family, without flinching once, is a man I want to know."

Taylor shook her head and laughed lightly. "I think you all took him by surprise, and he hasn't recovered yet."

Mr. Ashe smiled warmly at his only daughter. "We may have taken him by surprise. *You* took him by storm."

Taylor continued to look hopefully at her father. He was determined to make light of the current unexpected circumstances. She was not. She knew her parents were not judgmental or necessarily biased. Even after the fiasco with Michael they'd not been condemning, but had only wanted to comfort her and be there for her as family.

Mr. Ashe correctly read the doubt in Taylor's eyes, the same color as his own, and he grew serious, leaning forward to gently pat her cheek.

"You tend to do things so quickly, I guess I'd better tell you now. I like Dane. What I can see of him. I think he's a strong man and an honest one. I think he's mature and experienced, and quite frankly, I'd love to hear about some of his adventures someday."

Taylor smiled.

"I know that he's someone in whom you've placed a great deal of your trust, and probably your heart, and that he was the one person who was able to get to the bottom of this thing with Michael. I know he's a careful man. Thoughtful. Quiet. Private. Reminds me a lot of Quinn. Now, is that what you wanted to know?"

Taylor nodded. "Yes. It was."

"Not that you needed my blessing."

"And you see all of that about him in just one day?"

Mr. Ashe settled back into his lounge chair and began again to open his paper. "Why not? You apparently knew that you loved him quickly. How long does it have to take?''

Of course it was somewhat academic, since Taylor had only the scantiest of information from Dane as to how he felt about her. He *had* made the trip from London, and she realized it was a big step. But so far she had little to go on or build on.

As they left Mark Richards's office the day before, Taylor had taken bold first steps. But on the drive up the West Side Highway, up the Henry Hudson Parkway and Highway 87 into Westchester and on into Putnam, she'd wondered what Dane would have done, what he would have said if she hadn't taken the initiative. What if all he felt only amounted to sexual attraction, and she'd misconstrued every action and reaction from him while in London?

Taylor had felt nervous driving with Dane as a passenger, but only because her awareness of him physically—an awareness that seemed to have sharpened in their two-month separation—and the unexpected, jolting recognition that she'd missed him, and that her feelings had not changed. She'd tried to concentrate on the road, but had been tempted nonetheless to look at him, to examine his chiseled profile and hard features—hard to believe that he'd come, after all. On the other hand, his purpose in New York in Mark Richards's office was very specific. What if she were about to make a fool of herself again?

Taylor turned her attention back to the road at the same time Dane's arm shot out across her chest. ''Look out!'' he said abruptly.

Taylor slammed on the brakes, and the sudden stop jerked them both forward against their seat belts. The car in front had slowed, and she hadn't been watching. Taylor's hands were shaking, and she gripped the wheel harder.

"I—I'm sorry," she mumbled contritely. She slowly accelerated and came up to the speed of the traffic around her. Dane removed his arm from her chest.

"You were right about New York drivers," he said dryly.

Taylor shrugged. "I'm usually pretty levelheaded," she defended herself.

Dane looked at her briefly. "Do I make you nervous?" he asked softly in his gravelly voice. Taylor could feel the texture of it physically . . . right along her spine.

"Yes," she whispered honestly.

Dane turned his darkened eyes to her. There was almost a smile on his lips. "Good," he answered caressingly.

That incident had been an odd first clue, but Taylor tried to see it as promising. Others had come later. By the time they'd reached her parents' home, it was almost dinnertime. Her father had gotten home from his job as dean of the science and mathematics department at Sarah Lawrence. Quinn had stopped by unannounced to have dinner, as he frequently did, and Holly had already been dressed for bed in her sleeper, which looked amazingly to Dane like a bunny rabbit costume, covering the toddler all over except for head and hands.

No one seemed surprised by his sudden appearance; at least they were too polite to say anything. But he had been quickly disabused of that idea when, after being breathlessly and nervously introduced by Taylor to four members of the family, conversation had continued quite naturally, as if he'd been one of them. Mr. Ashe had immediately relieved Dane of his leather jacket and whisked it away to a closet. Mrs. Ashe had frowned and said that she hoped he liked broccoli, because she'd probably cooked too much. Quinn had noticed Dane's dark glasses and had unobtrusively dimmed the light over the dining-room table.

All of which Taylor had to admit Dane had taken in silently, but remarkably in stride. Of course, he'd been given no opportunity to object or even to feel doubtful. But at some point there were just Dane and Taylor—and Holly.

The toddler, having already been fed, waited only to be hugged by her mother and put to bed for the night.

"Come here, sweetheart. I want you to meet some-one." Taylor bent and held out her arms. Holly, who'd been scribbling with a crayon in a coloring book, eyed Dane with open fascination, but got up from the living-room floor in her comical night ensemble and trotted into her mother's arms. Taylor slowly stood straight under the weight of her daughter and settled her on her narrow hip.

The little girl stuck a finger into her mouth and shyly regarded Dane, resting her dark curly head against her mother's shoulder.

"Holly, I want you to meet Dane. He's a friend of Mommy's." Holly continued to contemplate Dane, but didn't respond. Taylor anxiously watched for Dane's re-action as well, but as usual, so much was hidden, except for a quick tightening of his jaw muscles.

"She's . . . she'd not used to . . ."

Dane briefly turned his shrouded eyes to Taylor and then back to Holly, who was still gnawing on a chubby finger.

If she so innocently was feeling shy, it was nothing compared to the abject fear that had suddenly taken hold of Dane. "To strangers?" he supplied quietly, but in a voice that was gentle and nearly devoid of the usual rough edge.

Holly suddenly straightened in her mother's arms and began to squirm to be released. But when Taylor would have stood her on the floor, Holly reached out her arms to Dane, who quickly transferred her weight to his own arms.

Holly, who was showing no fear of this giant stranger, stared openmouthed at Dane's face. Dane, for his part, was so taken by surprise that he was afraid to move, lest he somehow hurt her. He couldn't believe how tiny she was.

"Hi," Holly whispered. Then she pointed to Dane's dark glasses and quickly pulled back her hand.

"You don't need glasses inside the house," she reasoned simply.

Dane looked so comically dumbfounded that Taylor had to suppress a smile. He adjusted Holly's weight more comfortably on his strong forearm.

"My eyes will hurt if I don't wear them."

"Oh," Holly murmured, still staring in awe, then let out a stiff yawn.

Dane slowly extended a large hand and gently stroked Holly's hair. He was equally fascinated. He felt some regret, but looking at this small, exquisite person there was also incredible relief. His eyes turned to the slender, watchful woman next to him.

"She looks just like you," he whispered. "She's beautiful."

A small smile of relief curved Taylor's mouth. She reached out a hand to stroke her daughter's silky-smooth cheek.

"Holly is why I couldn't look for Michael right away. I didn't want to leave her." Dane nodded in understanding.

Taylor had been more than relieved that the three of them had gotten over the first essential meeting. She'd silently taken Holly once more and carried the little girl to her room. When she'd returned to the living room, Dane and Quinn were getting better acquainted and didn't acknowledge her presence. Delighted by how well things seemed to be going, Taylor had joined her mother in the kitchen.

But in her desire to build on a very small beginning she'd not taken into account how this sudden re-Americanization was affecting Dane. In the comfortable quiet of the guest room later that night, when all in the Ashe household had settled down, Dane reviewed those hours since Taylor had walked into Mark Richards's office. Everything had gone as expected—until she'd walked into the room. One look at her petite figure in a cream-colored spring dress, and Dane had felt his throat go dry and a funny constriction in his chest. These two little physical responses told him quite clearly where his emotions lay. He hadn't known until that instant if he'd hoped he'd feel nothing but warm affection for Taylor Ashe, and satisfaction that he'd put together the pieces of the puzzle for her, or if he'd need confirmation that he felt much more. He'd gotten the latter and was no longer in doubt. He did love her, and when she'd entered Mark's office, his whole body told him so.

Getting here to New York had been the easy part. Not knowing, until he actually saw Taylor, how he was going to feel, had left Dane unprepared for what would happen, once the meeting was through. Being back on familiar ground among family might have changed her feelings. He would have known that, the instant their eyes met, and would simply have left. But he'd seen the bright spark of recognition in Taylor's eyes, and read into the look what he needed to see—that she'd missed him.

Dane hadn't expected that she'd want him to stay as a guest. But that was all right. Taylor was the kind of woman for whom family was important, and it stood to reason that he'd have to pass inspection. For the new hope he nurtured, Dane was willing to fight against feeling like a fish out of water. He had been rewarded with a genuine welcome and acceptance. But he hadn't been concerned by the reception from the adults. He would hope that they could accept him as he was and for what he was, and feel that Taylor's judgment about him had been based on her own information, experience and instinct, and could be trusted. It was Taylor's daughter that had concerned him the most. If the natural wholesomeness of Ann and Taylor had shaken up his concept of womankind, he had absolutely nothing to go on, nor did he know what to expect of a child.

Meeting Holly had been easier than he'd thought, but he'd been so nervous when Taylor had summoned the toddler that he'd stood stiffly, with his hands pushed into his pant pockets. For some reason, Dane had taken it into his head that the child would probably start screaming and running for cover at the first sight of his harsh features. But she hadn't. And Dane had to admit now that if the truth were known, he'd been more afraid of meeting her.

Yet as he lay in the dark, an overwhelming sense of displacement and rootlessness attacked him, a feeling of not belonging here. For all her good intentions of bringing him into the warm bosom of her family, Taylor had inadvertently pointed out once again the emptiness of his life. Dane spoke to his father in Colorado two or three times a year from wherever he happened to be in the world. But he hadn't seen him in nearly five years.

Dane had had a childhood anger at his father for not recreating the emotional stability he'd craved after his mother died, for not being there. Instead his father had pursued his military career. Dane had been an adult before he could let go of his disappointment, and before he'd gained insight into the loss that his father had also suffered when his wife died. The constant moving around and other responsibilities had replaced feelings. It was not an earth-shattering revelation to Dane that he'd conducted his own life in the same way as his father had, for the same reasons—so that he wouldn't hurt so much when he stood still and was alone.

When Dane had received word that Roger had married, even before he'd met Ann and seen that she was about to have a baby, he'd known that a part of his life had ended. Roger he would forever consider his best friend, and know that he could trust him with anything—even his own life. But Roger belonged to Ann and now to his son, and formed part of a unit that Dane knew he could never really belong to. It was called a family. It was called home.

The emotional attraction Dane had felt for Taylor from the moment he'd first seen her acted like a jump-start to his heart. Their circumstances had been made more difficult by the understandable assumption that Taylor was married. But as the facts presented themselves to both Taylor and himself that she might not be, Dane could feel the hope begin to churn within him. It was still a very tentative thing, but he'd grabbed at it like a lifeline—that and the acknowledgment that he wanted a home with her—that and the admission that he missed his father.

Since his return to the States, Dane knew that already his life had changed. He realized that he was no longer in control. Taylor was. And this transformation, back to being a civilian and normal, was going to be hard for him. He had no guidelines to follow other than the example of Roger. But it was important enough to try.

IT WAS HOLLY who made Dane smile for the first time. It had been the second full day of his visit. Taylor was taking her daughter to a local preschool, where she spent the mornings with other toddlers. In her none-too-subtle attempts to include Dane as much as possible in her daily activities, Taylor had suggested that Dane come along. It had turned into more of an adventure for him than he would have imagined.

First of all Holly had refused to be strapped into her special car seat, but had stated her intention of riding up front with her mother and Dane.

"I can sit in your lap," Holly had explained, even as she hoisted herself into the passenger side and crawled her way across Dane's knees.

"Holly..." Taylor had begun, not wanting to force this kind of closeness upon Dane. But he'd held up a hand and briefly shaken his head. Taylor had watched silently as the little girl comfortably settled herself against Dane's chest, her too-short legs hanging over his thighs.

Dane had bent his head toward Holly. "Are you comfortable?" he'd inquired with amusement.

"Mmm-hmm," was Holly's response as Dane harnessed the two of them with his seat belt.

He looked at Taylor. "Is this all right?"

She shrugged. "If it's all right with you." She saw a smile slowly curving his mouth.

All the way to the school Holly warbled a nursery school song whose melody and lyrics were mostly unintelligible, but vastly entertaining to both adults.

Dane's smile became full-blown when they arrived just ten minutes later at the school. With astonishing quickness Holly had climbed down from Dane's lap. Taylor was about to get out from the driver's side to walk Holly into the school, when she noticed her daughter chewing something.

"Holly, what have you got in your mouth?"

Holly stood stock-still, obviously aware she'd been caught in some transgression. She stopped chewing and stared round-eyed at her mother, her little cheeks puffed out from whatever she was eating.

"What is it?" Taylor asked sternly; Dane carefully studied the dynamics between mother and child.

"It's bubble gum," Holly managed brightly, obviously hoping to charm her way out of the situation. Dane quirked a brow at the ploy.

"Bubble gum! And where did you get it?"

"From Ry," Holly confessed, referring to her nine-year-old cousin Ryan.

"You just wait until I see your cousin." Taylor frowned, but there wasn't an ounce of serious intent in her tone. "Now get rid of it, quick."

Holly needed no second invitation to pull the pink blob from her mouth. She then promptly held out her hand to Dane, who automatically put his hand out, palm up.

"Here," was all she said, dropped the sticky mess and turned on her heels to run into the open school door, dark curls dancing.

Taylor's mouth fell open in consternation and embarrassment. She was about to say, "I'm sorry," but instead started to laugh. And that was when Dane's half smile became full-blown. Taylor stopped laughing, because it came to her that Dane was rather a handsome man when he smiled. The sight of him being as much amazed by Holly's action as she was made her mirth fade quickly; it was replaced by a catch in her throat. Her decision to love Dane had been right this time. It would have been difficult for him in any case.

When they left the school, however, Dane grew quiet—and pensive, and Taylor felt it would be wise not to push him to speak or express his feelings.

"Just drive for a while," was all he'd said, and nodding in understanding, Taylor began a meandering drive around the small quaint towns and villages of the Hudson Valley region.

It was a soothing trip, one that allowed Dane to take stock of things. At that moment he was still adjusting to the knowledge that he found Holly quite enchanting. Having her sit so comfortably in his lap had made Dane almost as nervous as on the first evening he'd met her. But Dane had to admit that the experience had been enlightening. She was so light, so precious against him that Dane could never have admitted his delight in knowing that Holly liked him. He was absolutely enthralled with this little person who was charming, affectionate and funny. Holly was a total reflection of Taylor, and the two of them together were a powerful package.

Dane took a deep breath, rolling down his window to the rushing green of spring in the valley. He'd truly forgotten how beautiful parts of this country could be. The landscape was so sturdy, so sane and peaceful that Dane felt a sudden surge of joy shoot through him. He turned his eyes from the window to watch Taylor as she drove. He suddenly believed that anything was possible with her. Then he thought of Maddy, and even had a fleeting mental glimpse of her, smiling, with her wild red hair about her. But that was it.

Dane reached out a hand and stroked Taylor's hair, letting his fingers sink through the silky strands to her scalp. In surprise Taylor turned to glance at him, a smile of puzzlement on her mouth at his open touch.

"What is it?" she questioned, swinging her gaze back to the road.

"Pull over," Dane ordered.

Taylor's frown deepened; again she glanced briefly at him. She signaled, then slowed and pulled onto the narrow dirt shoulder. She put the car into Neutral.

"Dane, what's wrong?" Taylor asked anxiously. She could tell he was looking at her carefully through the dark glasses.

Dane slowly shook his head. His fingers were urging Taylor toward him, and he met no resistance; only her bright eyes indicated her concern. When Dane bent his head to her, the look vanished, and she let him quickly take her mouth. It was a possessive move, so that he could assuage the feelings that were unexpectedly rushing over him.

Dane's free hand cupped Taylor's chin and jaw, tilting her head more comfortably and allowing his tongue to rush hungrily into her warm mouth. Taylor's hands pressed against his hard chest, and she felt the strong pumping of his heart.

The kiss was demanding, but gentle. He seemed to want to imprint himself on her, to claim her. But there was also a giving that stirred and exhilarated her. The erotic fusion of their tongues made Taylor dizzy; she felt an instant ignition of long-held desire running hot through her body.

Taylor had dreamed about this—dreamed about the last, too-brief times they'd been together and the tantalizing passion that had sparked between them. She hoped that he remembered just as vividly. But already Dane's exploration of her mouth was gentling; he was slowly easing up, and his fingers loosened in her hair. Their lips separated reluctantly on a moist, heated sigh.

Taylor's eyes fluttered open. She felt slightly dazed as she searched his face. Her small hand lightly stroked his cheek. "Dane?" she questioned yet again.

"Nothing's wrong," he whispered, and gently kissed her again.

"Then what was that all about?" she asked softly.

Dane expelled a deep lungful of air, briefly focusing his eyes out the windshield. He didn't know if he should say it yet. Then his gaze settled once more on Taylor's pretty face. "That was about hope," he replied.

Ironically, Dane's visit in New York had lasted the same length of time as Taylor's in London. Both visits had had the same effect on them. And therein lay the problem. They had come together and seemed close, yet there was still something keeping them apart. Taylor was sure now that it was not her family, nor a fear on Dane's part of being accepted by them. It was no longer her being married, since it had been proved and documented that she wasn't. And it wasn't the fact that she had a daughter. Rather than being put off by the presence of another man's child, of a man who'd proven to be a coward, Dane seemed to be both amused and amazed by Holly's innocence and childish antics.

It seemed to be some anticlimactic tension, some little bit of information that had been left dangling, the last piece of the puzzle that neither wanted to search for and put in its proper place.

In a way, Dane's stay in New York seemed to demonstrate, to offer final proof that that missing piece would make the difference; Taylor, at least, knew it would. She'd held something back from Dane. Certainly not out of malice, but rather out of a hope that when he came to her, the thing with Michael would be over and done with. But Taylor knew that it wasn't. After six days and nights in close proximity to Dane, she also knew that *he* knew.

It had to do with the two books that Michael had given her years ago. Taylor had not even begun to make a connection between those particular books, the four men in London and Michael until she'd been home for a full month. Even then she'd been afraid to look at them, afraid of what they'd tell her. So she'd ignored them and stayed away from the co-op in Riverdale, where she could be traced through her old job at Strafford House. Taylor wanted to believe that those two books had nothing to do with Dane or the chance of him loving and wanting both her and Holly. But it did matter.

It was Saturday, at the end of Dane's week in New York. The Ashes were having a full-blown family affair, and Dane was introduced to Patrick, his wife Sara and their two sons, Ryan and Joel. There was so much noise, laughter and activity that Dane was able to sit quietly and observe them.

The women had, of course, ended up with the chore of providing the food, but also of maintaining some order in the rambunctious play of the children outside. The men indulged in a harmless dispute over baseball spring training and hockey play-offs, none of which made any sense to Dane. He had no experience with any of it. He did enjoy talking with Quinn, and they seemed to have an

affinity for each other. They also had a mutual interest
in architecture, building—and quiet.

Quinn had offered earlier in the week to show Dane
some of his work, and had begun with a three-room
cabin he'd built alone, not only as a degree project for
school, but also as a place to get away to. He somehow
sensed that Dane would appreciate the uniqueness of it,
and he had. Actually it had done more than that. It had
inspired Dane to think of a house along similar lines that
he wanted to build when he got back to Colorado.

Taylor was putting pieces of chicken breast into a
marinade when she heard a crash, followed by the high-
pitched screech of her daughter. Taylor, Sara and Mrs.
Ashe instantly converged upon a window to see what the
commotion was.

Holly was screaming her lungs out, her small face
completely contorted, her mouth pulled down at the
corners as tears rolled from her tightly squeezed eyes.
She'd been accidentally pushed against a lawn chair and
had gone toppling over with it. When the two cousins
tried to help her up, she only cried harder and they awkwardly stood back. Both uncles went over to help while
Dane stood silent, although he took one hesitant step
forward.

"I'd better go see what's going on," Mrs. Ashe said
and chuckled. No one believed that Holly was hurt; she
was only startled by the fall.

Taylor caught her mother's arm. "No, Mother, don't."

Mrs. Ashe looked in question at her daughter, then out
the window again.

"I'm sure she's okay. Just asking for a little special attention," Sara offered wisely.

Holly ignored her uncles, too, continuing her vigor-
ous display of childhood angst. Then she pulled herself

up and, still screaming for all she was worth, trotted blindly over to Dane and buried her face against his leg. Taylor held her breath.

It took only a second for Dane to respond. He crouched in front of Holly and gently separated her from his leg. The decibel level of her crying had lessened, and Dane was murmuring something to her.

Satisfied that it was going to be okay, the boys went back to tossing a football, the uncles and Granddad went back to the discussion of sports. Sara asked if there was any butter, and Mrs. Ashe went off to get it. Taylor continued to watch the exchange between her daughter and Dane.

Although still sniffling, Holly had stopped crying and had snuggled into Dane's arms, forcing him to lift her. She stuck a finger into her mouth to suck but was obviously listening to the soothing, low words Dane was speaking as he paced back and forth with her for a moment. Dane strolled over to the picnic table and perched against an edge. He let Holly stand on the table next to him. From an inside pocket he removed a small object. It was a pin of some sort, and he attached it to the top of Holly's sweater. She smiled.

Even from her distant vantage point at the kitchen window, Taylor knew it was a red enamel heart—the one he'd taken from her in London on Valentine's Day. Then he reached into his other pocket for the little leather ball, showing it to Holly to further distract her. She clutched it possessively in her tiny hand. It was clear that Holly and Dane had attached themselves to each other.

Without even a second thought, Taylor knew that the time had come for all the cards to be placed upon the table.

# Chapter Nine

Dane stood in the open doorway to the yard. Twilight had just ended and night was settling in. It was quiet, clear, and the evening felt fresh because of the lush smells of spring. It was a much different experience from all his years in Europe. London especially had been a place where he'd lived. But this valley bordering one side of the Hudson River felt like home.

The week had been one of reacquaintance, and often Dane wondered if keeping him as a houseguest—almost part of the family, he had to admit—was a clever ploy on Taylor's part to demonstrate to him what he'd been missing. He certainly wouldn't put it past Taylor, Dane thought with a dry chuckle. And if it was, then she'd succeeded. For most of the week he'd been thinking of the open skies and mountains of Colorado—and his father.

The other thing that had been happening was that it was becoming difficult to maintain his resolve around Taylor. A house full of relatives and family on that one hand necessitated a certain decorum. On the other, that decorum was playing havoc with his inclinations. Being around Taylor had only strengthened Dane's feelings for her. He had always been attracted by her petite strength and determination, her naiveté and fearlessness. He had been attracted to her dark, delicate beauty, her wavy hair and large, expressive eyes that were honest and clear, her beautiful mouth, which—he now considered wryly—he'd not had a chance to kiss the way he really wanted to since he'd accompanied her to Holly's school.

In the ensuing days, Dane had also been drawn by Taylor's domesticity. She was warm and caring and made him very comfortable. It used to be that a good adventure, time with Roger, or fulfilling an obligation would make his day. Now it was arriving in the Ashes' homey kitchen in the morning to be greeted with warm smiles, a cheerful good-morning, and a huge cup of hot coffee.

Dane frowned into the dark night and stuffed his hands into the pockets of the faded denims he was wearing. They belonged to Patrick, who'd passed along a pair to Dane with the comment that if he was planning on hanging around, he had to look the part. The fact of the matter was, Dane felt good. He felt like "hanging around"—but he did have his own plans, too.

Dane heard a door close softly down the hallway, and he stepped back into the kitchen and closed the door. He walked slowly into the living room and arrived at the same time as Taylor. For a long moment they stood and just watched each other. Dane felt his heart turn over at the sight of her. He decided he most definitely had to be in love, because he felt so awkward and foolish when he was with her, suddenly not knowing what to do or how to behave. That *had* been a problem.

Taylor smiled gently at him, her eyes bright and sparkling. The jeans *had* changed him...but so had the week. He looked more relaxed and comfortable, although she realized he would never give up the turtleneck sweaters. Or the dark glasses. Taylor's appraisal grew even more

tender when she recalled the way he'd handled Holly's
continued curiosity about his dark glasses. It had been
after dinner one night, and Dane and Holly had wandered into the living room as Taylor helped her mother
stack the dishwasher. She'd given up being concerned
about how Dane was responding to Holly and vice versa,
since they seemed to accept each other with a natural
ease. But that evening Taylor, having finished in the
kitchen, followed the sound of her daughter's high-
pitched voice.

Dane had been seated on the edge of a chair, casually
assembling some of Holly's plastic Legos and looking
perplexed by the brightly colored blocks. Holly was patiently explaining how they worked. Then she looked at
Dane's face for a moment, before reaching to remove the
dark glasses. Dane made no move to stop her.

"Do your eyes hurt all the time?" she asked in a
childishly gentle tone, the Legos momentarily forgotten.

Taylor watched as Dane regarded the little girl, his
green eyes narrowed against the living-room light.

"Most of the time. Especially here and here." Dane
demonstrated by touching the surface of his eyelids and
temples.

"You should ask my mommy for aspirins," Holly ad-
vised. "It will make you feel better." And then she carefully replaced Dane's glasses, unassisted, although they
were slightly crooked when she finished.

Taylor had been relieved. Holly had been no more upset by Dane's scars than she herself had been.

As she watched Dane now, she, too, had an urge to see
his face, to be near him. She had a great desire to be quietly held by him. There were just the two of them.

"Is she asleep?" Dane asked.

Taylor smiled. "For someone who's never tired when you put her to bed, she falls asleep very quickly." She looked around and then back to Dane. "Where are Mom and Dad?"

"Across the road. I understand it's the weekly game of...is it Trivial Pursuit?"

Again Taylor smiled. Dane had never heard of the game before. "Yes." She started to explain that it was similar to the TV show *Jeopardy*, then realized he wouldn't know about that, either. Instead, Taylor turned off the lamp next to her father's lounger and made the room dark. Silently she walked to Dane. He was ready; his arms rose and closed around her, and their mouths connected with a slow, erotic intensity. Taylor boldly opened her mouth and welcomed the rough invasion of his tongue; his lips rocked across her mouth to find a satisfying position. Her arms circled his waist, her fingers probing through the jersey of his sweater; she felt impatient, thwarted by the clothes that separated them. Relishing the feel of Dane's arms around her, Taylor pressed her chest, stomach and thighs tightly to him, feeling anticipation in the start of his erection.

Taylor drew in a sharp breath. Every time that Dane had kissed and held her, Taylor had always been aware of the pleasure he took from it, and she'd always known he'd exercised a great deal of control over his feelings, actions and reactions. But this was the first time he'd shown her that his wanting her, his need for her was real. Taylor felt Dane's hand slowly slide down her back, pressing and squeezing at the indentation of her waist, rubbing her thigh before purposefully cupping his large hand around her bottom, lifting her against his growing hardness. All the while his mouth was urgent and possessive and Taylor felt her heart pounding with a need that begged to be fulfilled. The feel of his tongue, his hardening middle, the hands gently massaging and kneading—all made her grow limp in his arms; she wanted more.

When their lips separated, Taylor laid her face—her mouth—against his hard chest. She didn't want to move again—ever.

"I was afraid you'd changed your mind," she heard herself mumble.

After a long pause, Dane sighed.

"No, I haven't," he said thickly, the evidence of his arousal in his voice, as well.

Now Taylor sighed, running her small hands up Dane's body, feeling him stiffen, then relax again. "Then you must be as frustrated as I am."

"I don't know," Dane whispered, and Taylor could hear amusement in his voice. "How frustrated are you?"

Taylor drew back and looked up into his shadowed face. She reached up and removed the glasses, catching the gleam in his eyes as he blinked at her. "I want you to make love to me," Taylor said, keeping her gaze riveted to his face. His nostrils flared gently, and a muscle flexed briefly in his jaw. But Dane didn't answer. He seemed to be considering either her request—or his answer—and Taylor was confused.

Dane regarded her and began to frown as he fingered her hair and scanned her face.

Taylor swallowed. "Is it . . . is it Holly?" she asked.

"No," Dane said firmly. He quirked a brow and a corner of his mouth. "Holly is—wonderful," he said. "A surprise."

Now Taylor frowned. "But her being my daughter changes something. What? How?"

Dane stared at her.

Taylor stroked his jaw, running the tips of her fingers over his lips. "Dane, I'm a mother, yes. But I'm still a woman. It's still important that I'm attractive and desirable and sexy to someone. To you. Holly doesn't change that. If anything, she's made me more able to trust and to love again. So have you."

Dane slowly bent his head and kissed Taylor with a surprising degree of gentleness. The moment was brief but filled with warmth.

"When I first saw you in Roger's office, all I wanted to do was protect you. *Then* I wanted to make love to you. It happened very quickly. But I knew there was a mystery surrounding you that put you beyond my reach. Quite frankly, I'm glad the matter of Michael is finished. But there's still a mystery, Taylor, and it sits between us."

Taylor didn't pretend not to understand. She nodded. "I know. But there's more than me. I want you to tell me about Maddy."

Only a little surprise showed in Dane's face. The look was hollow and resigned, but there was no sadness, hurt or bitterness.

"How did you know about Maddy?"

"Ann mentioned her." Taylor shrugged. "She assumed I knew. But all she did was mention her. And...a baby." Taylor's voice grew hesitant. "Was she your wife?"

Dane nodded, averting his eyes for a moment before looking at her again. "Madeleine was French. I met her in North Africa. I was only twenty-three at the time, and fighting a war. But we got married and Maddy got pregnant."

Taylor was inadvertently stroking Dane's chest in both a comforting and encouraging way. "And she was killed?"

Dane nodded.

"Was it the explosion? The one in which you were injured?"

Again he nodded. Taylor let out a deep breath and closed her eyes. "Oh, Dane. Was she pregnant then?"

"Yes," he whispered.

Taylor hugged him. "I'm sorry. I'm so sorry...."

He squeezed her to him. "Shh. Don't be sorry. It was a long time ago. It's all over."

"Dane—I do love you," she whispered.

"Shh," Dane said again. Was he afraid of the words she wanted to speak? But Taylor had already resolved to eliminate the rest of the mystery that still stood between them.

The next day Taylor dropped Holly off at her brother Patrick's house, since Sara had offered to baby-sit for the day. And then Taylor drove Dane to her co-op apartment in Riverdale. It was a very orderly, residential county, containing private homes, apartment buildings and small parks. Dane liked the country setting farther north better, and was pleased when Taylor told him she was selling her apartment.

It was a charming one-bedroom with surprisingly large rooms and an airy, sunny feel. But it was evident that Taylor had not stayed here in a while, and Dane could easily guess why.

Taylor didn't really bother to show Dane around, but he could see that signs of her personality were everywhere, giving him surprising glimpses into Taylor's life. He reflected that he had precious little to show for his own life, except some scars and memories. But it was fascinating to see what Taylor had surrounded herself with.

The rooms were very simply but comfortably furnished. In the living room stood a drafting table and a series of baskets in graduated sizes that contained materials—fabric, leather and paper—for binding books. One shelf of a bookcase that went from floor to ceiling contained a collection of pop-up children's books. Another shelf was crammed with infants' toys, and books belonging to a younger Holly. On another table were two book presses of different sizes and stacks of books in varying stages of repair.

On the windowsill stood two ceramic bowls, one filled with seashells, the other with pebbles. A memory jolted Dane. His mother used to collect seashells.

Dane wandered into the bedroom and found Taylor standing on a stool to reach the top shelf of a closet. She climbed down, clutching a white box tied with red string. Taylor stood there in her stocking feet and looked at Dane across the bed.

"I think you'll want to see this. I think . . . the men in London would want to know about this."

"What is it?" he asked, although he knew.

"The two books of poetry that Michael gave me. This is the end of the mystery."

Taylor left the wrapped box on the bed and went to the living room. When she returned she held an Exacto knife, a bone folder, a brush and tweezers. She and Dane sat down on the side of the bed, facing each other with the box in between. Taylor took a deep breath.

"None of this made any sense to me until everyone kept asking me if Michael had left me anything. I never seriously thought of these books until I came home, because there's no intrinsic value. But something *in* the books must be worth something—or why was Michael killed?''

Dane raised his brows, relieved and pleased that Taylor had thought it all out, but even more so that she was openly sharing the moment with him. He himself had reasoned after the warehouse incident that Taylor *must* have something from Michael that would pull everything together. He also knew that it was only a matter of time before the motley group from London would hazard a visit to Taylor to find out what. Dane didn't like the thought. If they had been capable of killing Michael, they would not think twice about harming Taylor.

"What do you think it is?" Dane asked.

Taylor shrugged and shook her head. "I really don't know." She gave Dane a mischievous smile. "But we are about to find out."

With that, Taylor opened the box and removed two tissue-covered volumes of poetry. She handed one to Dane and opening the other, she began to gently leaf through the pages.

"Perhaps there's something between the leaves," she murmured. But after ten minutes they knew this possibility could be eliminated, along with the idea of there being a code on the printed pages.

Then Taylor, using the Exacto knife, meticulously cut an opening in the end pages and the gutter of the book. Working very slowly, she removed and cut away paper. Taylor was then forced to apply an alum and flour paste mixture to soften the animal glue that had been used to attach the endpapers to the cover boards, as well as to the leather. When the paste had done its job, Taylor then used a tiny metal spatula to lift away paper and leather, while using the bone folder to scrap away dissolved glue.

It took her an hour, working mostly in silence, occasionally murmuring little comments or explaining each step. Then Taylor lifted off the leather covering the book boards and discovered a thin sheet of acid-free tissue. Under that were two printed sheets of folded paper, one each at the front and back of the book. She carefully lifted one, unfolded it then, unable to make sense of it, gave it to Dane. Dane had only to glance at it to recognize what it was. He raised his brows and looked at Taylor's puzzled face.

"It's a bearer bond. The face value of this one is $25,000. The other is probably worth the same."

"What's a bearer bond?"

"It's a negotiable bond, redeemable by the person in possession of it." Dane read the bond copy carefully, his lips pursed in speculation.

"You mentioned that Michael worked in banking. My guess is that he'd been stealing these and selling them overseas to the highest bidder. That way he didn't have to deal with them himself. But he first had to get them out of the country.

"Philip Mayhew Johns is a banker, and he collects rare books. I'm willing to bet he thought up the idea of passing the bonds in the binding of the rare books."

"But what would *he* do with the bonds?" Taylor wanted to know.

Dane shrugged. "Use them to purchase something. It could be anything. Guns, drugs, bribery, blackmail. It's quite an open market."

Taylor's eyes grew round. "You mean, those books I delivered held these kinds of bonds?"

"Probably."

"But . . . why me?"

"Because you were totally innocent. They chose someone who wasn't going to question a thing and who would pass customs easily. After all, you are a book restorer and work for a legitimate antiquarian dealer. What they hadn't counted on was your meeting Michael, or on him marrying you."

The color drained from Taylor's face as the awful truth was made clear. Dane made no move to touch or comfort her. Not yet.

"You mean...I was just part of the plot? Just a convenience?" she asked in an appalled whisper.

With reluctance Dane nodded. "I believe so. I think Michael intended to start keeping some of the bonds from his cohorts. But he had to have a safe place to hide the bonds. You became his cover. He never told you what he was doing, of course. And he never told them about you. Eventually they must have caught on to the fact that he was cheating them twofold. That's why he was killed."

Taylor had lowered her gaze to fiddle with a delicate bookbinding tool. She'd sensed that Michael had been involved in something illegal. But it had never occurred to her that he might have had no feelings for her at all, but had only found her a handy cover for himself and what he was doing. And now she wondered with dawning horror if it had all been hilariously funny to him. Had he been laughing behind her back at what a little idiot she was? So gullible and naive?

"I see," she said almost inaudibly, recalling being pregnant alone, anxious to find Michael and let him know about Holly, or at least to find out if he still wanted her. Well, now she knew.

Taylor wondered what would have happened had Michael *not* been killed. Would he eventually have come back to claim the books with their hidden surprise, and left her for good? Would he really have wanted to have a wife and a daughter? To be a family?

"Taylor..." Dane began gently because he could see the bewildered hurt in her face and the droop of her shoulders. "There was no way you could have realized what was going on. Believe me, these men are way out of your league. And they don't play fair."

Taylor suddenly got up and walked to the narrow window. She just stared, not bothering to adjust the venetian blinds so that she could see out. She hugged herself.

Dane knew every emotion she was going through, every nuance of pain and humiliation. She didn't bow under the truth. She wanted to cry, but Dane knew she wasn't going to let herself. It would be like conceding defeat. And if there was one thing Taylor had learned from her bizarre relationship with Michael Evans, it was how to pick up the pieces and go on.

"What do we do now?" she asked absently, thinking of Holly who, thankfully, had nothing of Michael in her.

"We see what's in the other book. My guess is we'll find two more bonds." Dane got up and quietly came to stand behind her. "Then you can turn them in to the authorities, and that will be that."

There was a long pause. With her back still to Dane, Taylor picked up the implication. "Or?" she questioned.

"Or we can call Mark Richards at the State Department and try to bring these guys down. You don't have to be involved. In fact, it will probably be dangerous. But we can do it."

Slowly Taylor turned. Her eyes were overly bright and her mouth looked grim, but her chin was up proudly and she met Dane's gaze. "Call Mark Richards."

"Are you sure?"

"Yes. Positive."

Again he wanted to touch her, but didn't. Instead Dane walked to the phone on the nightstand next to Taylor's bed. He dialed Mark's number.

When they were finally connected, Dane outlined briefly what he and Taylor had found and offered a suggestion as to what they might do next. Taylor stopped listening after a moment, too immersed in her own surprise and grief to really care; another thought had just occurred to her, adding more pain to her emotional injury.

Fifteen minutes later Dane was off the phone. Taylor took a deep breath and faced him. "What did he say?" she asked in a strangely controlled voice.

Dane could sense her withdrawal, and realized Taylor was angry. "He wants you to send a wire to Bolton's in London. Let the manager there know you found a bond. Tell him you were repairing one of the books. Ask if he knows anything about it. Give him your phone number and address here. You won't stay here, but Mark will arrange surveillance until you get an answer back."

"You're going to try and trap them?"

"If we can. Mark would like to trace it back to Johns and expose him to the British authorities. Don't worry. It will be easy to keep you uninvolved."

Taylor turned away impatiently. "There's no way you can do that. I'm the only one they're going to deal with. As you say, so far they think I'm completely naive," she said tightly.

Dane reached out to touch her. "Taylor..." She jerked away.

"It's true, isn't it? I'm just a silly little female who thought she was in love." Her eyes began to fill with tears. "And those bonds are why you're really here, aren't they, Dane? Were you right when you said you were no different than Michael?''

Dane's mistake began to dawn on him, and he wondered how he was going to convince her that she hadn't been wrong to trust him.

''In some ways perhaps I'm not. But I didn't come because of the bonds. I didn't know about them. I just knew that Michael left you something that those warehouse men wanted. Sooner or later they were going to come after it. And you.''

''And you wanted to be here to catch them, right?'' Taylor said, her voice warbling with hurt and disappointment. ''I was just a—a pawn.''

''No,'' Dane said. ''I wanted to be here, so nothing would happen to you. I was trying to protect you....''

''Stop!'' Taylor moaned, covering her ears. ''Isn't anyone paying attention? *I don't need protection.* I just need...'' She drew her bottom lip between her teeth to control herself, fighting not to cry.

The action reminded Dane of the cut on her mouth from Bick Rafferty, and of the horrible fear that had come over him at the thought of losing her. He loved her, and *that* was what had brought him to New York. *That* was what she wanted from him now.

''Taylor...'' Dane tried again, grabbing her arm. And although she resisted and tried to pull away, Dane yanked her into his arms and held her tightly against his chest.

''I want your love, Taylor. But I had to make sure you were free and safe to give it,'' Dane confessed hoarsely.

At those words, Taylor grew still in the circle of Dane's arms. He had her head pressed to his chest. Slowly she freed her arms and wrapped them tightly around Dane. ''Dane...'' she sobbed.

"Yes, I came to protect you. But don't you understand? That was the only way I could have you...after this was all over." Quietly he held her close for a very long moment; they both needed reassuring. Then Dane began to feel her leaning against him; he loved the slightness of her in his arms. He didn't want to hurt her. He never wanted anything to hurt her again. It felt strange to care for someone so intensely.

"God..." he muttered through clenched teeth. He was losing it. He wanted her so badly. Weren't they close enough yet to "this" being over?

Dane moved his hands to her head and lifted it to meet his desperate kiss. Something gave way inside him, and he knew there was no turning back. He had to show her how much she meant to him. He had to give her what she wanted so that he, too, could have it for himself. There was enormous relief in the admission of love; it allowed him to feel an equally enormous surge of passion and desire.

Taylor felt her mouth ravaged by his, and loved it. The sensation of his tongue was wonderful and she responded freely. Taylor's breathing quickened, and her hands sought to hold him and bring him as close as possible. Two insignificant books of poetry had just freed them. Now they could be together.

Taylor began tugging Dane's dark sweater from the waist of his pants and put her hands beneath it to touch his firm, supple skin. Her cool, feathery touch made him grunt in surprise. Taylor's fingers glided over his chest, making the sweater balloon out with the motion of her hand. Taylor's fingers encountered puckered skin on his right side and breast all the way to his throat, and she pressed little kisses to his chest through the sweater.

Her breath was hot and sweet. It was so incredibly sensual that Dane had to gently pull her hands away. But he quickly removed the dark glasses and pulled the sweater over his head, tossing both to a soft-cushioned chair behind Taylor.

Then Dane reached for her sweater and repeated the movement, loving the moment when her head came free from the sweater neck and her hair cascaded in a soft tumble to her shoulders.

Taylor pushed her way back into his arms, her hands and mouth stroking and kissing his chest, traveling fearlessly over the damaged skin, exciting Dane to a fever pitch. He reached behind her for the clasp of her bra, then slowly inserted his large hands beneath the lace until his palms completely covered the soft globes of her breasts. Taylor let out a small sound and came up on tiptoe, her mouth searching for his. Their lips fused and for long delicious moments they satisfied one elementary need, while preparing themselves for another.

Dane's erection was obvious now, and when Taylor inadvertently rubbed her hips against him, he moaned into her mouth.

Taylor broke the kiss and stepped out of his arms to remove the open bra and the rest of her clothing. Dane just stood and watched until she was naked, her skin pale in contrast to her dark hair. He swallowed as he took in her slenderness, enjoying the pert upward rise of her breasts and their turgid rosy nipples. He reached out a hand to gently cup a breast, to run his thumb over the nipple. Dane felt as if he could burst just from the joy of finally touching her.

"Taylor..." he began, perhaps to warn her, perhaps to see if she wanted to stop, perhaps because he was afraid she would vanish into thin air.

"Don't talk," she whispered, and took control again. She reached for the fastening on his pants and tugged from the sides to bring it down with his shorts. Then she, too, just stopped to look at and admire him.

Dane had a lithe, hard build, narrow in the hips, with clearly defined muscles and sinews. The burns on his chest, arm and neck had changed the color and texture of his skin. Taylor did not see it as ugly or disfiguring, but rather as a poignant reminder of another time in his life, by which he'd been marked forever. There were other scars, some on his thighs and hips, his rib cage, but Taylor only saw how beautifully he was proportioned and how strongly built.

He was completely erect, large, the hair surrounding him dark and thick. She reached out to close her hands around the hard smooth shaft, and felt him surge against her palm.

But Taylor's curious exploration was too stimulating, and Dane had to gently pull her hands free as he led her to the bed. "Later..." he said hoarsely as he put an arm around her and brought Taylor down to the bed with him. Dane stretched out next to her and bent over her body to kiss her breasts tenderly before slowly pulling at one nipple and finally sucking at it, causing a rush of bubbling warmth to Taylor's stomach as a tension began twisting and swirling inside.

Dane kept her like that, then let his hand travel down her silky-smooth body until he found the thatch of dark hair and gently buried his fingers in the strands between her legs.

Taylor gasped and cried out; her breathing grew short. She held Dane's head to her breast as her hips rose to meet the intoxicating exploration of his fingers. They stroked and rubbed so tantalizingly that Taylor thought her breathing would surely stop.

She felt a heaviness in her abdomen, a tumultuous rumble of sensation that was growing and moving faster in response to the pressure from Dane's hand. Taylor was caught between wanting him to stop so that he could join her, and wanting him to go on, so that the pulsating beat would continue. The indecision lasted just long enough for the tension to peak; it burst, and Taylor tumbled headlong into a pumping rhythm that left her suspended, while her body just responded. Then the slow descent with the last weak throb allowed her to start breathing again, albeit raggedly, with deep, satisfying sighs.

Dane rested his hands lightly on her thighs while he kissed her tenderly, and she weakly lifted her arms around his neck.

"Dane..." she said in a thin voice, kissing his chest, his throat.

Dane gently pushed her back against the pillows. "No...stay still." He'd wanted to make sure she was ready, so that he wouldn't hurt her. Stretched out next to him, she looked so small. "Just let me..."

Dane's kisses were once more replacing Taylor's lassitude with desire, and she let her hands wander until she found Dane and closed them around him. She could feel the changes in his body with each touch.

Dane had meant to wait a little longer to enjoy the lively response of Taylor's body, to learn the ways that made her feel good, but knew he couldn't. He pulled her hands away again and lifted himself over her.

"I'll go slowly," he whispered, settling at the tender spot with the barest contact, then thrusting forward with his hips.

Taylor moaned, but closed her legs around him. Dane thrust again, pushing deeper, joining them totally. He lay still for a moment, just enjoying the exquisite closeness. Dane kissed Taylor's damp forehead, her flushed cheeks and finally her mouth. And then he began a rhythmic rocking, a thrusting and withdrawal that made Taylor appreciate what he had given her moments before. For now her whole body, inside and out, was sensitized by the movements Dane was making with the weight of his chest and the surging of his hips. With his exploring tongue and mouth on hers, his hands stroking her thighs, molding themselves to her bottom to lift her to him, her lungs were stripped of all air, and blood began pounding at her temples as the delicious tension began building once more.

Taylor didn't think she could stand it again so soon, but felt she would have died if Dane had stopped now.

But quickly, in fact, he groaned deeply, thrusting hard, holding himself still inside her. It was the feel of his release that triggered hers a second time, and Taylor buried her face in his neck, their skin damp and hot, until it was over and she loosened her manic clutch around his neck and hips. She smiled dreamily when his body softened within her and her thighs grew limp. After a time Dane lightly stroked her thigh, then ran his hand into her hair to massage her scalp.

Slowly Dane lifted himself onto his elbows and gazed down into her face with heavy-lidded green eyes. His hair was wild and out of place, framing his face, and Taylor used her hands to try to smooth it back. He kissed her briefly, his thumbs smoothing over her flushed cheeks.

"That was inspired," he whispered. "I think it was a mistake to have waited so long. Should I be sorry?"

Taylor ran a hand over his right shoulder, over the burned skin. "Probably not," she said a bit shyly. "It was worth the anticipation."

Dane watched her carefully and raised a brow. "Why do I have the feeling you had this in mind when we arrived this afternoon?"

"I'm not talking," she said with lowered lashes. "I will say this. You're not the only one who's clever."

Dane grunted, brushing her hair from her forehead. "I grant you that's probably true. On the other hand, I didn't put up much of a fight."

Taylor smiled languidly. "Mmm... It didn't go exactly the way I thought. I wish, too, there weren't any more mysteries. But the results were perfect."

Dane kissed her. "I agree."

She looked at him with meltingly soft eyes and touched his cheeks. "Dane? About Holly..."

His kiss silenced her. "I know. I'm glad, too."

## Chapter Ten

"No!" Dane exploded. His features were set and stern and his mouth looked uncompromisingly firm. "I don't like that idea."

Taylor had never actually seen Dane angry before. He didn't rant or rave or gesture or demonstrate. He simply paced slowly, flexing his right fist. Taylor, however, was getting a glimpse of a Dane she'd not witnessed before. Commanding, in charge, determined, and—once he'd made up his mind and taken a position—a force that was not going to be easily dissuaded, if at all.

Mark Richards sighed easily, not disturbed by Dane's posturing. Taylor was concerned. She didn't want Dane upset or angry, but even she knew that Mark was right. When the courier arrived from London, she had to face him alone.

"Come on, Dane," Mark said reasonably, his dark, handsome face tilted as he watched his friend. "You of all people know how this is done and why."

Dane stopped in front of Mark's desk and glared down at him through his tinted glasses. "That's right. I do. And you and I both know it doesn't always go the way it's planned. Things go wrong all the time."

Taylor got up from her chair and moved to stand in front of Dane. She looked up at him, her eyes, expression and tones of assurance for him alone. "Dane, you know he's right. The person they send—whoever it is—is going to be interested in the books, not me. This should be easy. And I'll be fine."

Dane looked down at her for a second. Even through the glasses Taylor understood the look, although she would never have told him. It was more than anger at what Mark wanted her to do—what she had agreed to. It was stark fear again, and it was more devastating than ever before. Now Taylor knew that the basis for it was his love for her.

Dane understood full well himself, of course. But he'd never imagined that love could make so much difference. He'd been in love with Maddy, and he'd agreed to her following him around the field in circumstances much more serious than those being proposed for Taylor. He'd lost Maddy, and that had hurt a lot. Taylor was a different person, this was a different time, and if anything happened to her, he honestly didn't know if he could recover and go on—or if he'd want to.

"I'd rather just give the damn books to Mark and let him take care of it. Yes, I'd like to catch those bastards, but not if you're the bait." He swung his attention back to Mark. "The answer is no."

"I'll do it," Taylor interrupted in a voice of surprising authority and strength. And then she looked again at Dane before he could respond. "I'm going to do it."

Dane turned away from them both and uttered an oath. He knew she wasn't going to change her mind. In an odd way, Dane was impressed. The circumstances were untenable, and Dane would cheerfully have killed Michael Evans for putting them where they now found themselves, if someone else hadn't already done so. But that was his frustration reacting. He didn't care a damn about Michael. He only wanted to take care of Taylor, but it was clear that it was not his play to call. It was hers.

When they'd first discovered the hidden bonds and Dane had suggested calling Mark, he had done so with the intention that he and Mark would orchestrate the details, keeping Taylor out of it and in the background. He hadn't expected and wasn't prepared for her to virtually take over, with plans and ideas of her own about cornering the London group. Dane knew Taylor's was a better idea, but that was beside the point. For the first time in a long while, Dane wasn't willing either to be logical or to use the superior insight and cunning he was more than capable of, and which had always guided his life. Right now he could only feel, and what he was feeling was almost paralyzing in its intensity. He just couldn't risk anything happening to her.

Dane took a deep breath and combed his fingers through his hair. Quietly, confidently, Taylor was once more outlining her thoughts to Mark, who was listening intently and nodding in agreement. Dane had already heard it more times than he cared to.

They had done as Mark said, sending a telex to Mr. Neery, the manager at Bolton's. Taylor had worked hard to keep the information short and, more importantly, the phrasing simple and clear. She had to make it sound innocent, as if she were totally surprised by her findings. And she had to make it seem as though she had complete confidence that Mr. Neery, being a friend of Michael's, could take care of it.

They had to assume and hope that greed would outbalance the little loopholes and breaks in logic that would have made someone above Mr. Neery's intellectual level much more suspicious. Dane and Taylor had also to assume that the people in London were sufficiently convinced of Taylor's innocence and lack of knowledge of Michael's business to believe that she would not go to anyone else with her findings. But just in case all of these assumptions were wrong, Taylor had to be the only contact, the only way for them to get the bonds and books. She had to be involved. And Dane knew it.

The answer that came back two days later was equally benign. It stated that Mr. Neery had no knowledge of the bonds, and that they were probably worthless, in any case. He then expressed a flattering interest in the books themselves, adding that he could always find a buyer for even the most esoteric book of verse. That was it. There had been no formal offer or instructions—just expressed interest. But Dane knew that someone would contact her again and suggested that she be available in her apartment to take the call. Taylor did not disagree; an unspoken ulterior motive hung between them.

The truth was that their discovery of physical bliss that first afternoon had only stimulated a need to be together all the time. It had sealed a relationship founded on other elements, one that had been held in check by circumstances beyond their control. And what control remained had given way to the need for mutual comfort, reassurance and love.

Dane had been rather overcome and humbled by the intensity and explosiveness of their lovemaking. With women he'd known since Maddy, sex had certainly been satisfying. But with Taylor it had meant much more; the experience had been deeper. It had also been a commitment. Her small body was surprisingly responsive and emotionally pleasing. Dane had also enjoyed the way she curled around him afterward as they lay together, mel-

low and sublime. He loved the way she had stretched out
on his chest with easy familiarity and quietly listened as
he talked about his father, answering her soft, curious
questions about himself. She'd absently shifted and
readjusted her body on his for comfort, innocently
smoothed a finger along his jaw and chin as he talked
until the feel and weight of her, the curve of her breast
and the feathery lightness of her hand had aroused him
rather quickly and they'd made love again. Only the setting of the sun and the need to get Holly had forestalled
a third display of their passion for each other.

So yesterday they'd returned to the apartment. Taylor
had decided not to tell her parents what was going on,
and Dane had agreed that the less they knew, the better.
But she had wanted to tell Quinn, just in case a need de-
veloped later on for her family to be involved. Quinn had
not asked as they left his cabin and prepared to drive
down to Riverdale, but Dane had nonetheless assured
him.

"She'll be all right with me."

Quinn nodded. "I know that. I'm not worried."

When they reached the apartment, it was with the intention of waiting for the call they both were anticipat-
ing. But Taylor had other things on her mind, and Dane
had no objection. He loved her boldness in maneuvering
them both to the bedroom. He was amused by her playful seduction as she stripped off her clothing, and deeply
aroused as she removed all of his, her slender hands and
her smiling lips leaving a trail of kisses and caresses that
led to Dane lifting Taylor laughing into his arms, her hair
flying out behind her thrown-back head. Her laughter
died when he put her onto the bed and lay on top of her,
and proceeded to make love to her so deliberately and
expertly that she lay limp and trembling and supremely

satiated afterward. Taylor later had a drowsy thought that being mischievous and teasing certainly had its pay-off.

When the phone rang it was nearly six. Dane had signaled her to let it ring several times before answering. When she did, Dane started a recorder and Taylor contrived to sound vague and calm. There had been a pause, as if the caller were assessing her voice.

"Is this Taylor Evans?"

"Taylor Ashe," she corrected automatically, then clutched the phone and quickly added, "Evans was my married name. Who's this?" She glanced at Dane, who was standing nearby, alert and able to hear the caller.

"I'm an associate of Mr. Neery. I understand you have some books you want to sell."

Taylor's eyes widened and she looked at Dane. He nodded. "Well, yes. But Mr. Neery and I didn't discuss any price. The books are only—"

"Five thousand dollars," the man interrupted.

"What?" Taylor said weakly.

"Mr. Neery is offering five thousand dollars." Again Dane nodded.

"Oh, that's wonderful!" Taylor effused brightly. "I can certainly use the money."

The male voice stayed neutral and to the point. "When can I get the books?"

Taylor frowned in confusion. "You mean, can I send them?"

Dane shook his head, wanting her to avoid that option. Luckily the caller disagreed, as well.

"No. I'll pick them up."

"Oh. When?"

"Soon. Within the next few days." Taylor looked at Dane for guidance. He shook his head and made a cutting motion.

Taylor hesitated. "Ah...well...actually, it will have to be before Friday. You see, I'm invited away for the weekend," she improvised.

There was no response. Taylor laughed nervously. "I hope that's okay. I mean, I didn't expect to hear from Mr. Neery so soon and—"

"Okay. Thursday. I'll call to let you know when."

"That will be—"

The line went dead. Taylor turned to Dane. Her hands were shaking. He turned off the recorder, took the phone out of her hand and replaced it. He soothingly rubbed her upper arms.

"You did fine," Dane said calmly. "Tomorrow we'll go see Mark and see if he can get some people here to cover for you."

But Taylor had not been in favor of that idea, and neither had Mark. Now, as Taylor explained why he had no other choice, Dane was hard-pressed to disagree with her. His reasons would only have been between Taylor and himself, in any case.

Behind him, Taylor sighed and put a hand on his back. She could feel the stiffness in him; every nerve was protesting her decision.

"Dane, all of those men saw me in London. They know who I am. You can't put another woman in the apartment. You yourself said they aren't stupid, they're going to be looking for the possibility of a trap. Well...there won't be one. I'll give whoever shows up the books. If you're right about him wanting to get out of the country as quickly as possible, you can follow him at that point to the airport. I still think the best thing to do is what Mark suggested. Let this courier think all is well, but nab him at Customs in London. The books are over one hundred years old, so you can use the excuse that he needed special documentation for removal of antiques from one country to the next. That's the truth.''

Still Dane would not turn around, and Taylor could see the reflexive action of his jaw, telling her he was not yet willing to give in. She looked at Mark with a helpless expression. It was the only way, and she'd never expected that Dane would draw such a hard line.

Mark could also see they weren't making any headway. But he also understood why. He raised his brows at the realization that Hawk was very much in love with Taylor Ashe. He almost chuckled. Love was the only thing he knew of that made men foolish and stubborn, even men as smart as Dane Farrow.

Mark knew he was never going to be able to change Dane's mind to agree to the plan. That left it up to Taylor, and he had to trust that she was clever enough to do so.

Mark lazily got up from his chair.

"Look... I can at least start lining up surveillance on the building, and have a car ready to tail the courier to the airport. The Customs setup is good. I'll call Roger and see if he can help.''

Neither of the other two adults responded, and with a silent chuckle at their predicament, Mark left the office.

After a moment's silence, Taylor walked around Dane to stand directly in front of him, so close that she could feel his body heat—and his disapproval. She tilted back her head to look into his face. Taylor knew he was angry and that he was looking at her none too kindly through his glasses.

"You can't do it alone," he said.

Taylor stayed calm. "Oh, yes, I can.''

"No, you can't,'' he countered through clenched teeth.

"Dane, I'll be fine. They don't want me. They want what I have. We all agree on that." When she started to walk away, Dane quickly grabbed her arm, swinging her around to face him again.

"Have you forgotten that warehouse in London? Have you forgotten what almost happened there? And they didn't even know anything about you!"

Taylor blanched and gnawed her lip. How could he imagine that she'd ever forget that day? "This is different. They wouldn't dare start anything here."

"You don't know that for certain," Dane said roughly, brushing her logic aside.

Taylor sighed. "I have to do this my way. I don't want you or anyone else to do it for me."

Dane turned away. "Dammit, Taylor. You refuse to understand."

"I understand you don't think I can handle this," she answered, annoyed. "Everyone thinks I'm so incapable of dealing with a crisis, trouble or a difficult situation. Doesn't anyone realize I've been dealing with Michael for more than three years?"

Dane didn't answer, and Taylor couldn't understand why he had so little faith in her ability to help.

"Don't you realize what it did to me, *not* knowing what was going on or why? *Not* being in control of my own life?" she whispered emotionally. "It's *my* life, and I'll never give up control again. I have to do this, Dane. Those books and those bonds are the last things tying me to Michael. I want this over, once and for all, so that maybe...we can have our future. Together."

Slowly Dane turned his head to look down at her. Taylor smiled gently and came over to him. Then unexpectedly she pressed a kiss to his chest through the dark turtleneck sweater. Dane ran his hand under her hair and gently massaged her nape. He loved it when she touched him that way.

"I've learned a lot from the London trip," Taylor said dryly. "I promise to be careful. And Mr. Richards will have people in the background."

"I don't know if that's good enough," Dane answered, still not willing to compromise.

Taylor's eyes widened in surprise when Dane's hand squeezed her neck. She could feel his strength, but in his face she saw again, not anger, but fear. Taylor had never imagined there was anything in life that could make Dane afraid.

"Taylor..." he began, making his voice rough to hide his emotions. "I don't want anything to happen to you."

She stared, suddenly understanding, and her heart fluttered with happiness. She felt strong and in charge, and she felt Dane's care and love. She pushed herself into his arms and he held her tightly for a long moment.

Taylor pulled back to look at him again. He had his control back, the little show of emotion veiled. Her eyes sparkled. If she'd never gone after Michael Evans on a misguided but understandable mission to London, she would never have met a man of Dane's caliber and integrity—a man who truly wanted her.

Dane looked down at her with an expression that would have seemed threatening and dangerous to anyone else, but she was not the least intimidated, and it showed.

Dane cocked a brow and pursed his lips. "You can forget it. I agree that you have to be the one to hand over the books. But I plan on being there. That's the deal."

Taylor stroked his chin and tried not to smile. "You drive a hard bargain."

Dane grabbed her hand and held it tightly. "I have a lot at stake."

Taylor was just coaxing a kiss from Dane when Mark Richards came back into his office, holding several files. When he saw the two in an embrace, he began to laugh softly, mentally awarding Taylor ten points.

"Good! I see you've come to an understanding!"

TAYLOR KNEW there were at least four men carefully placed in the vicinity of her building, but for the life of her she couldn't imagine how or where. Mark had not bothered replacing the doormen, because that would have been too obvious, and he didn't want questions that couldn't be answered thrown at any of his men. The idea was to keep things as familiar and routine as possible.

Mark and Dane both agreed that the pickup person would probably not call, even though he'd said he would. He wasn't going to give any more information than he had to.

Unlike Ann, Taylor found nothing about what she was doing exciting. She was too nervous that she'd do something wrong, or the pickup would guess what was going on. But she would never have admitted it to either Mark or Dane, and luckily neither asked. She wouldn't have been a good liar.

That had been proved when Taylor gave her parents the world's flimsiest excuse for having to stay in the apartment for at least twenty-four hours. Her parents had exchanged blank looks, and her father had commented that it was a good thing her nose wasn't too long, so it would have room to grow.

After all was said and done, Taylor was very happy that Dane had been insistent on staying in the apartment with her. His physical presence was reassuring, even though he'd insisted that she not talk to him at all, and that she go about some activity as if he weren't there. Taylor had thought all these precautions silly, until she realized that Dane was serious and wouldn't respond to her.

Taylor had been too restless to read, watch TV or stare at the walls. She'd been too keyed up to sleep much the night before, and although she quickly became exhausted, couldn't take a nap now. They had no idea when the courier would show up, and could only wait.

After a time Taylor settled down at her drafting table with a book that needed the signatures resewn and the cover reattached. The work required concentration, and she was soon genuinely involved with the details.

Twice the phone rang. The first time was a local carpet-cleaning outfit with a special springtime sale. The second time it was a wrong number. Both calls set Taylor's nerves on edge, but Dane remained in the background, virtually invisible.

Dane's tactic was for Taylor not to rely on his presence. He wanted her to behave as if she'd been alone for hours—all day—so that anyone else talking with her would get the sense that she was alone. If she felt put out, so much the better. People got impatient and frustrated, just waiting, and that was how he wanted her to respond, because it was natural. And he knew the second call was a contact call. He stayed confined to the darkened bedroom, and the wait was only marginally easier for him.

At exactly six-thirty there was a knock on her door. Taylor looked up from her work, curious that the doorbell had not been used. She only briefly thought of Dane in the bedroom, deathly silent and invisible, before she got up and slowly approached the door.

"Who is it?" she called out quietly.

"I'm here to make a pickup from a Taylor Ashe," came a young male voice. Taylor frowned. It didn't sound like the man she'd spoken to over the phone.

She looked over her shoulder toward the bedroom, then slowly unlocked the door and peeked through a small opening. On the other side a young messenger waited patiently. Taylor opened the door a little wider, expecting some magical phrase or code name to be spoken.

"Well, where is it?" the young man asked.

"What?" Taylor asked dumbly.

"Lady, I have a call to pick up a package of books for Bolton's. In return I'm to give you this envelope. Do you have the books, or what?" the messenger asked sarcastically.

Taylor assessed him a moment longer. "Just a moment. I'll get it."

When Taylor returned with the books, the messenger gave her a legitimate receipt, had her sign it, and gave her a thick envelope.

"That's it. 'Night," he said with a nod and turned away.

Taylor closed the door and stood leaning against it until Dane appeared ghostlike from the bedroom. "Did you hear that? It was a messenger service." She handed him the receipt and the envelope.

Silently Dane took both and headed for the phone. He quickly dialed a number.

"Get Richards on the box," he ordered and while he waited, read the receipt and looked into the envelope. There were easily five thousand dollars inside. "Mark? A messenger made the pickup. Yeah, it looks legit."

Taylor came to stand next to Dane.

"I agree with you. It'll probably take forty-five minutes from here. Do you have the flight schedules? Good." He looked briefly at Taylor. "Fine. We're on our way out right now." He hung up.

"Dane? Did I do the wrong thing? Should I have given him the package? I really wasn't sure, and—"

"Take it easy," Dane soothed her, giving Taylor a brief hug before walking to the drafting table. He took the money out of the envelope, and Taylor gasped.

"It—it's cash!"

"Mmm," Dane said absently. "It can't be traced."

"Dane, what's going on?"

Dane looked at her. "Our man was a bit more clever than we thought. He wasn't taking any chances. He had a messenger pick up the books, and then they'll probably be delivered to him somewhere else."

"But where?"

"I'm willing to bet he's waiting at the airport. As soon as he gets the package, he's on a plane out. Mark is going to have the messenger followed. But the trick is to figure out which flight tonight our man is going to try and catch."

"Well, what do we do now?"

Dane came over and put an arm around her shoulder. "We do nothing but leave. Get out of here. Our part is over."

Taylor blinked. "You mean...that's it?"

Dane smiled. "You sound disappointed."

"Well...I guess I am, a little."

"Believe me, Taylor. The 'exciting' part you don't want to be around for. It gets serious and scary. Don't worry. Mark will let us know what happened. In the meantime, it's over."

In a way Taylor felt let down. She would have liked the instant gratification that catching the man tonight might have provided. She would have liked to learn that he wasn't so smart, after all, and had been caught red-handed. Most of all, she would have liked to experience some just revenge for what they—particularly Michael—had put her through. But it was not to be. For all of her straightforward approach to the problem, the solution was still going to be shrouded in mystery. And the very best she could do was walk away from it and forget.

Dane saw her disappointment. He also saw she was overly tired from the anticipation. But for better or worse, for her it all ended right here and now.

"Taylor, sometimes we don't get the answers we want."

"I suppose. But if we leave here, where do *we* go?"

"Quinn gave me the keys to the cabin, with the message that there are clean sheets on the bed and at least three days' supply of food in the fridge."

Taylor blushed. "It sounds good to me."

Dane stood close to her and cupped her face to look intently into her eyes. "I know this may not be much at the moment, but you're one hell of a brave lady, Taylor Ashe...and I love you."

Taylor blinked and tried to smile. "I needed to hear that," she whispered. "Are you always so accommodating?"

Dane gathered her into his arms. "I'm never accommodating," he reminded her with a soft chuckle.

"Why don't I believe you?" she murmured against his chest.

"You're not supposed to."

DANE LOVED THE CABIN. It was exactly the sort of house he'd had in mind many years ago, when he'd thought of building a home in Colorado. The plans, vague at the time, had been tabled as impractical and too much of a fantasy. But now he no longer thought so.

He opened the front door, which Quinn had cleverly placed to face southeast, and stood facing the soft quiet beginnings of dawn. He could feel the morning dampness and hear the faint rustle of the new day coming to life. Dane let the cool sweet air sweep over his naked flesh.

He'd want his house to be bigger, with more rooms and windows that allowed for sunlight, but he could begin with something like this. He could supply all the materials and equipment needed. Quinn could interpret his ideas and plans. He and Taylor could live in it.

Two days completely alone with Taylor had started Dane thinking along the lines of home—probably because he now couldn't imagine one without her. She had surrounded him with so much hope, so much love that Taylor had become his way home. He'd called his father, and they'd had a conversation of tentative reaching out to one another. They both recognized that an unnecessary amount of time and space had separated them, and were both ready to bridge the gap. Dane had been surprised by his father's welcoming, forgiving tone and by his anxiousness for his son to come home. It made Dane realize how little he'd understood his father's choices years ago, how much he might not have understood him then, and how much he missed him now. Dane told his father of his desire to settle down on the land he owned.

"So, you're finally going to build that house," his father had said. "Will you be coming alone?"

Dane had hesitated. Sometimes he still thought Taylor was a wish his heart had dreamed up. But she'd taken his hand as he spoke to his father, and she'd smiled reassuringly at Dane.

"No. I won't be alone," he could finally say.

Dane heard the soft movements behind him and looked over his shoulder into the cabin interior as Taylor approached. She was wearing one of her brother's T-shirts, and it swamped her, making her look like a little girl. She slowly approached Dane, blinking away recent sleep and putting her arms around his naked middle, hugging into his side. Dane held her silently against him, stroking her body.

Knowing that he hadn't slept very deeply Taylor had heard him get out of bed. She'd been concerned until she realized he was just a light sleeper. Taylor had also thought that perhaps something was troubling him and he wanted to be alone. They were still so new to each other that she didn't understand all of his ways. On the other hand, the last two days had allowed for endless, exquisite exploration of a physical nature. She loved the masculine perfection of him, injuries notwithstanding, and smiled secretly at the ways his body pleased her. It amazed her what a man and woman were capable of doing together.

Taylor tilted her head. The subtle morning shadows sharpened the planes and angles of his face, the deep sockets of his eyes without the glasses. He hadn't bothered to shave since they'd been alone, and looked rather like a renegade with his longish hair and growth of beard. He looked dangerous. But Taylor smiled knowingly.

"Are you okay?" she questioned in a whisper. Dane's mouth lifted in a slight smile.

"I'm fine. I'm sorry I woke you."

"I missed you next to me," she said simply.

They regarded each other quietly. The morning chill breezed through the open door to touch Taylor's skin. Under his hand Dane could feel her breast tighten and her nipple grow stiff. He gently rubbed it through the cotton shirt, and drawing her back inside the cabin, closed the door. He turned to face her, to enjoy the slimness of her small frame, its fragile appearance a lie to a startling show of passion not so long ago.

"I got restless," he said.

"I know the cabin's not so comfortable, but..."

Dane smiled, his eyes searching over her face. "It's not that. I was thinking about Colorado."

"Oh," Taylor said. "You mean home."

Dane shook his head. "It's not home yet." He grew hesitant. "It will be... if you come with me."

Taylor blinked at the implication. "Is—is this a proposal?" she asked weakly. "Or are you afraid to face your father alone?"

Dane arched a brow. "Afraid I'll lose you," he said with poignant honesty. "I don't have much to offer, Taylor...."

"Do you love me?" she queried softly.

"You know I do."

"Then that's all I want. Yes, I'll come." She hugged him close, wishing she were just a little taller, so her lips could reach his neck. "We can use the money to get started," she offered.

Dane frowned and looked down at her. "What money?"

"The five thousand dollars in cash from Bolton's. The twenty-five-thousand-dollar reward for the recovery of the bonds. Once the books were taken at Heathrow, I thought we'd heard the end of it. And you did promise

you'd tell me what's going to happen to the men involved. As long as Mark said I'm entitled to the money,
we might as well put it to good use."

"No."

"No? What do you mean, no?"

"I mean no, I can afford to build our home. The
money is for Holly's education. It's the least Michael
Evans can do for her," Dane said tightly.

Taylor was silent and thoughtful for a moment as she
absently stroked Dane's flank. She pulled away from him
and, taking his large hand in hers, headed back to the
very small bedroom and the double bed, which took up
all the space.

"Dane, there's enough money to put two kids through
school," Taylor offered quietly.

Dane stopped walking, pulling Taylor up short. He
pulled her slowly back into his arms and kissed her tenderly, with love—and gratitude.

"School's more expensive than you think. We'll worry
about it when the second one gets here."

"Would you like—?" she began shyly.

Dane cupped her face, looking deeply into her eyes. "I
like...very much." His rough voice caressed her. "I also
think I should adopt Holly, so she'll have my name.
What do you think?"

Taylor couldn't speak around the sudden lump in her
throat. She merely nodded. "You're about to change
your life completely. A house, an instant family, staying
in one place. Won't you miss the excitement and freedom of the past?"

Dane regarded her for a moment. In answer he began
pulling her T-shirt over her head and carelessly tossed it
aside. He slowly drew her warm, bare flesh against him,
aligning her comfortably. He kissed the top of her head.

"I had nothing to compare my life to, until Roger married Ann and I saw how happy they were. Or until I met you. Sometime I'll tell you exactly what the difference is." Dane kissed her and slowly began lowering Taylor to the bed.

She sighed, running her hands down his chest to his taut stomach and below. Taylor's hand closed around the evidence of his desire.

"What are we going to do in the meantime?" she whispered. Dane leaned over her to caress a breast. "I think we'll begin on the second one. Isn't that what you had in mind?"

Taylor chuckled seductively, reaching her arms up to him.

# Epilogue

When the group turned the corner, the head nurse looked up over the high counter of her workstation. She raised her brows and smiled as the three adults and one small child made the slow journey down the hospital corridor. There was quiet talk among them and even gentle laughter as they passed her desk and continued on the family outing.

The two men were of the same height. One was a bit stouter, no doubt because he was older and had lacked hard activity in recent years. Retirement sometimes did that to people. He had thick hair that was almost completely gray, and from the shape of his head and angles of his face anyone could tell he was father to the younger man at his side. But while the older man had a benign, grandfatherly look, and the comfortable sagging of someone who'd lived a long life and long ago made peace with the course it had taken, the younger man was still alert and in his prime.

With his turtleneck sweater and dark, concealing glasses he'd seemed somber, in control, even intimidating to the hospital staff, but the nurse remembered his attention to the petite, attractive woman being wheeled in front of him and knew there was in this man a fierce loyalty, gentleness and love for her. The nurse felt a jolt of envy as she witnessed the protective, loving bond that existed between them.

The dark-haired young woman seated in the wheelchair laughed lightly at the animated chatter of the little girl who sat perched on her knees, clasping a book and held securely around her middle by her mother. The group reached the end of the corridor and stopped.

The head nurse let her smile soften and went back to making notes in her log. The Farrow family was visiting the new baby....

Everyone stopped talking, and even Holly was awed into silence as she slid from her mother's knee and approached the large glass viewing window. But Holly was too short to see anything. She turned to Dane and reached up.

"Daddy, I can't see," she complained, and Dane bent to lift her into his arms. He moved closer to the window, and she anchored a short arm around his neck, the other still holding her book. There were only five occupied cribs in the room beyond the glass. Poking her finger into her mouth with shyness, Holly saw her little brother for the first time. Dane, Taylor and Lt. Col. Tim Farrow, retired, watched.

"Which one is ours?" Holly warbled around her finger.

Dane gently pulled it from her mouth. Then he pointed to the window. "The one in the middle."

"What's his name?"

"We don't know yet."

Holly thought for a moment. "We could call him Kermit."

"Kermit?" Dane asked blankly.

"You know. From the Muppet show."

Dane could hear Taylor and his father struggling not to laugh. He felt at a loss. Naming his first son Kermit, after a frog, was not what he had in mind. "I don't think Kermit would like that idea," he said wryly.

Holly looked for a long moment at the baby, her mouth slowly opening into a circle of surprise. She leaned to whisper into Dane's ear. "Is he sleeping?"

Dane smiled slowly. "Yes," he nodded, his gravelly voice expressing tenderness.

Holly shrugged her shoulders. "Doesn't he know it's time to get up? It's morning," she reasoned.

Dane extended his right hand, and Taylor placed hers in his callused palm.

"He and Mommy worked very hard last night. I think he's still tired," Dane improvised easily.

Holly didn't answer, but quietly studied the tiny sleeping infant with his waving fluff of dark hair and tightly curled fists.

"That's why I brought Mommy to the hospital last night, so that he could be born," Dane said softly, squeezing Taylor's hand, still in awe himself at the event that had given him a son. He looked down at Taylor, and his lips moved into a smile—a gesture of the love that he held only for her.

Holly was tapping his cheek to get his attention. "But how did he get born? How did he get out of Mommy's tummy?"

Dane couldn't think of a single thing to say, and for one of the very few times in his life stood speechless.

There was a deep sputtering behind him from his father that quickly turned into a half attempt to smother laughter. To his right, Taylor could be heard giggling.

"You come with Grandpa, Halfpint, and I'll explain," Tim Farrow chuckled, reaching to take the willing Holly from Dane's arm.

"Dad..." Dane began hesitantly, but his father waved him into silence.

"Don't worry, son. I'll keep it simple."

The older man turned and deftly diverted Holly's attention with the unorthodox bribe of a donut from the hospital commissary.

For a moment Dane and Taylor watched the two walk away; both were thinking the same thing. What a difference there was in Dane's father now, from when they'd arrived in Colorado eighteen months before.

Tim Farrow had welcomed his son home with some hesitancy. Not from a lack of desire to have him home, but from a lack of knowledge of what his son would be like after so many years. The emotional and filial schism between them was not that deep, but neither knew how to bridge it. It had taken Holly's curiosity, cheerfulness and innocence to get things rolling, for she accepted Tim Farrow's place in her new life as readily as she'd accepted Dane as her father—with the trusting instincts of the very young.

It took no time at all for Tim Farrow to succumb to Holly's charm, to warmly welcome her, and Taylor as new family, and to say how glad, *really* glad, he was to have his son home again....

Taylor was still holding Dane's hand and turned her gaze back to him. Dane's attention was riveted on his son, who was sleeping just beyond his reach. In spite of his dark lenses, Taylor could sense his fascination, his pride, even his disbelief at this gift they shared. It was much the same look he'd shown just ten hours earlier, when the doctor had given him the squalling, damp in-

fant to hold for the first time, thirty seconds after he'd
entered the world.

Taylor slowly pulled herself up from the wheelchair
and stood by Dane's side. Together they looked at the
baby.

"I love you," Dane whispered, and Taylor felt a thrill,
and overwhelming love in return.

She smiled and rubbed her cheek against the sleeve of
Dane's sweater.

"And thank you for our son."

"I had a lot of help," Taylor whispered softly.

"It's really amazing to think—"

"A miracle?" she supplied.

Dane nodded. "Yes. Now I understand how Roger
felt."

"Have you called them yet? And Trudy?"

"And your mom and dad. This morning, before driving over."

Dane led her back to the wheelchair. Taylor allowed
herself to be wheeled back to her room.

Taylor's mother was arriving for a two-week stay to
help out while everyone adjusted to the baby's schedule.
They would wait awhile before planning a reunion trip to
London. Holly had begun kindergarten just that fall, and
there was still work to be done on the new house. So
many changes had come so quickly; Taylor reflected on
the excitement that had been generated since she and
Dane married.

Quinn had done the architectural design of their house
as a wedding gift, and Dane had supervised the contrac-
tors. Tim Farrow had indicated that he was not interested in moving into the large new home of his son and
daughter-in-law, not only because of his own independent bent, but also because he was wise enough to let his

son and family live their own lives. He was a frequent, welcomed visitor, however, and Taylor especially enjoyed seeing Dane on more comfortable terms with his father.

Their lives had become normal and grounded, like those of most families. Dane had adjusted quickly, perhaps too quickly to a life completely different from what he'd been used to. The most significant move, from world traveler and troubleshooter to husband and father, had seemed easy for him. Even when Holly tested his authority and her own independence, he was firm but gentle.

Dane's demonstrations of his love for Taylor were powerful and constant, his passion a very tangible thing that she was aware of even without intimacy, though she delighted in their lovemaking, too. She was happier than she'd ever thought to be—and she had also never been so scared.

It had not occurred to Taylor that Dane would have to continue to travel. But after all, he did own his own legitimate international business, and it was business as usual. It was different from her experience with Michael in that she knew quite a bit about Dane's work, and always knew where he'd be. But she lived in dread that something would happen to him while he was in Europe, and she'd never see him again.

Taylor's fear was due in part to the news from Roger, almost at the beginning of her marriage to Dane, that Philip Mayhew Johns had protected himself better than anyone had thought possible. Although his ring of smugglers and thieves was broken and arrests were made, he could not be touched, and he slipped, under a cloud but still unfettered, back into the easy life of the privileged.

Taylor didn't care about him, but she knew that Bick Rafferty had not been caught, and was still on the loose somewhere in Europe. Taylor did not have to think long and hard to figure out that Dane spent part of his trips to London in meeting with Roger, exploring all the leads that came in on Rafferty's whereabouts. They wanted him badly.

As Dane wheeled Taylor into her private room and closed the door, there was silence between them. Dane understood the silence. When Taylor continued to sit, he reached an arm beneath her knees and lifted her out of the chair, then sat in another chair with Taylor across his lap. He kissed her forehead and held her comfortably. She had never complained, and had never said one word about the trips that had been necessary during the past year. It was, in a sense, ironic, but Taylor was afraid that he, too, might disappear from her life. Not like Michael . . . but actually because of him. But Dane had no intentions of letting the shadows of Michael Evans's past trail them for the rest of their lives.

Dane remembered all too well the trip that had not only led Roger and himself to Rafferty—hiding in a dismal little town in Germany—but the one that had also finalized the sale of his own company's holdings overseas. The rest he would operate from Colorado. The trip had taken two days longer than he'd planned. When he'd gotten home it was to find Taylor pale with fright and anticipation, which had finally manifested itself in a flood of fears when they were alone in the privacy of their room. In those dark hours their son had been conceived. Oddly, with the baby's birth Dane's odyssey—and the fear from the past—had ended.

"I have a present for you," Dane said in a low voice.

Taylor smiled. "I've already got one, thank you."

"This one is different," Dane said. "This one is to close the files on London."

Taylor looked up with fear in her eyes. "Do you have to go back?" she asked, her voice betraying her anxiety.

"Not anymore," Dane said, reaching into a pocket. He handed her the telegram. Interpol had found Bick Rafferty. Unfortunately someone else had gotten to him first.

Taylor read the letter over and over; the tension visibly disappeared. On a deep sigh, she closed her eyes and hugged Dane closely.

"I'm glad. I don't care. I—I just didn't want anything..."

He squeezed her. "I know. I didn't want anything to happen, either. I didn't want to take the chance that his vindictiveness would reach out to us here."

"Oh, Dane—" Taylor breathed.

"And there's something else," he said, reaching into the other pocket and pulling out another paper.

Taylor opened up an official-looking document that listed the name of his company and its holdings, now to be operated from Colorado, U.S.A.

"From now on, if I do any more traveling, we do it as a family."

Taylor looked up at him; tears filled her eyes and spilled. Dane gently wiped them away. "I was afraid maybe you missed all of that. I thought that was why you traveled."

He shook his head. "The choice was easy, Taylor. Having you and a home and a family, or always being alone. There was no contest. This is where I belong. With you, Holly and our son."

Taylor smiled through her tears as she stroked his cheek. "We're going to have to stop calling him 'our son' and find a name for him."

"I like Christopher," Dane said somewhat shyly. Every now and then it struck him anew that he was a father, that he had a son.

"I like Christopher, too. Or we could let Holly name him," she teased.

Dane grimaced. "That's risky. Holly's range of names is limited to Disney and Muppet characters."

Taylor laughed merrily. In the last year Dane had been re-Americanized, and his reactions to American television and current pop culture had been amusing to watch. But she had to agree that naming their son Kermit did not appeal to her, either.

There was a soft knock on the door, and Dane shifted Taylor back to her bed, kissing her briefly before she said, "Come in."

Tim Farrow entered the room, holding Holly by the hand. He could see from the bright spark in Taylor's eyes and the relaxed attitude of his son that their few private moments together had been needed, and well spent.

"This little miss has a prodigious appetite," he chuckled. "Two jelly donuts and a glass of chocolate milk. And then I read her her book. Again." He sighed.

Holly ran to her mother's side, and Dane lifted her to the bed.

"I know what we can name my little brother."

Dane and Taylor exchanged cautious looks.

"What, sweetheart?" Taylor asked, holding her breath.

"After him," Holly said, holding up the book. "See . . . Christopher Robin," she explained.

For a long moment there was silence, then the three adults began to laugh.

"That's an excellent idea," Dane said to Holly. "I'm so glad you thought of it." He smiled at Taylor.

"Me, too," she said.

**H A R L E Q U I N**

*American Romance*

## COMING NEXT MONTH

### #329 BEST WISHES by Julie Kistler

Known as the Grande Dame of the Rockies, The Stanley Hotel had its share of legends. But when a mysterious stranger gave front desk manager Hayley Austin a golden apple, she didn't know she was about to make hotel history. When she met Mason Wilder, the man of her dreams, Hayley wondered if the apple was truly magic, or was it sheer coincidence?.

BEST WISHES introduces a three-book series called ROCKY MOUNTAIN MAGIC. In March 1990 don't miss #333 SIGHT UNSEEN by Kathy Clark, and in April 1990 look for #337 RETURN TO SUMMER by Emma Merritt.

### #330 SURVIVORS by Judith Arnold

Nursery-owner Paul Tremaine grew stately oaks and graceful birches—but the humid jungles of Vietnam plagued his dreams. Bonnie Hudson taught her son that his father was a hero, an antiwar activist who'd died for his beliefs. But it was the terrible truth about those years that challenged them to put the past to rest—and save their passion for living.

### #331 OUTSIDE IN by Beverly Sommers

At twenty-seven, Jill was masquerading as a high-school senior to find the truth about her sister's death. She was also causing quite a commotion, snubbing the cheerleaders and hanging out with the jocks. And giving her Civics teacher the fright of his life. Poor Doug Lacayo had no way of knowing that his provocative, attractive pupil wasn't a teenager.

### #332 MEMORY LANE by Vella Munn

Though she'd been brought back by duty and responsibility, Kim Revis had promised herself to enjoy her visit to her childhood home. But Kim's grandmother's handsome lawyer, Mark Stockton, had made promises of his own. His presence kept luring her away from the deceptive pleasures of the past and warning her of the danger of the present.

You'll flip . . . your pages won't!
Read paperbacks *hands-free* with

# Book Mate·I

**The perfect "mate" for all your romance paperbacks**

**Traveling • Vacationing • At Work • In Bed • Studying • Cooking • Eating**

Perfect size for all standard paperbacks, this wonderful invention makes reading a pure pleasure! Ingenious design holds paperback books OPEN and FLAT so even wind can't ruffle pages – leaves your hands free to do other things. Reinforced, wipe-clean vinyl-covered holder flexes to let you turn pages without undoing the strap . . . supports paperbacks so well, they have the strength of hardcovers!

Pages turn WITHOUT opening the strap

SEE-THROUGH STRAP

Reinforced back stays flat

Built in bookmark

BOOK MARK

BACK COVER HOLDING STRIP

10 x 7¼ opened
Snaps closed for easy carrying, too

A compelling novel of deadly revenge and passion
from Harlequin's bestselling international
romance author Penny Jordan

# POWER PLAY

Eleven years had passed but the
terror of that night was something
Pepper Minesse would never
forget. Fueled by revenge against
the four men who had brutally
shattered her past, she set in
motion a deadly plan to destroy
their futures.

**Available in February!**

 **Harlequin Books** ®

HPP-1A